THREATS and PROMISES

**Center Point
Large Print**

**This Large Print Book carries the
Seal of Approval of N.A.V.H.**

BARBARA DELINSKY

THREATS and PROMISES

CENTER POINT PUBLISHING
THORNDIKE, MAINE

This Center Point Large Print edition
is published in the year 2003 by arrangement with
Harlequin Books S. A.

Copyright © 1986 by Barbara Delinsky.

All rights reserved.

The text of this Large Print edition is unabridged.
In other aspects, this book may vary from the original edition.

Printed in the United States of America.

Set in 16-point Times New Roman type.

ISBN 1-58547-344-8

Library of Congress Cataloging-in-Publication Data

Delinsky, Barbara.
    Threats and promises / Barbara Delinsky.--Center Point large print ed.
    p. cm.
    ISBN 1-58547-344-8 (lib. bdg. : alk. paper)
    1. Large type books. I. Title.

PS3554.E4427T46 2003
813'.54--dc21

2003048573

PROLOGUE

The dark of night lay thick in the garden of the lavish Hollywood Hills estate where two shadowed figures conversed in low tones. Both were men. One was tall, broad and physical; the other was smooth, arrogant and cerebral.

"Are you sure? Absolutely sure?" the smooth one demanded, sounding less smooth than usual as his eyes pierced the darkness to bead mercilessly at his companion.

"She wasn't in that car," the tall one insisted quietly.

"You said she was. I buried her."

"You buried ashes of what we thought was her. We were wrong."

The smooth one's nostrils flared, but he kept his voice low. "And how can you be sure it wasn't her?"

"One of our men heard talk around the coroner's office. There was no evidence of a body, charred or otherwise. A burned purse and shoes, but no body. Unofficially, of course. Officially, at least as far as the heat's concerned, she's dead."

The arrogant one cursed under his breath. He pulled a pack of cigarettes from his pocket and barely had time to raise one to his mouth when the underling snapped a match with his thumbnail and lit it.

"No body," he muttered, squaring his shoulders. "So she got away."

The physical one had enough sense to keep still. He knew what was to come, knew he had his work cut out for him.

"I want her found," the smooth one growled. "I want her found *now*."

Still the physical one remained silent.

"She didn't have any family, at least none she ever told me about. She wasn't in touch with anyone else, and her friends were mine." A long drag on the cigarette momentarily brightened its glowing red tip. "She must have had help." Smoke curled out with the words and dissipated into the air. "New identity, new location, money. . . . Damn it," he gritted out as the wheels of his mind turned, "she sold the jewels. There wasn't any burglary. The bitch took the jewels herself and sold them!"

"I'll find her."

"Damn right you will. Half a million in diamonds and rubies, not to mention another hundred thou in furs—no woman can steal like that from me!"

"Do you want me to bring her back?"

The tall man's boss pondered that as he stroked the closely shaved skin above his lip. When he spoke, his voice was low once more and as dark as the night. "She's a thief. And a traitor. I've given her a funeral fit for a queen. I won't suffer the embarrassment of having her materialize from the grave." He paused for a moment before continuing smoothly, arrogantly, cerebrally, in his own perverted way. "She's dead. That's how I want her. Make her squirm first. Let her know that I know what she's done. Get the jewels and whatever else you can from her. Then see that she's buried, this time with an unmarked stone."

Tossing the cigarette to the grass, he ground it out beneath the sole of his imported leather shoe. Then he straightened his silk evening jacket, thrust out his chin and walked calmly, coolly, back toward the house.

CHAPTER ONE

Lauren Stevenson looked at herself in the mirror. And looked. And looked. "It doesn't matter how long I stand here," she said breathlessly. "I still can't believe it's me!"

Richard Bowen grinned at her reflection. "It's you, and if I do say so myself, it's smashing."

She slanted him a shy glance. In the weeks during which she'd come to know this man, she'd grown perfectly comfortable with him as her doctor. But she couldn't ignore the fact that he was attractive; hence his compliment was that much more weighty. "I'll bet you say that to all the women you've worked on."

"Not necessarily. Some only look good. Some only look better than they did before. For that matter," he added with a wink, "some looked better before the surgery."

"You don't tell them that, do you?" she chided.

"Are you kidding? If it's vanity that's brought them down here, I'm not about to make an enemy for life. But it wasn't vanity that brought you here, Lauren Stevenson, was it?"

She shook her head. "It was sheer necessity." Once again she eyed herself in the mirror. "I'm amazed, though. I knew there'd be an improvement . . ." She faltered. Narcissism was foreign to her nature. Her cheeks grew red, her voice humble. "I didn't expect half this."

Richard's laugh was filled with intense satisfaction.

"Cases like yours are the most gratifying. You had the makings of a real beauty when you walked in here. All it took was a little rearranging."

Very lightly, she ran her fingertips down her straight nose, then along her newly reformed jawline. "More than a little." Her hand fell to graze her hip as she turned back to Richard. "And I've put on ten pounds in as many weeks. Funny, but I would have thought that having my jaws banded together and drinking through a straw would make me lose weight."

"You couldn't afford to have that happen, which was why I put you on a high-calorie liquid diet. And now that you can take in solids, I want you to follow the regimen I gave you to the letter. You could still use another five pounds on that slender frame of yours, which means you'll have to work at eating. Remember, you'll be able to chew just a little at a time until the muscles of your jaws regain their strength. How's it been since we removed the bands?"

"A little sore, but okay."

"It's only been three days. The soreness will ease off. You're talking well. In some cases we have to bring in a speech therapist, but I don't think you have to worry about that." He rose from where he'd been perched on the corner of his desk. A soft breeze wafted from the open window behind him, bringing with it the gentle rustle of palms and the fragile essence of frangipani blossoms. "So what do you think? Are you ready to go home?"

Her sigh was a teasing one, and her eyes twinkled. "I don't know. Ten weeks in the Bahamas . . . body wraps, massages, manicures . . . sun and sand and sipping all kinds of goodies through straws. . . . It's not a bad life."

"But the best is ahead. When does your plane leave?"

"In two hours."

"Nervous?"

"About my debut?" She sent him a helpless look of apology. "A little."

"Will someone be meeting you when you land in Boston?"

"Uh-huh. Beth."

He squinted and raised a finger, trying to keep names straight. "Your business partner, right?"

Lauren smiled. "Right. She's dying to show me everything she's done since I've been gone. She rented the spot we wanted in the Marketplace, and from what she writes, the renovations are nearly done. We've got prints and frames on order and have been in close contact with the artists we'll be representing, so it's just a question of getting everything framed and on display."

"For what it's worth, Lauren, you strike me as a patient but determined woman. I'm sure you'll be successful." He threw a gentle arm over her shoulders as she started for the door. "You'll drop me a line and let me know how things are going?"

"Uh-huh."

"And you've got the name I gave you of the specialist in Boston in case you have a problem?"

"Uh-huh."

"And you'll be sure to eat—and eat well?"

"I'll try."

Releasing her shoulder, he turned to study her face a final time. His gaze took in the symmetry of her nose, the graceful line of her jaw and the now-perfect alignment of her chin before coming to rest with warmth on her pale gray eyes. "Smashing, Lauren. I'm telling you, you look smashing."

"Thank you. Thank you for everything, Richard."

"My pleasure, sweet lady." He gave her hand a tight go-get-'em squeeze, then turned back to his office. The last thing Lauren heard him say was a smug but thoroughly endearing "Good work, Richard. You done us proud this time."

Laughing softly, she retrieved her suitcase from the reception area and headed for the airport.

"You . . . look . . . *smashing!*" was the first thing Beth Lavin could manage to say through her astonishment when, after Lauren had grinned at her for a full minute, she finally realized that it was indeed Lauren Stevenson who stood before her.

The two women hugged each other, and Lauren laughed. "You sound like my doctor."

"Well, he's right!" Beth's eyes were wide. Hands on Lauren's shoulders, she shifted her friend first to one side, then the next. "I don't believe it! Your profile is gorgeous, and you've filled out, and your eyes look huge and wide-set, and you had your hair cut. . . ."

In a self-conscious gesture, one of pure habit, Lauren threaded her fingers into the hair above her ear to draw the thick chestnut fall forward. Then she caught herself. With a concerted effort, she completed the backward swing, letting her hair swirl gently around her ears so that her face was free of the cover she'd hid behind for years. "I really look okay?" There was honest anxiety in her voice.

"You have to ask?"

Lauren gave an awkward half shrug. "I look at myself in the mirror and see a new person, but in my mind I'm the way I've always been."

"I'm no psychologist, but I'd say that's normal." Beth's expression brimmed with excitement and the touch of mischief Lauren knew so well. "A different person—think of the possibilities! What if you were to bump into someone you'd known before, someone like Rafe Johnson—"

"Macho Rafe?"

"Macho Rafe, who would never have thought to look at either of us, but all of a sudden he sees this gorgeous woman and makes his play. You could string him along, then reveal your true identity and cut him off dead. Ah, the satisfaction!"

"You're awful, Beth."

But Beth was staring at her again, this time with a touch of awe. "Maybe. . . . God, you look marvelous," she said, moments before her face twisted in mock horror. "And *I'm* going to look positively plain next to you!"

"Fat chance, Beth Lavin." Lauren hooked her elbow through her friend's and started them both toward the baggage pickup. She knew that Beth was attractive;

she also knew that Beth had worn her dark brown hair in the same long, straight hairstyle for fifteen years and that her clothes—the round-collared blouse, wraparound skirt and flat leather sandals she wore now being a case in point—were as down-country as Lauren's own had always been. "Neither one of us is going to look plain by the time we're ready to open that shop. I learned a lot down there, Beth. There were seminars on hairstyling and makeup and dressing for success. I took tons of notes—"

"You would."

"So would you, so don't give me that," Lauren teased gently. "Tell me, what's the latest with the shop?"

Beth took a deep breath. "I finally got the ad to look the way I wanted it. It'll appear in the next issue of *Boston*. The workmen should be done in another day or two—which is good, because the prints have started arriving. Not to mention the order forms, sales slips and stationery. And the frames and hooks, wire and labels. I've got everything stashed in my apartment."

"How *is* the apartment?"

"I like it. It's compact and within easy walking distance of the shop. Beacon Hill is exciting." Beth paused to ogle her friend again. "I can't believe you!"

"In another minute I'm going to put a bag over my head."

"Don't you dare. I'm thoroughly enjoying riding on your coattails. For that matter, I still wish you'd let me take a bigger apartment so we could room together."

"Rooming together *and* working together, we'd get on each other's nerves in no time. Besides, you want the city, while I want the country. Lots of room, wide-open spaces, trees, peace and quiet."

"You're thinking of that farmhouse."

"Uh-huh."

"You'll be isolated!"

"In Lincoln?" Lauren crinkled her nose. "Nah. I'll only have three acres. When the trees are bare, I'll be able to see neighbors on either side. And the commute will be little more than half an hour."

"But that farmhouse is a wreck!"

"It's simply in need of loving."

"Tell me you've already put in an offer."

Lauren grinned. "I've already put in an offer." At Beth's moan, Lauren delivered an affectionate nudge to her ribs. "When I couldn't get the place out of my mind, I called the realtor. The purchase agreement is ready and waiting to be signed."

"Lauren, Lauren, Lauren, what am I going to do with you?"

Lauren's eyes twinkled. "You're going to put me up at your place tonight. Then, tomorrow morning, you're going to take me on a grand tour of our pride and joy. After that we are both going shopping on Newbury Street."

"Oh?"

"Uh-huh."

"Could be expensive."

"That's right," Lauren agreed remorselessly.

Beth hunched up her shoulders and gave a naughty

chuckle. "I love it, I love it." Then she abruptly narrowed her eyes and flattened her voice to a newspaper-headline drone. "Country bumpkins take city by storm. Effect transformation reminiscent of Clark Kent."

"Clark Kent?" was Lauren's wincing echo.

"Or Wonder Woman, or whomever. Of course, you know we're both a little crazy, don't you?"

"We're twenty-nine. We deserve it."

"I'll tell that to the creditors when they come calling."

Lauren Stevenson wasn't worried about the creditors. She wasn't a spendthrift, but she'd finally come to the realization that life was too short to be lived in a cocoon of timidity. Thanks to her saving prudently and the legacy she'd received when her brother had died nearly a year ago, Lauren had enough money to buy and renovate the farmhouse, pay what little wasn't covered by insurance for the corrective surgery she'd had, get a wardrobe befitting the new Lauren and establish the business.

"Here we go," she said as her luggage appeared on the revolving carousel. "Did you drive over or take a cab?"

"I drove. Your poor car was so glad to see me, I swear it got all choked up."

Lauren grunted. "Must need an oil change. On second thought, it needs to get out of the city. See, *it* wants to live in the country, too."

They left the enclosure of the terminal and headed for the parking lot. "Will you be driving north this weekend?" Beth ventured.

"To see my parents? I guess I'd better."

"I'd think you'd be excited—the new you and all."

Lauren grimaced. "You know my parents. For ultra-liberals, they're as narrow as a pair of shoelaces. They didn't see the need for facial reconstruction. They thought I was just fine before."

"But medically, you were suffering!"

"I know that and you know that, and one part of them must know it, too. They're both brilliant, albeit locked in their ivory towers. I think they associate plastic surgery with vanity alone, and vanity isn't high on their list of admired traits. They said they loved me the way I was, and I'm sure they did, because that's what being a parent is all about. But let me tell you, I feel so much better now, even aside from the medical issue, I'm not sure they'd understand."

"Of course they would."

Lauren didn't argue further. Her trepidation about seeing her parents went far beyond the reconstructive surgery she'd had. She was starting a new life, and much of that life was being underwritten by her brother's bequest. Her parents resented that. Brad had been estranged from the family for eleven years pre-ceding his death. Colin and Nadine Stevenson had nei-ther forgotten nor forgiven what they'd considered to be their only son's abdication from the throne of the literati.

Lauren sighed. "Well, whatever the case may be, I'll see them this weekend. It may be the last time I'll be able to in a while." Lips toying with a smile, she darted a knowing glance at Beth. "I have a feeling that the next few weeks are going to be hectic."

"Hectic" was putting it mildly, though the pace was interlaced with such excitement that Lauren wouldn't have dreamed of complaining. With the completion of the redecoration of the shop, she and Beth began transferring things from Beth's apartment. Prints were framed and hung on the walls. Large art folders, filled with a myriad of additional prints and silk screens, were set in open cases on the floor for easy browsing. Vees of mat board in an endless assortment of colors were placed on Plexiglas stands atop the large butcher-block checkout counter, behind which were systematically arranged frame-corner samples, each attached to the wall with Velcro to facilitate their removal and replacement. Bolts of hand-screened fabric were attractively displayed beside bins containing unstained-wood frame kits; matching pillows were suspended from the ceiling like bananas from a tree.

Lauren signed the agreement on the farmhouse in Lincoln and, since it was already vacant, moved in a short week later. Her enthusiasm wasn't the slightest bit dampened when she saw at firsthand the amount of renovation the place would need. She had only to stand on her front porch and look across the lush yard to the forested growth surrounding her, or to smell the roses that climbed the porch-side trellis, or to listen to the birds as they whistled their spring mating ritual, to know that she'd made the right decision.

And, more than anything, she had only to look in the mirror to realize that she'd truly begun a new life.

In keeping with that new life, she and Beth did go shopping. They bought chic slacks, skirts, bright summer sweaters and lightweight dresses. They bought shoes and costume jewelry to coordinate with the outfits, all the while feeling slightly irresponsible yet enjoying every minute of it. Neither of them had been irresponsible before in their lives, but now they had earned the luxury.

Three weeks after Lauren returned from the Bahamas, the print-and-frame shop opened. It was the second week of June, and the fair-weather influx of visitors to the Marketplace kept a steady stream of shoppers circulating. With sales brisk, Lauren and Beth were ecstatic, so much so that on the first Friday night after closing, they took themselves to nearby Houlihan's to celebrate.

"If business continues this way, we'll have to hire someone to help," Lauren suggested. They were sitting at the crowded bar nursing cool drinks while they waited for their table.

"Tell me about it," Beth complained, but in delight. "There isn't enough time during the day to do bookkeeping, so I've been taking care of it at night. And you're going to need time to work with printmakers and the framer."

"I'll call the museum. Maybe they'll know of someone who'd be interested. If not, we can advertise in the newspaper."

In slow amazement, Beth shook her head. "I can't

believe how good things were this week. We really lucked out with the location. There are people all over the place."

"Summer's always a busy season, what with tourists in the city. The Fanueil Hall is one of *the* spots to see."

"Wintertime's supposedly as good. At least, that's what Tom next door—you know, at the sports shop— told me."

Lauren's lips twitched mischievously. "So you've befriended Tom, have you? See what a new hairdo and clothes can do?"

Raking a hand through wavy black hair that had newly been cut to shoulder length, Beth wiggled her brows. "Look who's talking. That guy over there hasn't taken his eyes off you since we walked in."

"He's probably in a drunken stupor and I just happened into his line of vision."

"That's a crazy thing to say. You don't believe how good you look!"

Beth was right. Lauren had been accustomed to being practically invisible where men were concerned, and old habits die hard. Now she dared a quick glance in the mirror behind the bar to remind herself of the woman she'd become. Even her smart cotton sundress of crimson and cream was an eye-catcher.

With a conspiratorial glimmer in her eyes, she turned again to Beth. "Tell me about him. I don't want to be obvious and stare."

Beth had no such qualms, but she spoke in little more than a whisper. "He's of medium height and build and is wearing a brown suit. His hair's dark, a little too short. He's got aviator-style glasses—must be an affectation, since they don't go with the rest of him." Her voice suddenly frosted. "Oops, there's a wedding band." She instantly swiveled in her seat and stared straight ahead. "Forget him. He'd only be trouble."

Lauren grinned. "Forgotten."

"Doesn't it bother you? I mean, I'm sure he'd make a play for you if you flirted a little, and the bum's married."

Shrugging with her eyebrows alone, Lauren took a sip of her drink. "I think you're making too much of it. I was probably right the first time. He's probably in a fog."

Beth grew more thoughtful. "We're going to have to do something about this situation."

"What situation?"

"Our love lives."

"What love lives?"

"That's the point. They're nonexistent. We have to meet guys."

"We have. There's Tom from the sports shop, and Anthony from the music store across the way, and Peter, who sells those super hand-painted sweatshirts, and your neighbors, those three bachelors . . . We could always reconsider and go to one of their parties."

Beth snorted. "We'd probably get high just walking into the room. I'm sure they're on something. Whenever I run into them, they seem off the wall. I'm telling you, we were smart to chicken out last time.

We're so naive that the place could be raided and everyone would run out through the back and leave us holding the bag."

"Hmm. Maybe we'd meet a cute cop."

"I don't know, Lauren. I still think you should have gone out with that guy who came in on Wednesday."

"He was a total stranger, just browsing around."

"He was nice enough. And he did ask you out for drinks. For that matter, the fellow who came in this morning was even nicer and better-looking."

"He was a pest—trying to be so nonchalant about asking where I come from and where I live and, by the way, what my astrological sign is. I don't know what my astrological sign is. I've never been into that."

"You're scared."

Lauren hesitated for only a minute. "Yup."

"But why? You've dated before."

"That was different."

"You're right. This is supposed to be a new life you're leading!"

"On the outside it is. On the inside, well, I guess it'll take me a little longer to catch up. I don't know, Beth. Those guys seemed so . . . fast. So slick and sophisticated."

"You look slick and sophisticated."

"*Look*, not *am*. You know me as well as anyone does. I've lived a pretty sedate life. What dates I had were with quiet men, more serious, bookish types."

"Bo-ring."

"Maybe. But I'm not a swinger."

"Maybe you're gonna have to learn."

The hostess called their table then, but Beth picked up the conversation the instant they were seated in the glass-domed room just below street level. "Maybe we should try a singles bar, or a dating service."

"If we didn't have the guts to go to your neighbors' party, we'd never have the guts to go to a singles bar. And blind dates give me the willies."

"Blind dates gave the 'old' you the willies. The 'new' you doesn't have anything to worry about. Besides, it's not really a blind date if you go through a dating service. You get to express your preferences and pick through the possibilities."

"Just like they get to pick through us. Uh-uh, Beth. I don't really think I'm up for that."

"Well, we have to do something. Here we are, two wonderful women who are bright and available, and we should be having dinner with two equally as captivating men."

"Maybe we should put an ad in the paper," Lauren joked, then promptly scowled. "Only problem is that we're cowards. All talk, no action." Her eyes grew dreamy. "They say that good things come to those who wait. I'm more than willing to wait if one day some gorgeous guy who is bright and available and gentle and easygoing will walk up to me and introduce himself."

"According to women's lib," Beth offered tongue-in-cheek, "we shouldn't have to sit back and wait. We can take the bull by the horns."

Lauren glanced over Beth's shoulder toward the table at which a lone man sat, just finishing his dinner.

He wasn't gorgeous, but he was certainly pleasant-looking. When he looked up and caught her eye, he smiled. Curious, Beth turned also; he shared his smile with her.

"There's your chance," Lauren coaxed in a stage whisper filled with good-humored challenge. "I don't want him, so he's all yours. Go ahead. Take the bull by the horns."

Turning back to their own table, Beth opened her menu and concentrated on its contents. Lauren followed suit. Neither woman noticed when the lone man took his check from the waitress and headed for the cash register.

CHAPTER TWO

The second week of the shop's existence was as promising as the first had been. Just as Lauren was wondering how she and Beth would be able to cope with the continued pace on their own, a freelance photographer came in, peddling his wares. He was a young man—Lauren guessed him to be no more than twenty-five—and his pictures were good. He was also looking for part-time work to pay for the increasing costs of his materials and equipment. She hired him instantly, and neither she nor Beth regretted the decision. Now they could take an hour off here or there—albeit separately—to do paperwork, go out for lunch or shop through downtown Boston.

On one such occasion, a week after Jamie had signed on, Lauren returned to the shop with a new sweater in a bag under her arm and a faint pallor on her face. Beth quickly joined her in the back room. "Are you okay?"

Setting the bag on the desk, Lauren sank into a chair. "I think so. You wouldn't believe what just happened to me, Beth. I'd bought this sweater and was walking back along Newbury Street when a car lost control and veered onto the sidewalk. I was daydreaming, feeling on top of the world, looking at my reflection as I passed store windows. I mean, I was so caught up in being happy that I wasn't paying attention to what was going on around me. If it hadn't been for some stranger who grabbed me out of the way in the nick of time, God only knows what would have happened!"

"Don't think about that. You're safe, and that's all that matters. Was the driver drunk?"

"Who knows? He regained control of the car and went on his merry way again. Didn't even bother to stop and make sure no one was hurt."

"Bastard."

"Mmm."

"The stranger who saved you . . . was he cute?"

"He was a she," Lauren snapped, but her annoyance was contrived. "And what kind of question is that to ask at a time like this?"

"Have to restore a little humor here. Just think how romantic it would have been if you'd been snatched from the hands of death by a tall, dark and handsome stranger. You could have fainted away in his arms, and he'd have lifted you, holding you ever so gently against his rock-hard chest while he gazed, smitten, upon your lovely face."

Lauren rolled her eyes. "Oh, God."

Beth wagged a finger at her. "Someday it might happen. Miracles are like that, y'know."

"Is this the same woman who was putting in a plug for women's lib not so long ago?" Lauren asked the calendar on the wall, looking back at Beth only when she felt a hand on her arm.

"Are you okay now?" The question was soft and filled with concern. "Want a cold drink or something?"

Taking a deep breath, Lauren shook her head. "I'm fine. It was after the fact, while I was walking, that the shakes set in. But I'm better now. I'd really like to get back to work. That'll keep my mind occupied."

It did, and by the time Lauren arrived in Lincoln that evening, she'd pretty much forgotten the incident. By the next day, it was lost amid more important and immediate activities relating to the shop.

That night she went home, changed into a T-shirt and jeans and made herself dinner, dutifully following the guidelines Richard Bowen had given her. It was an effort at times, since she seemed to be eating so much, but she'd gained three of the five pounds Richard had prescribed, and she had to agree that they looked good on her.

What with the time demands that the shop had made since her return from the Bahamas, she'd had precious little opportunity to organize her thoughts with regard to renovating the farmhouse. Now, pen and paper in hand, she walked from room to room, making lists of what she wanted to have done. The realtor who'd sold her the house had given her the names of a local contractor, a carpenter, an electrician and a plumber. Though she wasn't about to hire any one of them without checking them out further, she wanted to have her thoughts together before arranging preliminary meetings.

After more than an hour of taking detailed notes, she put down the pen and paper and went out to the front porch. The night was clear, the moon a silver crescent in the star-studded sky. On an impulse, she wandered across the yard and stopped at its center, then tipped her head back and singled out a star to wish on.

But what did one wish for when life was already so good? She was totally healthy for the first time in many years. She had a new look, which she adored. She had a new business, and it was well on its way to becoming a success. She had a home of her own, with potential enough to keep her happy for a long, long time.

What did one wish for? Perhaps a man. Perhaps children. In time.

Lowering her head, she started slowly back toward the house. A sound caught her ear. She stopped and frowned. It was a sound of nature, yet odd. It had been distinctly unfriendly.

When it came again, she whirled around. A low growl. She cocked her head toward the nearby trees, then narrowed her eyes on the creature that slowly advanced on her. A dog. She breathed a sigh of relief. Probably one of the neighbors' pets.

Pressing a hand to her racing heart, she spoke aloud. "You frightened me, dog. Is that any way to greet a new neighbor?" As she took a step forward to befriend the animal, it bared its teeth and issued another growl, this one clearly in warning. Lauren held her hands out, palms up, and said softly, "I won't hurt you, boy." She lowered one hand. "Here. Sniff."

Rather than approaching her, the dog growled again, accompanying the hostile sound with a crouch that suggested an imminent attack.

"Hey, don't get upset—" She barely had time to manage the tremulous words when the dog was on her, knocking her to the ground, snarling viciously. Struggling to fend off the beast, she put her arms up to protect herself and kicked out. But as quickly as it had lunged, the dog retreated, galloping toward the trees and disappearing into the dense growth.

Trembling wildly, Lauren pushed herself up to a seated position. Then, not willing to take a chance that the dog might return, she stumbled to her feet and made a frantic beeline for the house.

Once inside, she leaned back against the firmly shut door, closed her eyes and dragged in a shaky breath. When the worst of the shock had subsided, anger set in. Had it not been so late at night, she would have called the Youngs, her neighbors on the side from which the dog had come. Then again, she realized, perhaps it was lucky it was too late to make a call. Furious as she was that anyone would let such a savage animal loose in even as rural an area as this, she was apt to say something she might later regret.

She'd met Carol Young only once. She didn't want to alienate the woman, or her husband, or one of their teenaged boys. Better to let herself calm down. She'd call tomorrow.

Hence, from work the next morning, she dialed the Youngs' number and was relieved to hear Carol herself answer the phone. "Carol, this is Lauren Stevenson. We met several weeks ago when I moved in next door."

"Sure, Lauren. It's good to hear from you. How's it going?"

"Really well. . . . I hope I'm not dragging you away from anything."

"Don't be silly. One of the luxuries of working at a computer terminal out of my house is that I can take a break whenever I want. The boys have gone to visit their grandparents in Maryland for a week, so I've got more than enough time for a phone call or two. How's the house?"

"Pretty raw still. I've been so busy here at the shop that I haven't had much of a chance to look into hiring workers to fix things up. But that's not why I called." Lauren chose her words carefully, striving to be as diplomatic as possible. "I had an awful scare last night. I was walking out in the yard sometime around eleven when I was attacked by a dog."

"*Attacked?* Are you all right?"

"I'm fine. The dog jumped me, bared its teeth and made ugly noises, but it ran off before it did any harm."

"My God! I didn't think there were any wild dogs

around here!"

"Then . . . it's not yours?"

"God, no. Is that what you thought?"

"It came from the trees on your side. . . . I'm sorry, I just assumed . . ."

"You should have called us last night. We might have been able to help you track it down. What did it look like?"

"It was big and dark. Short-haired. Maybe a Doberman, but it was too dark out for me to see the dog's exact coloration, and besides, I was too terrified to notice much of anything."

"You poor girl. I'd have been terrified, too." Carol paused, thinking. "To my knowledge, no one in the neighborhood has a dog like that, certainly not one that would attack a person. Sometimes strange animals do wander into the area, though. Maybe you should call the local police."

Lauren was lukewarm to that idea. As a new resident, she hated to make a stir. "I—I don't think that's necessary. As long as I know the dog wasn't from the immediate vicinity, I feel better. It's probably a watchdog that escaped and got lost. And it didn't hurt me, much as it looked like it could have."

"Listen, we'll keep an eye out for it, and I'll mention it to some of the other neighbors. But if you catch sight of it again, you really should file a complaint. There's no reason why you should be frightened to walk on your own property."

Lauren sighed. "I'll be on guard in the future. Thanks, Carol. You've been a help."

"I wish I could do more. Let me know if something comes up, okay?"

"Okay."

As Lauren hung up the phone, Beth straightened up from where she'd been leaning unnoticed against the door. "A dog? First a car, now a dog. Lord, the new you is attracting some pretty weird elements."

"Go ahead," Lauren teased, "have a good laugh at my expense."

"I'm not laughing." Beth rubbed her hands together in anticipation of high drama. "Maybe someone's out to get you . . . someone who lived in that old farmhouse a century ago and whose ghost will never be laid to rest until the rightful owner of the place returns."

"Beth . . ."

Beth held up a hand. "No, listen. Suppose, just suppose, the ghost is determined to run you out of town, so it plots all kinds of little 'accidents' designed to scare you to death—"

"Beth!"

"And then some gorgeous hunk arrives and just happens to have a secret weapon that can zap even a ghost and reduce it to—to a shredded sheet. . . ."

Lauren sat back in her chair, helpless to contain the beginnings of a grin. "Are you done?"

"Oh, no. The best part comes after the ghost is shredded and you and the gorgeous hunk fall madly in love and live happily ever after."

"Why aren't you working?"

"Because Jamie's working."

"I think *you* should be working." Lauren pushed herself out of her seat. "I think *I* should be working." With a fond squeeze to Beth's arm as she passed, she returned to the front of the shop.

Several days later, Lauren knew that she had to do something about starting the renovation work on her house. The garage door had unexpectedly slammed to the ground when she'd been within mere inches of it. Ironically, if the garage had been nearly as old as the farmhouse itself, its doors would have swung open from the center to the sides, and she would never have been in danger of a skull fracture. But the garage had been added twenty-five years before. Apparently, she mused in frustration, it had been as neglected by recent owners as the house.

She made several calls, setting up appointments to discuss repairs with the men whose names she'd been given. None of them had impressed her on the phone, though she reasoned that there was no harm in meeting with them before she sought out additional contacts. She wanted her home to be perfect, and she was willing to pay to make it so.

With that settled in her mind, she sat down on the living room floor, using the low coffee table as a desk, to write up orders for the framer. But she was distracted. Repeatedly her pen grew still and her gaze wandered to the window. It was dark as pitch outside. She was alone. Anyone could see in, watch her, study her.

Cursing both Beth for her fanciful imaginings and

herself for her own surprising susceptibility, she returned to her work. But that night, to her chagrin, she fell asleep wondering if one-hundred-year-old ghosts were capable of sabotaging twenty-five-year-old garage doors.

Shortly after noon on the following day, Lauren saw him for the first time. She was working in the front window of the shop, replacing a framed picture that had been bought that morning, when she happened to glance toward the bench just outside. He was sitting there, quietly and intently. And he was staring at her.

With a tight smile, she looked quickly away, finished hanging the new print, then took refuge in the inner sanctum of the shop.

Fifteen minutes later, during a brief lull in business, she glanced out to find that he hadn't moved. One arm slung over the back of the bench, one knee crossed casually over the other, he appeared to be innocently people-watching—until his gaze penetrated the front window once more.

Again Lauren looked away, this time wondering why she had. There was nothing unusual about a man sitting on a bench in the Marketplace; people did it all the time. And this man, wearing a short-sleeved plaid shirt, jeans and sneakers, looked like a typical passerby. Though he wasn't munching on fried dough or licking an ice cream cone, as so many of the others did, she assumed he was enjoying the pleasant atmosphere. Or waiting for someone. Or simply resting his legs. The fact that he kept looking into the shop was understandable, since it was smack in front of him.

A telephone call came through from one of the print-makers she'd been trying to reach; then customers occupied her time for the next hour and a half. She'd nearly forgotten about the man outside until she left the shop to buy stamps, and even then she was per-plexed that she should think of him at all.

He was nowhere to be seen.

At home that night, Lauren was strangely on edge. She didn't know why, and for lack of anything better, she blamed it on the two cups of coffee she'd had that afternoon.

With a critical eye, she looked around the kitchen as she waited for the bouillabaisse she'd bought at a gourmet take-out shop to heat. She intended to do this room in white—white cabinets with white ash trim, white stove and refrigerator, white ceramic tile on the floor. The accent would be pale blue, as in enamel cookware, patterned wallpaper, prints on the wall. Perhaps she'd order a pale blue pleated miniblind—not that she'd originally planned to put anything on the windows, but it occurred to her that she might like the option of privacy for moments like these when the night seemed mysterious.

She was edgy. Too much coffee. That was all.

The following morning, the man was back. Wearing a crisp white polo shirt with his jeans, he was sitting on the bench again, this time with his legs sprawled before him.

"Remarkable, isn't he?" Beth quipped, coming up beside Lauren.

"Who?"

"That guy you're looking at. Have you ever seen such gorgeous hair?" It was light brown with a sun-streaked sheen and was neatly brushed, but thick and on the long side.

"No."

"Or such long legs?"

"No."

"Wonder who he is."

"I don't know."

"Probably just another tourist. Why is it the good ones are here today, gone tomorrow?"

"This one was here yesterday."

"What?"

Lauren blinked once, dragging her gaze from the man to her friend. Absently she wiped damp palms on her slim-cut green linen skirt. "I saw him here yesterday."

Beth's eyes widened. "You're kidding! Do you think he's waiting for . . . us?"

"Come on, Beth. Why in the world would he be waiting for us?"

"Maybe he heard about these two terrific ladies who own the print-and-frame shop, and he's come to investigate."

"If he had any guts, he'd come in."

"If we had any guts, we'd go out."

"Well, we don't, and apparently he doesn't, either, so that's that." As the two watched, the man got to his feet and ambled off. "That's that," Lauren repeated, not quite sure whether to be relieved or disappointed. There had been something fascinating about the man, not only his legs and his hair but also a certain sturdiness. She wondered if he'd ever owned a black dog that snarled. Then she promptly pushed that thought from her mind, along with all other thoughts of the man—until she caught sight of him again that afternoon.

At first he walked slowly past the shop without sparing it a glance. A few minutes later he returned from the opposite direction, this time pausing near the door before heading for the bench. When Lauren saw him sink onto it, leaning forward with his knees spread and his hands clasped between them, she couldn't help but grow apprehensive. There was something definitely suspicious about the way he glanced toward the shop, then away, then back again.

"Who *is* that man?" she whispered to Beth, who promptly looked up from the VISA charge form she was filling out to follow Lauren's worried gaze.

"So he's back, is he?" Beth resumed writing but spoke under her breath. "He's a little too rugged for my tastes. You can have him."

"I don't want him," Lauren grumbled from the corner of her mouth, "but I would like to know why he's been loitering around here for two days straight."

"Why don't you go and ask him?" Beth murmured, then, smiling, handed the charge slip and a pen to her customer. "If you'll just sign this and put your address and phone number at the bottom . . ."

Lauren whispered back in a miffed tone of voice. "I can't just walk out there and *ask* him! He's probably got a very good reason for being there, and I'd feel like a fool."

"Then stop worrying. I'm sure he's harmless."

Lauren wasn't so sure. The man was too intent in his scrutiny of the shop, and she felt the touch of his gaze too strongly to forget him.

When a customer approached her to buy a piece of fabric and have it stretched onto a frame, Lauren welcomed the diversion. When another customer selected a print and needed advice on its framing, she was more than happy to oblige. When a third customer entered the shop in search of several prints to coordinate with swatches of fabric and wallpaper, she immersed herself in the project.

By the time the closing hour drew near, Lauren was tired. She was in the back room, dutifully updating inventory cards and looking forward to a leisurely drive home, a quiet dinner and what was left of the evening with a good book.

"Lauren?" The low urgency in Beth's voice brought Lauren's head up quickly. "He's here, asking for *you*."

"Who—"

"Him." Beth's eyes darted back over her shoulder. "The guy from the bench."

Lauren put down the cards. "He's asking for *me?*"

"By name."

"How did he . . . he must have . . . where is he?"

"Right here," Beth mouthed in a way that would have been comical had Lauren been feeling particularly confident.

But she wasn't. This man was different. Not boring-looking. Not slick and sophisticated-looking. Very . . . different.

Beth made an urgent gesture with her hand.

"I'm coming. I'm coming," Lauren murmured unsteadily. She stood up, smoothing the hip-length ivory cotton sweater over her skirt and squared her shoulders. Then, praying that she looked more composed than she felt, she slowly and reluctantly left her refuge.

CHAPTER THREE

He was much taller close up than he'd appeared through the shop window. And broader in the shoulders. And more tanned. What was most surprising, though, was that he seemed just a little unsure of himself.

"Lauren Stevenson?" he asked cautiously.

She'd come to a stop several feet away and rested her hand on the butcher-block table. "Yes?"

As he studied her more closely, his puzzlement grew. "It's really strange. You're not at all as I expected you to be."

Lauren held her breath for a minute, then asked with a caution of her own, "What had you expected?"

"Someone . . . well, someone different."

If he had some connection to her past, she realized, not only was his puzzlement understandable but his tact was commendable. Still, she couldn't deny her wariness. The man had been staking her out for two days. "Do you know me? Should I know you?"

For the first time, he smiled. It was a self-conscious smile, endearing in its way. "My name's Matthew Kruger. Matt." He hesitated for a split second. "I was a friend of your brother's."

Lauren wasn't sure what *she* had expected, but it hadn't been this. "Brad's friend?" She was unable to hide either her surprise or her skepticism.

"That's right. I was with him just after the accident. I'm . . . sorry about his death."

"I am, too," she returned honestly, her brow lightly furrowed as she studied Matthew Kruger. He didn't quite fit into the mold she'd constructed of Brad and his friends. Strange that she'd never heard of him. Then again, perhaps not so strange. She hadn't been any closer to Brad before his death than her parents had been. "But . . . it's been a year since he died." Silently she asked herself why this so-called friend of Brad's had waited this long to contact her.

"I know you weren't close, but Brad did mention you to me several times, and since I had to come east on business, I thought I'd look you up."

"What kind of business are you in?"

Another split second's hesitation. "I'm a builder. The development firm I work for has just contracted to do some work in western Massachusetts. I'm here to set things up—to get the ball rolling, so to speak."

She nodded. A builder. Given the pale crow's feet at the corners of his eyes, he was not a builder who directed things from his desk. He was a builder who got his hands dirty. And whose body was well-toned through hard physical labor. *That* she could associate with the image she'd formed of her brother's new life and friends, though if her parents' opinion had been valid, she would have expected someone far coarser. On the surface, at least, Matthew Kruger didn't appear to be coarse. "Clean and all-American" was a more apt description. Could the surface appearance be deceptive?

"I see," she said. Then, feeling uncomfortable, she averted her gaze. In truth, she'd known little about her brother and his way of life . . . and then there was the matter of this man's physical presence. He intimidated her. "Have you, uh, have you been in Boston very long?"

"A week."

She nodded.

"I'm staying at the Long Wharf Marriott."

"If your work is in the western part of the state, wouldn't it be easier to stay out there?"

"I have been, but our investors are here and there's some paperwork to do, so I decided to take a few days to sightsee." When he suddenly looked beyond her, Lauren swung her head around.

"I'm going to lock up," Beth whispered, darting a curious glance at Matt as she started to pass.

Lauren reached out and caught her arm. "Uh, Beth, this is Matthew Kruger. He is—was—a friend of Brad's." Lauren still had her doubts about that, but saying it simplified the introduction. "Matt, Beth Lavin."

Beth had known Brad Stevenson before he'd struck out on his own, and since she wasn't a member of his immediate family, she'd been more objective about his departure. Hands clasped tightly before her, she smiled shyly at Matt. "I'm pleased to meet you."

"The pleasure's mine," Matt said, returning her smile. His gaze quickly grew apologetic when it sought Lauren's again. "I don't want to hold you up if there's something you should be doing now."

Lauren opened her mouth to say that she really did have work to finish, but Beth spoke first. "Oh, you're not holding her up. We were pretty much done for the day when you came in. I finished the inventory cards, Lauren. Why don't you and Matt take off? I'll close up."

The last thing Lauren wanted to do was to take off with Matt. She wasn't convinced he was who he said he was, and even if it was so, they were on opposite sides of a rift. Besides, he hadn't asked her to "take off" with him.

As though on cue, he did. "How about it, Lauren?" He paused, then took a quick breath. "I heard there was a sunset cruise around the harbor. If we hurry, we can make it."

"Uh, I really shouldn't. . . ."

"Go on, Lauren," Beth coaxed. Subtlety had never been her forte. "You haven't been out much. It's a beautiful night. The fresh air will do you good."

"I'd really like the company," Matt urged softly.

His last words trapped Lauren. If he'd come on strong, she might have easily refused. But he sounded sincere, and she caught a drift of the same unsureness she'd seen when she'd first faced him. Though large and rugged-looking, he had an odd gentleness to him. His eyes were brown, warm and soft. At that moment they hinted at vulnerability; above all, Lauren Stevenson was a sucker for vulnerability.

Releasing the breath she'd subconsciously been holding, Lauren acknowledged an internal truce. "I'll get my things," she whispered.

Soon after, she and Matt were walking side by side toward the waterfront. He was as quiet as she, casting intermittent glances her way, and she wondered if he felt as strange as she did.

In an attempt to break the silence, she asked the first thing that came to mind. "How did you know I was in Boston?"

"Your parents told me."

"My *parents!*"

He sent her a sidelong glance. "Shouldn't they have?"

"No—yes—I mean, I'm just surprised. That's all."

They walked a little farther before he spoke again. "You're thinking that they wouldn't have willingly given your address to any friend of Brad's."

"I . . . guess that says it."

A muscle in his jaw flexed. "At least you're honest."

She shrugged. "How much do you know about Brad's reasons for leaving?"

"Only what Brad told me—that your parents couldn't accept his wanting to work with his hands rather than with his mind, that they flipped out when he left college and pretty much washed their hands of him."

Perhaps Matt had known Brad after all. "Spoken that way, it sounds cruel."

"It was, in a way. Brad was badly hurt by the split."

"So were my parents, yet none of the three tried to mend it."

"And you, Lauren? Did you do anything?"

Her gaze shot sharply to his, then softened and fell. "No," she admitted quietly. "I think I might have in time. Then time ran out."

"You regretted the distance?"

"Brad was my only brother. We had no other siblings. He was four years older than I, and his interests were always different. We weren't close as kids, but I like to think that we might have found common ground as we'd gotten older."

They had reached Atlantic Avenue. Matt put a light hand on her elbow as they trotted across to avoid an onrushing car. He dropped it when they reached the median strip, where they waited for a minute before finishing the crossing.

"Then you were seventeen when Brad left."

Lauren blew out a breath. "You really *do* know about Brad, don't you?"

"He told me he was twenty-one when he dropped out. If you were four years his junior . . ." Matt's voice trailed off and his features tensed. "Did you think I was lying about being his friend?"

"No. Well, maybe. I have to take your word for it that you knew him, since he can't verify it, can he?"

"Are you always distrustful?"

She looked him in the eye. "Only when I see someone lurking outside my shop for two days before coming in."

"Oh. You saw me."

"Yes." Was that a sudden rush of color to his cheeks? She wondered if it was guilt, or embarrassment. In case it was the latter, she softened her tone. "I assume you weren't trying to hide."

"Actually," he confessed, "I was trying to get up the nerve to come in."

That was a new one in her experience. "Why ever would you have to get up the nerve to approach *me?*"

"Several reasons. First, I knew there were hard feelings where Brad was concerned and I wasn't sure how I'd be received. Second, I wasn't sure if it was really you." His gaze slid from one to another of her features. Again that puzzled look crossed his face. "You look so different. Very . . . very pretty."

Lauren clutched the shoulder strap of her bag more tightly. "Brad had a picture."

"An old one. You were sixteen at the time."

For reasons she wasn't about to analyze, she didn't want to go into the matter of her reconstructive surgery. "It was a long time ago," she said quietly. "People change."

"I'll say," Matt drawled. "Still, it's amazing . . ." He seemed about to go on, and for an instant Lauren wondered just how much Brad had told him about her. She was saved when he looked up and announced tentatively, "I think this is it."

She followed his gaze toward where the wharf and its cruise boats loomed. "Looks like it. This is really the blind leading the blind. I went to college in Boston, but that was a while ago. I haven't been back for very long."

"Are you living here in the city?"

The glance she sent him held subtle accusation, but there was a whisper of amusement underlying her words. "What did my parents tell you?"

Reading her loud and clear, he fought back a grin. "Just the name of the shop. I assume they wanted to keep things on a strictly business level."

"I'm sure they did."

"And you?"

"And me what?"

He was suddenly serious. "Would you put me down because I don't have a Ph.D. in some esoteric subject?"

"I don't have a Ph.D. in *any* subject."

"You have a master's degree in art. I never went to college."

"But you're successful in what you do. At least, if you're traveling across the country, the firm you work for must be doing well . . . you must be valued." Having doubted his story such a short time ago, she amazed herself by coming to his defense. Suckers for vulnerability weren't always the most prudent. She took a deep breath. "No, Matt. I'm not like my parents. Brad wasn't the only one who had differences with them. It's just taken me a little longer to act on those differences."

Their conversation was cut short when they arrived at the ticket booth. Matt paid their fare, and they boarded the boat. Wending their way through the other groups that had gathered, they climbed to the top deck and found an empty place by the rail to look back at the city skyline.

"I love Boston," Lauren mused after several minutes of silent appreciation.

"Explain."

"It's bigger than Bennington and that much more exciting, yet smaller than New York and that much more manageable. You can understand it, get to know it. It's livable."

"You have an apartment?"

"A farmhouse."

"In the *city*?"

"In Lincoln—" She caught herself and scowled at him. "That was sneaky. You took advantage of me when my defenses were down."

He grinned amiably. "Sorry about that. Do you really own a farmhouse?"

Somehow further prevarication seemed silly. "Uh-huh. It's old and needs a whole load of work before its potential can be realized, but it's on a great piece of land and has charm, real charm."

"Old places are like that. History adds character. That's one of the reasons *I* like Boston. Wandering around, seeing where the Boston Massacre took place or where the Declaration of Independence was first read—it gives you goose bumps." He paused, staring at Lauren. "Why are you grinning?"

"You and goose bumps. You're so big and solid. It seems a contradiction."

"No," he said gently. "The goose bumps I'm talking about have an emotional cause. Big and solid don't necessarily mean unfeeling."

"I didn't mean—"

"I know." His point made, he left it at that.

They lapsed into silence, watching as the gangplank was drawn up and the boat inched away from the dock. Soon the engines growled louder. The boat made a laborious turn, then picked up speed and entered the main body of the harbor, moving at a steady, if chugging, pace.

"Would you like a drink?" Matt asked.

Lauren drew herself back from her immersion in the scenery. "No—uh, make that yes. A wine spritzer, if they can handle it, or lemonade. Something cool."

With a nod, he made his way back across the deck and disappeared down the stairs leading to the lower level. Following his progress, Lauren had to admit that he was as attractive as any other man in sight. It wasn't that he was beautiful in the classic sense; his chin was too square, his nose a shade crooked, his skin too weathered. But he exuded good health and strength and competence. He'd crossed the shimmying deck without faltering.

The wind whipped through her hair as she turned to face the sea once more. She concentrated on the sights—the Aquarium, the Harbor Towers, the piers with their assortment of fishing boats and tankers, the waterfront restaurants. Only when Matt returned and she smiled did she realize how much nicer the setting seemed with him by her side.

"Two lemonades." He handed her one. "The spritzer was beyond the bartender, and the other drinks were heavier. There were some hot dogs down there, but they looked pretty sad." He took a bag of potato chips from under his arm, opened it and held it out. She munched one, then washed it down with a drink.

"Tell me about Brad," she surprised herself by saying.

Somber-eyed, he studied her expression. "I'm not sure you really want to know."

She attributed his hesitancy to her own obvious ambivalence. "You may be right. But . . . I guess I really am curious. I've never met anyone who knew him after he left. I'm not sure I should pass the opportunity by."

Matt tossed several chips into his mouth. "What do you want to know?" he asked between stilted bites.

"Did he work for your company?"

"No."

"Had he always been in San Francisco?" She knew that was where he'd died.

"He started out in Sacramento."

"As a carpenter."

"That's right. By the time he came to San Francisco, though, he was doing a lot of designing."

"Designing what?"

Matt hesitated for an instant. "Houses, mostly. Some office parks. As an architect, he was a natural."

"Is that how he was viewed—as an architect?"

"No. He didn't have the credentials. He was like a ghost-writer, presenting rough sketches to the company's architect, who then embellished and formalized the sketches."

"Were you familiar with his company?"

"We were competitors."

The words were simple and straightforward, yet something about the way they'd been offered gave Lauren the impression that Matt hadn't particularly cared for Brad's outfit. "But still, you were friends. How did that work?"

Matt seemed to relax somewhat. "Very comfortably. Our respective superiors held the patent on rivalry. Brad and I rather enjoyed fraternizing with the enemy."

"How did you meet?"

"In a bowling league."

Her expression grew distant. "Funny, I can't picture Brad bowling. But then, I can't picture him sweating on the roof of a house, either." She tore herself from her musings. "What else did you do together?"

"Ate out. Sometimes double-dated. We vacationed together—there were six of us, actually. We rafted down the Colorado, went on horseback through parts of Montana. It was fun."

"Very macho," she teased and was rewarded by a sheepish grin from Matt.

"I suppose."

Her smile lingered for a minute before fading. "Brad never married." She'd learned that when she'd been informed by the lawyer that she was the sole beneficiary of her brother's estate. "I wonder why."

"Maybe he never met the right girl, one who could accept him as he was."

"Have you ever married?" she asked on impulse. Matt stared at her for a minute, then shook his head. "Why not?"

"Same reason."

She pondered his answer quietly. "I can understand it in Brad's case. He grew up in an atmosphere in which intellectual excellence was the only valid goal. He struggled to keep up for a while, then simply threw in the towel. Neither my parents nor their circle of friends could accept his behavior. Long before he left, he was labeled a misfit. I'm sure he was sensitive about it."

"We all have our sensitivities."

"What are yours, Matt? Why would a woman have trouble accepting you as you are?"

He chomped several more potato chips and would have seemed perfectly nonchalant had it not been for the ominous darkening of his eyes. "I'm blue-collar all the way. I don't have a pedigree, or a series of fancy qualifying initials to put after my name. Over the years I've done well in my work, but that doesn't mean I aspire to own my own company, or that one day I won't decide to chuck it all and go back to building log cabins. If a woman thinks she's getting a future real-estate tycoon in me, she'd better think again."

Lauren couldn't miss the bitterness in his words. "You've been burned."

"Several times." He looked out over the water and his tone gentled, growing apologetic enough to defy arrogance. "I've always attracted women pretty easily. But physical attraction isn't enough. Not by a long shot."

"The grass is always greener . . ." she said softly. "There are those of us who'd *love* to have looks that would attract."

Matt eyed her as if she were crazy. "But you *do!* I can't believe there isn't a line of men waiting to take you out!"

It took Lauren a minute to realize what she'd said and why Matt had answered as forcefully as he had. She'd forgotten. That happened a lot. A slow warmth crept up her neck. Compliments were still new to her, and from as physically superb a man as Matthew Kruger . . . "I don't know about a line," she said simply.

"Then there's one man?"

She shook her head.

"You're a beautiful woman, Lauren. Surely you've had offers."

Again she shook her head, this time with a self-conscious half smile.

"Why not?"

At his bluntness, she burst out laughing. "You're almost as undiplomatic as Beth."

"I'm sorry. I was just curious." He held up a large, well-formed hand. "Not that I'm saying you should be married. You're only, what, twenty-nine, and you're obviously building a career for yourself." A new thought hit him, and he frowned. "You said you haven't been in Boston for very long. Then the shop is a recent thing?"

"We've been open barely a month."

"And before that?"

"I worked in a museum back home."

He rubbed his forefinger along the rim of his paper cup. "Back home. That could explain it. Brad told me about back home."

"What did he say?"

"That it was stifling. One-dimensional. You were either an artist or an academician affiliated with the college."

"He was being unfair. Bennington's a beautiful place. Some fascinating people chose to live there. Brad just didn't."

"Nor did you, apparently. Why did you leave, Lauren?"

"Because I wanted to open the shop."

"But you could have opened a shop in Bennington."

She shook her head. "Too small a market."

"So you're going for the big time."

"I want the shop to be a success, yes," she said on a defensive note. "I may not aspire to put out one profound treatise after another the way Mom and Dad have, but that doesn't mean I can't aim to do what I do well."

There was a wistfulness to Matt's smile. "Now you *do* sound like Brad. He was so determined. . . ." A flicker of uncertainty crossed his brow.

"So determined. . . ?"

It was a while before Matt finished his sentence, and then it was with care. "To be successful. Recognized. I'm not sure he realized it, or realized what was driving him, but as often as he claimed that he was doing his own thing and didn't care what his family thought, I think he was kidding himself."

"Was he happy, Matt?"

Matt had to consider that. "In a way, yes."

Peering down at the bits of lemon pulp clinging to the sides of her cup, Lauren spoke more slowly. "All we were told about the accident was that he was supervising some blasting and got caught in the mess. Was there . . . anything more to it?"

"That was it."

He'd answered quickly and with finality. Not knowing why, Lauren was taken aback. "You saw him right after?"

"At the hospital." His tone was clipped. As he went on, its harshness eased. "Brad was lucid for a time, but between the internal injuries and everything else—well, maybe it was for the best. If he'd lived—and the chances of that were slim from the start—he would have been a quadriplegic. I don't think he would have been able to bear that."

"No," she whispered, and when she looked up, her eyes were moist. "I feel guilty about it sometimes."

"Guilty?"

"Everything I have now—the shop, the farmhouse, this—" she gestured broadly toward herself "—has come from the money he left me. Did you know that?"

Matt put his hand on her shoulder and massaged it

gently. His voice was much, much softer, his focus shifted. "That was Brad's wish. I was the one who passed it on to the lawyer. Given the circumstances, Brad gained a measure of peace from it."

Lauren nodded, then somehow couldn't stop the overflow of words. "If it hadn't been for Brad, I'd probably still be back in Bennington. Even aside from the money, his death was a turning point for me. For the first time in my life, I stopped to think of my own mortality, of what I'd have to my credit when the time came, of what I'd be leaving behind. That was when I decided to move to Boston and open the shop. I only wish Brad could know how much better I feel about myself now."

"It's enough that you know, Lauren. If Brad were here to see you, I'm sure he'd be proud."

She looked timidly at Matt, then away, and took a long, shuddering breath. "It's too bad we can't have it both ways—too bad I can't have what I do and have Brad alive to see it."

Slipping his arm across her back, Matt drew her to his side. His warmth was the comfort she needed. "Life is cruel that way, filled with choice and compromise. Even those who reach the heights make sacrifices along the way. The best we can do is to decide exactly how much we're prepared to give up and move on from there."

As she raised her gaze to his, her cheek brushed his shoulder. It seemed a perfectly natural gesture. "But that's a negative view."

"It's realistic."

"Maybe I'm more of a romantic, then. I want to focus on the goals and face the hurdles as I come to them."

He shrugged. "And I want to be prepared for the hurdles. It's just a different approach. Who's to say which one is better?"

She didn't answer. Her gaze was suddenly locked with his, lost in his, and she struggled to cope with the intensity. He was a virtual stranger, yet she'd told him things she'd never told another soul. Was it the fact that he was a link to her brother, or that he was a good listener, or that he'd shared his own thoughts with her? She'd been wary of him at first; she still was, in some respects. And yet . . . and yet she was drawn to him. . . .

The sudden blast of the boat's horn made them both jump. They looked around to find the bulk of the passengers crowded on the other side of the deck, waving to a passing tall ship. Without releasing her, Matt moved to join them.

"Impressive," he breathed, taking in the towering masts and ancient fittings of the proud vessel. "Too bad she's not under sail."

"Mmm. It's almost disillusioning. There weren't any motors in the old days."

"Or Sony Walkmans." He pointed to the sailor perched on the rigging, headset firmly in place. Lauren smiled at the sight, then shifted her gaze to the airport.

"If I had a downtown office with a view of all this, I doubt I'd ever get any work done. I could sit for hours watching the planes take off and land."

"Not me. Even watching gives me the willies. I'm a white-knuckle flier."

Lauren stared at him in disbelief. "A big guy like you?"

"Big guys crash harder."

She suppressed a smile. "I suppose you've got a point. But you do fly."

His expression was priceless, a blend of revulsion and resignation. "When necessary."

"Which is far too often for your tastes."

"You got it."

Her eyes took on an extra glow. "I don't think I could ever fly too often for my tastes. Not that I've flown that much, but I've always been so excited about getting where I'm going that I just sit back and relax. That's about all you can do, y'know. Once you're in the air, you're in fate's hands. It's not as if you have control over anything that might happen to the plane."

His grunt was eloquent. "That's what bothers me. I *like* to be in control. Just like measuring hurdles. . . ."

Lauren narrowed her eyes playfully. "I'll bet you're the type who checks over every blessed inch of a new car before you venture to slide behind the wheel."

"I also sample the whipped cream, then the nuts, then the hot fudge, then the ice cream before I take a complete spoonful of a sundae."

"But where's the surprise, then?"

"The surprise is in the perfect blend of ingredients. The way I do it, y'see, I minimize the chance of disappointment. If something's not quite right, I can get it fixed, and if I can't do that, at least I'm prepared, so my expectations are on a par with reality."

"You're a man of caution."

"Quite."

"Another reason why you sat outside my shop for two days." She tipped her head. "Tell me, what would have happened if I'd looked exactly like that picture you'd seen?"

"I'd have come in the first day."

Lauren had wondered if he would ever have come in. "I don't understand. My looks made you *cautious?*"

"That's right."

"But . . . I look better than I did in the picture, don't I?"

"You look gorgeous."

"Then?" Mired in confusion, she made no protest when he turned her into him and crossed his wrists on the small of her back.

"Gorgeous women intimidate me. I've been burned, remember?"

His smile didn't ease her this time. Her eyes widened. "Do you think I'm after your *body?*"

He winced and shot an embarrassed glance to either side. "Shh."

She grasped his arms to push him away. When he held her steady, she whispered, but vehemently, "Is that what you think? Well, let me tell you, *I* didn't ask you to walk into my shop. I didn't ask you to take me on a cruise. I don't want any part of your body! And even if I did, that wouldn't be all I'd want. Before I ever got around to your body, I'd make sure that I wanted the rest." She snorted in disgust and turned her face away. "Of all the self-centered, arrogant—"

"That wasn't what I meant, Lauren. You're jumping to conclusions. Has it ever occurred to you that you can intimidate a man?"

"Me?"

"Yes, you. I'd expected to find a quiet—" he hesitated, then cleared his throat "—rather thin and plain-looking young woman living an equally quiet life in the country. At least, that was what Brad had implied. If he could only see you now! You own your own shop—in the city, no less. You're beautiful. You dress smartly. You're bright as all get-out. And you're sure as hell not falling at *my* feet." He took a begrudging breath. "Yes, I'm intimidated."

Lauren had felt suspended during his short speech. Now she realized how absurd her own attack must have sounded. "Funny," she managed to say in a small voice, "you don't look intimidated."

He squeezed his eyes together. Even before they relaxed and opened, a smile had begun to form on his lips. "I guess I'm not now, at least not as much as I was before. For someone who is beautiful and chic and super-intelligent, you're really pretty normal."

She smiled self-consciously, averting her gaze. "I think we're missing the sunset."

"I think you're right."

They returned to their own side of the boat, then switched when the vessel made a slow turn and headed back to the docks. Neither of them said very much. Lauren, for one, was lost in her own thoughts.

In spite of Matt's explanation, she still felt stunned that her looks had put him off. Initially her pride had been hurt. The thought that she'd drastically improved her appearance only to find that it kept men away was unsettling; hence she'd lashed out.

Or had she simply been searching for a wedge to put between Matt and her?

He was too attractive, too easy to be with, too firmly aligned with Brad and a way of life that she'd been indoctrinated to frown on. No, she wasn't exactly frowning now, but neither could she turn her back on the disappointment of Brad's long-ago desertion. And then came the guilt. She'd acceded to her parents' view of Brad as a failure, yet she'd accepted his money—lots of it. Did an architect masquerading as a carpenter earn that much money? Had he banked every spare cent for some eleven years?

She realized that there were many more questions she wanted to ask Matt about Brad. In hindsight, she wondered if he'd been evasive when talking about her brother's work. His answers had been short, his expression solemn. He'd opened up more about Brad's personal life, yet she couldn't help but wonder if there were some things he hadn't said.

The boat pulled alongside the dock, its lines were secured, and the gangplank was lowered.

"You must be starving," Matt said. "Want to catch a bite at my hotel?" The Marriott was only a short distance from where they stood, but Lauren quickly shook her head.

"I'd better be getting home. It's been a long day."

"Are you sure?"

This time she steeled herself against the cocoa softness of his gaze. She needed time to acclimate herself to his appearance in her life. He was a figure from Brad's past, yet the immediacy of him unbalanced her. What she craved was the solid footing of her own home.

"I'm sure," she said with a gentle smile. "But . . . thank you, Matt. This has been lovely."

"At least let me walk you to your car. It's pretty dark."

"And the path to my car is well lighted all the way. Really, I'll be fine."

Matt straightened his shoulders and nodded. "Well, take care, then."

She started off, half turning as she walked. "Good luck with your work. I hope it goes well."

He nodded again and waved, then turned and headed for his hotel. Lauren didn't look back until she'd crossed Atlantic Avenue, and by then he was gone.

The late-afternoon sun glanced brilliantly over the Hollywood Hills, but the shades in the study were drawn as its proprietor entered, strode across the tiled floor to the desk and picked up the telephone.

"Yes?"

"We're on our way."

"It's about time. I'd assumed I would have heard from you sooner."

"She's a clever girl. Covered her tracks like a pro—almost. I still don't know who helped her out of L.A., but you were right about the Bahamas. She went back to the same clinic she visited when the two of you were vacationing on the islands last fall. That was her only slipup."

"Then you've found her?"

"She had plastic surgery, just like you thought she would. Not much. Subtle changes. There was a phony 'before' shot stuck into the doctor's files and a bunch of misleading medical reports, but the 'after' shot had just enough similarity to the real thing to give her away. Her hair's different now, darker and shorter. And she's taken a different name."

"We knew she would. Where is she?"

"Boston. She just opened a little print-and-frame shop."

"With the money from the gifts *I* gave her. A print-and-frame shop. That's priceless."

"You'd be amazed if you saw her. She's the image of innocence. Dresses just so—stylish but understated, nothing flashy like before. Drives a Saab she must have picked up secondhand. Has this woman working with her who looks nearly as snowy-pure as she does, and a young guy who's probably eating out of—"

"What about the jewels? Have you located the fence?"

"No. No sign of the jewels at all. She may have started with the furs. They'd be easy to sell and nearly impossible to trace."

"Have you made contact with her?"

"Got a good man on it. She's already had a couple of little 'accidents'—nothing to hurt her actually, just set her to wondering."

"Is she?"

"Yeah. She's looking nervously around her front yard each time she leaves the house."

"The house?"

"An old farmhouse she picked up outside the city."

"With my money!"

"It'll all come back to you. Between the shop and the house, she's made investments that'll come back with interest."

"I want you to find the jewels."

"We're looking. She doesn't have them at home. I went through the place myself today."

"Ransacked it?"

"Nothing that obvious. Just moved little things here and there. She'll suspect someone's been snooping, but she won't be sure enough to call the cops."

"She wouldn't *dare* call the cops. She knows how long my arm is, and she wouldn't do anything to risk blowing her cover. So where do we go from here?"

"I've got a few more mishaps up my sleeve. You want her to squirm. I want her to squirm. She's gonna squirm."

"You're having fun, aren't you?"

"You could say that. I feel like I let you down before, and it was her fault. This is my revenge."

"It's *my* revenge, and don't you forget it."

"No way, boss. No way."

CHAPTER FOUR

Beth was lying in wait for Lauren when she arrived at work the next morning. "Well? How did it go? What happened? Your parents would *die* if they knew you were dating him, but I think it's great! A sunset cruise . . . I've never heard of anything so romantic in my life. He may be rugged, but he's got style. Was he nice? Did you invite him back to Lincoln after the cruise? I almost called you, but I didn't dare. *Tell* me, Lauren. Tell me *everything!*"

Closely shadowed by her friend, Lauren continued through to the back room and plunked her purse in the bottom drawer of the file cabinet. "How can I tell you anything if I can't get a word in edgewise?"

"Okay. I'll shush. Give."

Lauren only wished she could. She'd spent a good part of the night thinking about Matthew Kruger, and she still didn't know what to make of him. "Yes, he was nice. Yes, the cruise was nice. Romantic? Well, I don't know about that. And no, I did not invite him back to Lincoln."

"Why not?"

"Because it wasn't called for. And we weren't on a *date*. He was my brother's friend. That's all. We talked a little about Brad and a little about other things. Period."

"Did he explain why he'd been hanging around outside for so long?"

For the first time that morning, Lauren smiled.

Dryly. "If you can believe it, he was trying to get up his nerve to come in. Brad had shown him a picture of me. I wasn't quite what he'd expected."

"That's marvelous!" Beth's eyes grew rounder. "The handsome prince was so taken with your beauty that he was actually awestruck. I love it!"

Lauren screwed up her face and carefully enunciated her words. "Handsome prince? Taken with my beauty? Awestruck? What *have* you been reading, Beth?"

"Come on. I think this is great. Are you seeing him again?"

"I don't know."

"What do you mean, you don't know?"

"Just that. He didn't say anything about seeing me again, and I wasn't about to put him on the spot." Lauren reached for a can and began to spoon fresh coffee into a filter.

"'Put him on the spot.'" Beth snorted. "Straight from the mouth of the old you. The new you is sought-after. You'd be doing him a favor to *consider* seeing him again. . . . Well?"

"Well, what?"

"Are you?"

"What?" Lauren measured out water and poured it into the top of the coffee maker.

Beth sighed in frustration. "Considering seeing him again."

"I don't know."

As coffee began to trickle slowly into the carafe, Beth rolled her eyes and muttered, "This is absurd.

We're going in circles. Do you or do you not want to see the man again?"

Lauren turned toward her friend. "I don't know! Damn it, Beth, how can I give you a better answer if I don't have one myself? Yes, I liked him, and under normal circumstances I'd be glad to see him again. But these aren't exactly normal circumstances. In the first place, the man lives on the West Coast. He's only here doing business, most of which keeps him in the western part of the state. He'll be going back to San Francisco and he hates to fly. I don't exactly have the time to zip out to see him every weekend—not to mention the money, when there are so many other things I have it earmarked for." She sucked in a breath. "And in the second place, he was Brad's friend. You're right. My parents would go bonkers."

"You're an adult. They didn't want you to go to the Bahamas, but you did it. They didn't want you to leave Bennington or open this shop, but you did both. You don't need their permission. You can do whatever you want and see whomever you want."

Lauren sighed loudly. "I know that, Beth. I'm not asking their permission for anything. I have qualms of my own about seeing Matt again. He was a friend of Brad's. He sees me and my parents through Brad's eyes. And he's a confirmed bachelor who loves taking off with the guys and shooting the rapids for a week. So what's the point?"

"The point," Beth murmured, wiggling her brows, "is that he's single and gorgeous."

"I thought he was too rugged for you."

"For me, yes. For you, no. The two of you looked great walking out of here together last night. I'm telling you, see where it leads."

"You have a one-track mind," Lauren grumbled, brushing a wisp of hair from her low-belted, apricot jersey dress.

"And you're in a lousy mood. Where's your sense of humor? Hey, I'll bet Matthew Kruger would be the *perfect* one to ward off the ghost that's hanging out at your farm."

"Humph. I'm beginning to think I need something. That ghost was at work again."

Beth blinked once, then again. The coffee continued to trickle in the background, its rich aroma wafting from the carafe and spreading through the small room. "Excuse me?"

"That ghost. I swear it went through my things yesterday."

"Wait a minute, Lauren. There are no such things as ghosts."

"You're the one who's been touting them."

"I was teasing."

"Then I guess you've teased once too often. I'm almost becoming a believer."

"You're not serious!"

"Well, maybe not. But still . . . it was weird." She made a face accordingly. "I could have sworn I'd put certain things in certain places at home, and they were still there, just . . . shifted somehow."

Beth leaned back against the desk and crossed her arms over her chest. She might have been a psychiatrist for the indulgent tone of her voice. "I think you're going to have to be more specific. In what ways were they 'shifted'?"

"Small ways. A bottle of perfume turned around so that the sculpted bird faced the wall. A pair of shoes neatly set in the closet, with the right shoe on the left and the left one on the right. A pair of underpants perfectly folded, but inside out. I always turn them the right way before I fold them. *Underpants*." She shuddered, then whispered in dismay, "Can you believe it?"

"Maybe you should call the police."

"I thought about that, but I feel like a fool! I mean, it's not as if anything were taken. The locks on the doors were intact, and as far as I could tell, none of the windows had been jimmied open. Ruling out a breaking and entering, I'd say someone might have just walked in, except that I'm the only one with a key."

"How about the realtor who sold you the place?"

"I had the locks changed right after I moved in." Lauren gave a guttural laugh. "That's about all I've done, but it does preclude a human visitor." She took a deep breath. "So either it *was* a ghost, or I'm simply not as meticulous about things as I used to be. Maybe that's it. I mean, I suppose I have been preoccupied with the shop. It's very possible that I wasn't paying attention when I put the perfume bottle back or took the shoes off or folded the laundry." She looked beseechingly at Beth. "So what are the police going to say?"

"Mmm. I see your point. Maybe you should get a dog."

"One encounter with a dog on my property was enough."

"Then a burglar alarm system."

"A burglar alarm isn't going to stop a ghost. And it sure isn't going to improve my own absentminded-ness, if that's what it was." She reached for a clean mug and poured herself some coffee. When she looked up to find a smug smile spreading over Beth's face, she scowled. "Now what are you thinking?"

"That I was right all along. Matthew Kruger may be just the one to protect you. All you have to do is to coax him along. Before you know it, he'll be thinking of that farmhouse as his second home."

"Matt is going back to San Francisco. How many times must I tell you that? And even if he wasn't, I can't use the man that way."

"Seems to me he'd get something out of the arrange-ment."

"Humph. When—and if—I take a live-in lover, it'll be because I truly adore whoever he is, not because I need him as a bodyguard."

"You could truly adore your bodyguard."

Lauren sank into a chair and raised her mug. She spoke slowly and distinctly, as though her friend might not understand her otherwise. "I am going to drink my coffee now and gather my thoughts. Then I am going to face this new day with a bright smile and a free mind." She closed her eyes, brought the mug to her lips, sipped the coffee, then sighed.

Somewhere between the sip and sigh, Beth gave up on her and left the room.

The shop grew busier as the noon hour approached, and Jamie's arrival at one was a relief. Beth ran out to pick up sandwiches, returning shortly thereafter with news far more interesting than that the rye bread had caraway seeds.

"Have you looked outside lately?" she murmured excitedly to Lauren as she passed on her way to the back room.

Lauren had been helping a customer decide which of two silkscreen prints to buy. She glanced toward the front window.

Matt. Sitting on the bench she was coming to think of as his. Reading a book.

Reading a book? That was a novel approach! Not that she doubted he was a reader; he looked more than comfortable with the paperback in his hand. But reading a book in the middle of the bustling Market-place and on that particular bench? What was he thinking? What did he want?

She returned her attention to her customer, pleased that in the minute she'd been distracted he'd decided on the print she'd originally recommended. Decisions on its framing proved to be more difficult, what with so many different mat boards and frames to choose from, but Lauren didn't mind. This was the part of the job she really enjoyed, and the shop made far more money on matting and framing than on the sale of the prints themselves.

It was only after she'd written up the customer's order, taken a deposit and let her gaze follow him to the door that she glanced again at the bench outside.

Matt was still reading.

Beth, who'd finished her lunch and come to relieve Lauren, was perplexed. "What's he doing out there?"

"Reading, obviously."

"But what's he *really* doing?"

"Beats me."

"Aren't you curious?"

"Sure."

"Aren't you going to satisfy your curiosity?"

"I'm going to have lunch. I'm famished."

"You're hopeless, is what you are," Beth declared. Lauren merely shrugged as she headed for the back room.

"Hopeless" wasn't exactly the word for it. She was flattered. Matt couldn't have chosen that bench by chance. But she was also puzzled. If he wanted to see her, wouldn't he simply come into the shop?

Did she want to see him? She still wasn't sure. There was something intimidating about him, and she couldn't quite pinpoint its cause.

Unwrapping her sandwich, she ate it slowly, sipping occasionally from a can of Coke. By the time she was finished, her curiosity had risen right along with her energy level. She *did* want to know what Matthew Kruger was up to. What right did he have to monopolize that bench? What right did he have to distract her? What right did he have to make her feel *guilty* for not acknowledging his presence?

Without further thought, she crossed through the shop, breezed out the door and approached the bench. Matt didn't look up. She stood there for a minute, then quietly eased herself down on the bench several feet away from him, far enough to preclude any implication of intimacy.

While he continued to read, she studied him closely. Other than his eyes, which moved rhythmically from one line to the next, his features were at rest. His lean cheeks were freshly shaved. His tawny hair was clean and vaguely windblown, haphazardly brushing his forehead and collar. He wore his usual jeans and sneakers, but today he'd put on a pink oxford cloth shirt. If she'd ever thought pink was feminine, she quickly revised that opinion. With his sleeves rolled to just beneath the elbow, and with the bronzed hue of his forearms, neck and chin contrasting handsomely with the shirt, he looked thoroughly male. Almost rawly so.

Reaching out, Lauren removed the book from his hands. She caught a brief glimpse of his startled expression before she turned the book over, carefully holding his place with her fingers, and examined the cover.

"*A Savage Place,*" she read aloud. "It's a good one. But some of Parker's other books are set more in Boston. His descriptions of the city are priceless. You really should read them."

"I have," Matt answered. His liquid brown eyes caught hers when she lifted her head. "I've been a Parker fan for years."

Any indignance Lauren might have felt when she'd marched out of the shop had vanished. For that matter, she couldn't remember what doubts she'd had about Matt yesterday, last night, this morning. She couldn't seem to think of anything except the fact that his eyes were the warmest she'd ever seen and that his smile did something strange to her insides.

With a determined effort, she refocused on the book. "Like mystery and a little bit of violence, do you? Or is it Spenser's machismo that intrigues you?" The softness of her tone kept any sting from her words.

"Actually, it's Parker's writing style I enjoy. It's clean and crisp. Fast-paced. Filled with wit and dry humor."

She nodded. So it hadn't been an act, Matt's immersion in the book. He obviously knew his Parker and appreciated him.

"Why this bench?" Lauren asked suddenly. Her eyes had narrowed and were teasing in their way.

Matt stared at her, opened his mouth, then promptly shut it again. As she watched, his expression grew sheepish, filled with a boyish guilt that tugged at her heartstrings. When he finally did explain, she knew she was lost.

"I like this bench because it's close to your shop. I guess I was hoping you'd come out. What I was *really* hoping was that you'd take off with me for the afternoon and we'd rent a sailboat and join the others on the Charles. I got a view of the Basin from the thirty-second floor this morning. It looked so inviting." His voice fell, along with the expression on his face. "But you have to work. I know. It's not fair for me to come along and expect you to drop everything you're doing. You have responsibilities. I accept that, and respect it."

Lauren didn't know whether to hug him in consolation or hit him over the head with his book. "How can you *do* this to me, Matt? It's not fair!" That he should be a lovable little boy in a virile man's body. That he should be a stranger, yet so very familiar. That he should offer excitement in such a gentle and undemanding way. None of it was fair.

"Then you'll come sailing with me?"

"You were right the first time. I can't."

"But you would if you could."

"Yes."

He smiled and relaxed against the bench. "I guess I can live with that." Almost as soon as he'd sat back, he came forward again. "How about tonight? There's a Boston Pops concert on the Esplanade. We could pick up something to take out and eat while we listen."

Lauren knew that an hour later, or two or three, she'd find all kinds of reasons why she shouldn't go. At the moment, however, she couldn't think of one. "That'd be fun. I'd like it."

"Great! What time can you get off?"

"What time does the concert start?"

Matt's eyes widened. "I hadn't thought that far." He jumped up, staying her with his hand. "Don't move. I'll be right back."

She watched him sprint toward Bostix, the ticket and information booth adjacent to Fanueil Hall, where he managed to wedge himself through the crowd at the window. Within minutes, he had trotted back to her.

"Eight o'clock. They suggested we get there early for the best spots on the grass, but the music carries pretty far, so if you can't get away from the shop until later—"

"I think I can convince Jamie to give Beth a hand until the shop closes. If we want to allow time to walk over the hill . . . How about your coming by at, say, seven? I'll call in an order for dinner—"

"Let me take care of that. I'm on a quasi vacation, remember? My work is done for the day, while you've still got more to do."

With a shy smile, she stood up. "Okay, then. I'll see you later?"

"Sure thing."

She nodded and had started for the shop when Matt called out to stop her. "Uh, Lauren?" Brows raised in question, she looked back. His gaze dropped from hers to the book she still held in her hand. She blushed, hurried back and gave it to him.

"Sorry. I'd forgotten I was holding it."

"I hadn't. If I can't go sailing this afternoon, I'll have to keep myself occupied somehow. Even aside from Parker's style, I suppose there is something to be said for mystery and a little bit of violence. And as for machismo—"

"Don't say it," she interrupted with a teasing glint in her eyes. "I don't think I want to hear it. A girl can take only so much, y'know." She'd pretty much reached her limit already. Another minute or two, and she'd chuck the shop and run off to the Charles with Matt. And that she would certainly regret. The shop was lasting. Matt wasn't. She'd have to remember that.

It was hard for her to remember much of anything that afternoon—other than the fact that Matt would be coming by for her at seven, of course. Beth teased her mercilessly when she rang something up wrong on the cash register, then again when she began to stretch fabric on a frame backside-to.

She thought seven o'clock would never arrive, but it did, bringing Matt, a blanket "compliments of the Marriott" and a large brown bag filled with all kinds of promising goodies. They walked over Beacon Hill, past the State House, the Common and the Public Garden, then across to Storrow Drive and the Hatch Shell.

They weren't the first to arrive, but they found a patch of grass within easy viewing of the raised stage. In truth, Lauren could have sat half a mile off under a tree by the water. The fact of the concert was secondary to that of the pleasure she felt being with Matt. She didn't analyze it, didn't stop to wonder why she was letting herself get so carried away about a man who'd be gone before she knew it. She simply wanted to enjoy, and enjoy she did.

Matt doubled up the blanket and spread it on the grass; then, after they had both sat down, he pulled out one container of food after another. He'd brought spinach turnovers, chicken salad with grapes and walnuts, Brie and crackers, fruit and a tumbler of frothy raspberry cooler. Lauren wondered where they'd ever put such a feast and told him so. He merely laughed, then laughed again when they'd eaten nearly everything. The concert was well under way by that time. He stuffed the remains of their picnic back into the bag, then sat close to Lauren with one arm propped straight on the grass behind him.

The assembled crowd was far from quiet; esplanade concerts were that way, informal evenings geared toward lighthearted company and relaxation. Families with children, young couples, middle-aged couples, elderly couples, mixed groups—all shared the pleasure of an evening along the Charles with the sweet smell of the outdoors, the gentle breeze, the exquisite blend of strings, horns and percussion.

As the evening progressed, Lauren and Matt sat closer and closer together. Lauren couldn't remember ever having felt so replete, and the dinner was only partly responsible. Matt was with *her*. Not with the pretty blonde to their right or the adorable redhead to their left. He was with *her*. She had only to drop her eyes from the stage to see his strong legs stretching endlessly before him. He'd changed into a white shirt and a pair of tan slacks that were more tailored than the jeans but no less sexy. His thighs were solid beneath the lightweight cloth, his hips proportionally lean. She felt the warmth of his shoulder as it gently supported her back; felt the goodness of its fit and its strength. His arm cut a diagonal swath to her hip, beside which his hand was flattened. His hand . . .

long, tanned fingers, fine golden hairs, a well-formed wrist . . .

One song ended on a round of enthusiastic applause. When another began, the applause never quite stopped, for this song was a popular one with a heady beat, and the temptation to clap along was too great to resist. Too great, at least, for everyone but Lauren and Matt. They grinned along with the others, but neither seemed to want to disturb the physical closeness they'd captured. It seemed natural, and right, and very, very special.

Bidden by a silent call, Lauren turned her head to look up at Matt, and what she saw made her breath catch. His eyes were dark, drawing hers with a magnetic warmth, and his expression was one of gentle but insistent hunger. She might have been frightened by it, had her own body not been as insistently hungry. A glowing sun seemed to have risen inside her, radiating sparkles that speeded up the beat of her heart and her pulse and gave the faintest quiver to her limbs.

Lowering his head just the fraction that was necessary, he shadow-kissed her, openmouthed, not quite touching her lips. He drew back for an instant, dazed, then tipped his head and kissed her the same way, but from a different angle. The first kiss had been tantalizing enough for Lauren, but the second one was devastating. Acting purely on instinct, driven by the ache of desire, she opened her mouth in the invitation he'd been waiting for.

When he lowered his head this time, there was nothing shadowy about his kiss. It was full and binding, caressing her with a passion she'd never have believed mere lips to be capable of. She smelled the faint musk of his skin, tasted the fresh, fruity tang of his mouth, felt the sensual abrasion of his tongue as it swept through the moist recesses she offered.

She was about to turn into him, wrap her arms around his neck and draw him closer, when he dragged his mouth from hers and pressed it to her forehead. Though he didn't speak, the harsh rasp of his breath was eloquent and comforting, since Lauren was working equally hard to suck in the air she needed. Eyes closed, she gradually regained control.

Matt shifted and drew her back against his chest, fully this time, with her head resting on his opposite shoulder and his arms wrapped tightly around her waist. They stayed very much that way until the last encore was over. Then, with reluctance, they got up, gathered their things together and let the leisurely movement of the crowd carry them back the way they'd come.

Matt held the folded blanket under one arm. His other arm was draped over Lauren's shoulder. She held tightly to the hand that dangled by her collarbone.

They were nearly at the State House before he spoke. "I've got to be heading back to Leominster."

"When?"

"Tomorrow morning. Early. I have a nine o'clock appointment and probably should have driven out tonight, but I wanted to be with you."

She nodded, not knowing what else to say.

"I'll have to be there through Sunday. I'm sorry. It would have been nice to do something together on the weekend."

"That's okay. The shop's open seven days a week. I've forgotten what a weekend is."

"You have to have *some* time off each week."

"I will, once things get more settled. We weren't sure how soon we'd be able to hire extra help, but business has been going so well that we're trying to convince Jamie to work full-time so Beth and I can stagger days off for ourselves."

"That'd be nice. There must be things you need to do."

"At least a million. Sundays are a help—we're only open from one till six—but I'd really like a day off in the middle of the week once in a while. If I don't start hiring people to fix up my farmhouse, it's apt to give a final groan and crumble at my feet."

"Maybe I could help with that."

"With the farmhouse? But you're leaving."

"I've got some good contacts, and while I'm in Leominster I can check around for more. What do you need?"

"You name it. Plumber, electrician, roofer, carpenter. Actually, I was exaggerating before. The structure of the house is sound. I had that checked out before I bought the place. But I want to do extensive modernizing inside, and I need good people I can trust, since I won't be able to stand around and supervise."

He gave her hand a squeeze. "Got it. I'll see

what I can do."

They walked on in silence for a time. Lauren felt simultaneously content and unsettled, if that were possible. Finally she couldn't help but ask, "When will you be flying back to San Francisco?"

"Not for another week or two. I'll be here in the city early next week, then back in Leominster. . . . Where are you parked?"

She pointed in the direction of the garage. "You don't need to—"

"I insist."

"But it's out of your way."

"What else do I have to do?" he teased.

"Sleep. You'll have to be on the road very early to get to Leominster by nine."

"It's okay. I'll sleep tomorrow night."

All too soon, they had reached the garage, climbed to the third level and found her car. Reluctantly, she unlocked the door and opened it, only then turning to Matt. "Can I give you a lift back to the hotel?"

He shook his head. "It's out of your way."

"But this was out of yours."

"I'm on foot. It's ten times harder by car, what with one-way streets and all."

"I don't mind. Really—"

Any further words she might have said were stopped at her lips by the single finger he placed there. The dim light of the garage couldn't disguise the way his eyes slowly covered her face. They were hypnotic, those mellow brown eyes, and they conspired with the unmistakable vibrations from his body to suspend

Lauren's thought processes once more.

His finger slid to her chin, where it collaborated with his thumb to tip her face up. He kissed her once, then again, then brushed his lips over her cheeks, eyes and nose. Lauren was entranced. Her own lips parted, then waited, waited until he'd completed the erotic journey and returned home.

But if she'd thought what he'd already done was erotic, she was in for an awakening. The tip of his tongue flicked out to paint her lips in the rosy hue of passion, and if she hadn't been clutching the top of the car door, she might have collapsed. She'd never experienced anything as electric, and the hardest part to believe was that the only points where their bodies touched were his tongue and her lips.

When he severed that connection, she stood still, eyes closed, mesmerized by the lingering flicker of a sweet, sweet longing. With regret, she finally opened her eyes.

"Can I come out to see you when I get back to town?" he asked. There was a trace of hoarseness in his voice.

Clearly implied was that he wanted to see her in Lincoln. Without a second thought, she nodded. "I'd like that."

He smiled, then cocked his head toward the car. "Get in. I might not let you leave if you wait much longer."

"Is that a threat or a promise?" she quipped softly, but she was already sliding behind the wheel. One part of her was tempted to wait much, much longer. The other part knew that things were happening quickly and that there were too many considerations to be made before she dared Matt to follow through.

After he had shut the door, she locked it, then started the car and backed out of the space. Matt stood to the side, watching. He gave a short wave as she began the slow, twisting descent. Soon he was lost to her view.

Lauren smiled all the way down Cambridge Street. She was still smiling when she curved into Storrow Drive and was ebullient enough to ignore the harsh beam of headlights from a car following too close on her tail. When she crossed the Eliot Bridge onto Route 2 and the same car remained behind her, she indulgently assured herself that if she was patient, the car would turn off soon.

It didn't.

She passed through Fresh Pond, circled the far rotary and moved into the right lane of what was now a comfortable superhighway. The car stayed with her. She tossed frequent glances in the rearview mirror and frowned. The traffic wasn't heavy. Surely whoever it was could move to the left and pass her, rather than tail her at forty-five miles per hour.

The highway was well lighted. She could see that the car was a late-model compact and that the driver was alone. Some kid having fun? There was no weaving to suggest he was drunk. Neither was there any hint that he was trying to tell her something, such as that her car had a flat tire or was on fire. He was simply following her and succeeding in making her extremely nervous.

Lauren pressed her foot on the gas pedal, pulled into the middle lane and held steady. The other car accelerated, pulled into the middle lane and held steady. She moved back into the right lane. The compact followed suit. She pumped her brakes lightly in an attempt to signal the driver to pass her, but he only slowed accordingly, then resumed speed when she did. In a last-ditch attempt to free herself of the tail, she flicked on the signal lights, moved into the breakdown lane and came to a cautious stop, prepared to floor the gas pedal if the other car stopped.

It swung to the left and passed her.

Breathing a shaky sigh of relief, Lauren sat for several minutes to recompose herself. Since she'd realized she was actively being followed, her imagination had taken her to frightening places. Too many little things had happened to her lately—the near accident on Newbury Street, the vicious dog in her yard, the garage door's fall, the subtle suggestion that someone had been in her home—for her to dismiss summarily this instance as a prank.

Yet as she entered the driving lane once more, that was exactly what she forced herself to do. A prank. A dangerous prank.

Then she crested a hill and saw taillights in the breakdown lane. She passed them by, instinctively speeding up, but within minutes the same car was behind her once more.

She swore softly, but that did no good. The car remained in pursuit. Five minutes went by. She searched the road for a sign of a police cruiser she might hail, but there was none. Another five minutes elapsed, and her knuckles were white on the steering wheel.

She approached her exit and held her breath, praying that when she turned off, the driver of the compact car would consider the game not worth any further effort.

He exited directly behind her and proceeded to follow her along the suddenly darker, narrower road.

Praying now that her car wouldn't break down and leave her at the mercy of the nameless, faceless lunatic, she drove along the road as fast as she dared, heading directly for the center of town.

For the first time she blessed every chase movie she'd suffered through in which the dumb innocent was pursued up and down hills, around corners and through dark alleys without grasping at the simplest solution. Lauren Stevenson was no dummy. She had no intention of heading off into a side street, much less leading someone to her farmhouse, where she would be totally unprotected.

She headed for the police station.

What she hadn't expected when she pulled up in front was that the car that had been on her tail all the way home would swing smoothly—with no qualms or hesitation—into a space in the parking lot. Between two police cruisers.

Lauren quickly shifted into drive and headed home.

She was mortified. Apparently she'd imagined the worst for nothing. Yes, she was angry. For an officer of the law, plainclothes or otherwise, to have behaved in such an irresponsible fashion was inexcusable!

But what could she do? If she marched into the police station and complained, she'd be making a certain enemy. Policemen protected their own, and if what she'd read so often in the newspapers was correct, they weren't beyond administering their own subtle forms of punishment. Someday she might need them, really need them. Could she risk turning them off to her now?

Moreover, what could she say? That she'd been terrified because so many strange things had happened to her of late? They'd think she was nuts. A wild dog. A garage door that went bump. A ghost in her underwear. Maybe she *was* nuts.

No one was following her now, but then, she hadn't expected that anyone would be. Some cop had been playing his own perverse game, perhaps simply practicing up on the technique of the chase. It must be boring being a cop in as peaceful a town as Lincoln. No doubt he'd enjoyed the excitement of his little escapade. At that moment he was probably sitting in the back room with his police buddies, having a good laugh.

Lauren put the car in the garage, then all but ran for the side door of the farmhouse. No doubt about it, she was spooked. She'd left her pursuer at the police station. She'd reasoned away all of her other little near-mishaps. Still, she was spooked.

Coincidence and imagination were a combustible combination.

Turning on every available light, she walked from room to room before satisfying herself that everything was the same as when she'd left that morning. That morning seemed so very far away. And that evening had been so very special, but somehow tarnished by the terrifying experience she'd just been through.

After leaving a single bright light on downstairs, she went up to bed, thinking about the outside floodlights she would have put in when she finally found an electrician. Perhaps she *should* consider a burglar alarm. God, she hated that thought. One of the reasons she'd bought a home in the country was to avoid the stereotypical city fears.

She was making something out of nothing, she reminded herself for the umpteenth time as she lay in the dark of her bedroom, afraid to move. She was letting Beth's wild imagination get to her. She was letting her own wild imagination get to her. Maybe Beth was right. Maybe she did need a bodyguard. The thought of Matt Kruger—strong, capable of protecting her, capable of thrilling her with a kiss—brought some measure of relaxation, so that at last she was able to fall asleep.

That weekend, working around the hours when the shop was open, Lauren met with three different general contractors to discuss what she wanted to do with the farmhouse. None of the three impressed her.

The first was too traditional in his orientation. What she wanted wasn't exactly restoration, she tried to explain. Yes, she wanted the outside of the farmhouse to look much the way it always had. But she wanted the inside to be a modern surprise of sorts.

Unfortunately, number one didn't have much imagination when it came to modern surprises.

Number two was both patronizing and condescending. "I know exactly what you want," he informed her, then proceeded to tell her what he'd do to the farmhouse. It was exactly what she didn't want.

Number three was not only late for the appointment, but both he and his truck were filthy. That said a lot in her book. She could just picture hiring the man and having him show up for work when the mood suited him. He'd probably leave a mess behind every day for her to trip over, and then she'd have to hire a team of workers to clean up after him.

She'd gone to the contractors first in the hope of finding someone who would then issue subcontracts for things like plumbing and electricity. Now, having struck out, she debated calling the plumbers and electricians herself. Lord only knew she desperately needed to get the job done.

She decided to wait for Matt to return. He'd help her. And she trusted him. She'd never seen his work, but she somehow knew that any recommendations he made would be solid.

By Sunday night, she was thinking of Matt more and more, wondering when he'd be returning and what would happen then. She liked him—very, very much. She wanted to believe that his finest qualities—his gentleness, honesty and spontaneity—were indicative of the way Brad had been, too. She still wondered about Brad, still had questions for Matt to answer. But when she was with Matt she wasn't thinking brotherly thoughts. Matt intrigued her. He excited her. He seemed to take the best of both worlds—brain and brawn—and emerge superior. He wasn't quite like anyone she'd ever known before.

Nor did he kiss like anyone she'd ever known before. Not that she was anywhere near to being an expert on kissing. But she'd dreamed of feeling things in a kiss, and Matt had taken her far, far beyond those dreams—so much so that the restlessness she felt was no mystery.

Knowledge of the cause of a problem was not, however, a solution in itself. And since the solution was for the present out of reach, Lauren did the next best thing. Leaving a light burning in the living room, which had become a habit, she headed upstairs to treat herself to a long, soothing shower.

"Treat" was the operative word. As with most everything else pertaining to the farmhouse, the hot-water heater was small and outmoded. Even with its thermostat set on high, the "hot" was negligible. She'd quickly learned that she couldn't take a shower and then expect there to be enough hot water for the laundry. But she wasn't doing laundry that night, and she fully intended to indulge herself until the water ran cold.

Tossing her clothes into the hamper, she took a fresh nightgown from her drawer and went into the bathroom. The shower was little more than a head rigged high in the bathtub, but it served the purpose. She turned on the water, drew the curtain, waited until steam rose above it, then stepped inside.

Heaven. Just what the doctor ordered. Eyes closed, she tipped back her head and let the warmth flow over her hair, shoulders, back and legs. Soap in hand, she lathered her body, then turned, inch by inch, to rinse off. Relaxation seeped through her. She rocked slowly to the pulse of the water.

Then she heard a noise. Her head shot up and her eyes flew open. The slam of a door? Or was it her imagination? She lingered beneath the spray, listening closely. She thought she felt vibrations.

Without pausing to decide whether the vibrations were footsteps or her own thudding heart, she reached back and quickly turned off the water. Then she grabbed her towel and, with jerky movements, began to dry off. Under the circumstances, she did a commendable job, though her nightgown didn't realize that. It stuck so perversely to the damp spots she'd left that she was all but screaming in frustration by the time she finally managed to get it on properly.

Holding her breath, she peered around the bathroom door into the bedroom. When she didn't see anyone there, she dashed out to her closet and grabbed the first weapon she could find. The heavy, workhorse of a Nikon camera, which she hadn't used in years, would certainly serve as a makeshift club, particularly when heaved from its strap.

She tiptoed to the wall by the open bedroom door, flattened herself against it and listened. And listened. Nothing.

She took a deep breath, then yelled as forcefully as she could, "I've already connected with the police department and they're on their way! Better get out while you can!"

Silence.

Of course, she hadn't connected with the police department. They'd think she was a fool. Old houses made noises all the time, and she wasn't sure she'd lived long enough in this one to be able to identify all its characteristic moans and groans. No, she wasn't convinced there was an intruder.

On the other hand, she wasn't convinced there wasn't one, either.

Figuring that she'd need every precious moment if someone should storm in, she reached for the light switch and threw the room into a darkness that was broken only by a faint glow from the bathroom. Then, moving as silently as she could, given that she was more than a little unsteady on her feet, she wedged herself behind the bedroom door and peered through the crack, waiting for someone to creep up the stairs or emerge from one of the other two bedrooms.

No one did.

Noiselessly, Lauren sank to the floor, her gaze never once leaving the narrow slit of a peephole. She waited and watched and listened, growing stiff with tension but not daring to move. Five minutes passed, and there was nothing. Ten minutes passed, and she continued to wait, her temple now pressed wearily to the wall. By the time fifteen minutes had elapsed, she had to admit that she'd very possibly jumped to conclusions.

She wasn't convinced enough to leave herself unprotected, though. To that measure, she carefully closed the bedroom door, carried over a chair and propped it beneath the knob. Then, with the strap of the camera still wound around her hand, she climbed into bed and lay stiffly, listening, waiting. The only thing she was sure about as the hours crept by was that she very definitely would have a burglar alarm system installed when the house was sufficiently readied for it. Nights like this she didn't need.

Unless, of course, she had that bodyguard.

CHAPTER FIVE

When the phone rang early the next morning, Lauren jumped. She was in the kitchen, trying to force down a breakfast she didn't really want, and the unexpected sound jarred her already taut nerves. Snatching up the receiver after the first ring, she gasped a breathless "Hello?"

"Lauren? It's Matt."

Hand over her heart, she let out a sigh of relief. It wasn't that she'd actually expected someone menacing to be on the other end of the line but, rather, that the sound of Matt's voice was an instant and incredible comfort. "Matt," she murmured. "I'm so glad. . . ."

There was a slight pause. "Is something wrong?"

"No, no. Just me and my imagination." She put her hand on the top of her head and found herself spilling it all. "I had the worst time last night. I was in the shower and thought I heard a noise. It turned out to be nothing, but the weirdest things have been happening lately, Matt. You wouldn't believe it. After I left you the night of the concert, some car tailed me all the way home. Well, not all the way, but almost. And before that the garage door had missed me by inches, and the dog had attacked me, and the car had swerved into the sidewalk—"

"Whoa, sweetheart. Slow up a bit. It doesn't sound like it's all been your imagination."

"No, but my imagination has been connecting all these little things that have nothing to do with one another and could really have happened to anyone—"

"But they happened to you." His voice was low and distinctly grim. "When did this all start?"

"I don't know . . . maybe a week and a half ago. It's like every few days something happens. I never thought I was accident-prone, but I'm beginning to wonder. Beth thought it was a ghost—"

"A ghost? Come on!"

"I know, I know, but if someone's trying to scare me out of this farmhouse, he's doing one hell of a job."

Matt was silent for several long seconds. "Listen, I'm still in Leominster, but I'll be driving back later this afternoon. Why don't I meet you at home? If I get there before you do, I can take a look around."

Lauren was without pride at that moment, and self-sufficiency was a luxury she couldn't afford. "Would you? I'd be so grateful, Matt! I've never been one to be spooked, but I'm as spooked as they come right about now. I don't think I slept more than two or three hours last night, and that was with a chair propped against the bedroom door and a camera nearby."

"You were going to take pictures?" he asked in

meek disbelief.

"I was going to hit whoever it was over the head! My camera was the closest thing to a weapon I had. And then this morning I crept around the house looking for signs of an intruder. Crept around my own house in broad daylight—I must be getting paranoid!"

"Shh. Don't say things like that, Lauren. I'm sure there are perfectly logical explanations for everything that's happened."

"That's what I've been telling myself, but it's getting harder to believe. I mean, I can't deny that a car nearly ran me down, or that a dog attacked me, or that the garage door fell . . . but someone going through my lingerie?"

Matt cleared his throat. "Someone going through your lingerie?"

"See? You think I'm crazy, too!"

"I do not think you're crazy. Never that. You strike me as one of the most together women I've ever known."

"But you don't know me. Not really."

"Well, we'll have to do something about that, then. Tonight?"

"Promise you'll come?"

"I promise."

Lauren gave him directions; then, for the first time that morning, she smiled. "Thanks, Matt. I feel better already."

"So do I, sweetheart. See ya later."

Lauren arrived home from work that night to find a

car in the drive. It was a brown Topaz and had local· license plates. She assumed it was Matt's rental, but, seeing no sign of him, she felt a momentary tension. The car that had tailed her the Thursday before had been of a similar size, and though she'd had only glimpses of it when it passed beneath lights, she'd guessed it was either maroon or brown.

Staying where she was, safely locked inside her car with the motor running just in case, she leaned heavily on the horn. Then she waited. She seemed to be doing a lot of that lately.

This time she didn't have long to wait. Within a minute, Matt opened the front door of the house and loped out to greet her. The relief and sheer pleasure she felt upon seeing him eclipsed the fact that he'd somehow entered her house without a key.

Killing the motor, she scrambled from the car and threw herself into his arms. It seemed the most natural thing to do and, given the way Matt's arms wound tightly around her, he appeared to have no objections.

When at last he set her down, they exchanged silly grins.

"You look wonderful," he said. "A little tired, maybe, but a sight for sore eyes."

"I could say the same." Her hands were looped around his neck, her lower body flush with his. He looked positively gorgeous, sun-baked skin, slightly crooked nose, too-square chin and all. "Thanks for coming, Matt. I really needed you here. Did you have any trouble finding the place?"

"Nope. Your directions were perfect. I got here a

couple of hours ago. It's a nice place, Lauren. I can see why you bought it. It does have charm."

"But does it have ghosts? That's what I *really* need to know."

Taking her hand, he started with her toward the house. "No ghosts. Just lots of things that need repairing." He cleared his throat. "For starters, the lock on one of the back windows is broken. I had no trouble climbing inside."

So that was how he'd done it. Simple enough. "But I tested all the locks. I was sure they worked!"

"Oh, this one works, all right. Until you raise the window. The wood around the screws has rotted. The entire lock simply slides up with the window. Close the window and the lock is in place again." He paused. "Which means that there's good news and bad news."

"Mmm." She dropped her purse on the chair just inside the front door. "The good news is that there's no ghost. The bad news is that the moving around of things inside the house was caused by a human intruder."

"Right. Hey, don't look so down. Every other lock in the house is solid, so it's just a matter of fixing this one. I've already been to the hardware store and picked up larger screws and packing. That'll hold the lock until the wood can be replaced."

"Oh, Matt, you didn't have to."

"I did it for my own peace of mind, if nothing else. Besides, fixing things is my specialty." He eyed her apologetically as they entered the kitchen. "I'm not sure I did as well with dinner. I picked up some things in town, but I'm afraid I'm not all that good a cook."

"I could have taken care of that."

"You'll still have to. I made a salad and husked some sweet corn, but I didn't know what in the hell to do with the chicken. At home I douse it in barbecue sauce and throw it on the grill, but you don't have a grill, and for the life of me I couldn't figure out how the broiler in that stove of yours works." His eyes shot daggers at the appliance in question.

She laughed. "It doesn't. The stove has to be replaced along with the refrigerator, the hot-water heater, the furnace—I could go on and on."

"So what do we do with the chicken?" Opening the refrigerator, he removed the plastic-wrapped package.

"We bake it. And I've got a super sauce. You'll think you're eating the best of barbecue." She looked toward the single cabinet on the wall beside the sink, then down at her sleeveless beige jump suit. "I'd better change first. By the way, was that a bottle of wine I saw in the refrigerator?"

He nodded. "California's finest, already chilled. I'll pour while you change. Then we can talk."

Talk. For a minute she'd forgotten what they needed to discuss. She felt so good, so safe, with Matt that the last thing on her mind had been her series of recent misadventures. But she wanted to tell him. Matt was levelheaded and straightforward. She trusted that he'd be honest with her and let her know if she was making a mountain out of a molehill.

She trotted upstairs to her bedroom, changed into a pair of jeans and an oversize gray shirt that she knotted at the waist, then returned to the kitchen in record time.

Matt stood at the kitchen window, looking out at the field beyond. He spun around in surprise when she breezed into the room, then stared at her and swallowed hard.

"I . . . is something wrong?" She glanced down at herself.

"No. Not at all. It's just that I've never seen you in play clothes."

Lauren could have kicked herself for not having taken the time to touch up her makeup and brush out her hair. In the past those things had never mattered. She'd looked as good—or as bad—with or without the primping. She'd forgotten that she had something to work with now. But it was too late.

Self-consciously, she reached up to finger-comb her hair toward her cheek, but Matt crossed the room in two long strides and stayed her hand. "Don't. Don't do that." Releasing her hand, he used his own fingers as a comb to smooth the hair back. "You look so pretty. I want to see your face."

You look so pretty. I want to see your face. So hard to believe. So . . . strange. "I look tired. I should have done something."

"You look beautiful—and with only two or three hours' sleep." Dipping his head, he brushed a kiss on her cheek, another closer to her mouth, then another closer still. His hand was curved around her jaw by the time he reached her lips, though Lauren wouldn't have pulled away even if he hadn't held her. His nearness was drugging, his kiss intoxicating. His breath mingled with hers, seeming to bring her to life as she'd never lived it before. She forgot all else but the sweet sensation of closeness, of awareness, of longing that the caress of his mouth inspired.

"Ahh," he breathed against her lips at last, "your kiss takes me . . ."

"You have it . . . the wrong way around."

"Then it's reciprocal, which is why it happens to begin with."

"This is getting confusing."

"Mmm." He smacked his mouth to hers, then set her back and put his wineglass in her hand. She sipped the wine, perfectly content to drink from his glass while he laid claim to the second he'd poured. "Now, let me watch you make this super sauce of yours. I want to see what you put in it."

She grinned. "Cautious, Matthew. Hungry but cautious."

"Quite" was all he said, but the grin he gave her stole her breath almost as completely as his kiss had. Fearing for the state of her health, she quickly set to work mixing the ingredients of her super sauce, then indulged Matt by offering him the spoon for a taste.

"Mmm." He licked his lips. "Not bad. Not bad at all."

"Don't give me 'not bad.' It's *super*. At least," she added in a demure undertone, "that's what it was called in the cookbook I took it from."

"Ah, a cookbook reader." He glanced around. "But I don't see any cookbooks."

She flipped open the cabinet and pointed.

"Two cookbooks? That's all? A cookbook reader is supposed to have a huge collection."

"I'm, uh, I'm a little new at it." She unwrapped the chicken and rinsed it under the faucet.

"You didn't used to cook?"

"I didn't used to eat."

Matt chuckled and scratched his forehead. "That picture. I'd forgotten. You were pretty skinny back then—no offense intended."

"None taken. You're right, I was pretty skinny. It's just recently that I've been forcing myself to eat. I don't dare tell that to many people, mind you," she added, patting the chicken dry with a paper towel. "Most of them get annoyed."

"Jealousy, plain and simple."

She sent him a mischievous grin, then knelt down to remove a baking dish from the lone lower cabinet. That took some doing on her part. Pots were piled on top of pots, which were piled on top of pans, which were piled on top of the baking dish. "Top priority in this kitchen," she announced, rising at last, "is new cabinets, and plenty of them."

"Cabinets—easily done. What else?"

As Lauren dipped the pieces of chicken, one by one, into the sauce and placed them in the baking dish, she outlined her concept of the perfect kitchen, only to find that Matt's suggestions and additions made her plans more perfect than before.

"Why didn't *I* think of a center island?" she asked as she shoved the baking dish into the oven.

"Because you're not a builder."

"And you do this kind of thing?"

His shrug was one of modesty. "The development we're planning in Leominster is a cluster-home type of complex, a planned-community thing. Modern and elegant but also practical. Island counters in the kitchens are an option. They can be used for storage underneath and eating above, or for a sink and a stovetop. Lord only knows, this kitchen's big enough to handle an island."

"And you know people who can do this for me?"

He patted the breast pocket of his shirt. "Names and numbers, already checked out."

With exaggerated greed, she put out her hand. "Gimme. I'll make the calls tomorrow." She proceeded to tell him of the contractors she'd interviewed herself; well before she had finished, he'd closed her fingers around his list. She promptly secured the piece of paper with a decorative magnet on the refrigerator door, then reached for the foil-wrapped loaf of French bread Matt had brought.

He clasped her wrist. "Set the timer for twenty-five minutes. That'll be plenty early to put the bread in the oven." While she did so and then put a pot of water on to heat for the corn, he refilled their wineglasses. "Come on. Let's go out back. I want to hear more about your . . . escapades."

With vague reluctance, since she'd enjoyed talking with Matt about lighter subjects, Lauren led the way through the back door to the yard. A weathered bench under the canopy of an apple tree provided them with seats. Sunset approached; shards of orange and gold sliced through the trees and threw elongated shadows on the grass.

"Okay," he said. "Start from the top. I want to hear about each thing as it happened."

Encouraged that at least he was taking her seriously, she turned her thoughts to the days that had passed. "The first incident took place more than a week and a half ago, I guess." She related the Newbury Street story. "I don't know if the driver was drunk. I don't even know if it was a man or a woman."

"How about the car? Size? Color?"

She shook her head. "It came from behind. I don't think it was red or yellow. Nothing bright—that would have stuck with me. It must have been some nondescript color. As for the size, God only knows."

"Did you go to the police?"

"What could the police do? The car was gone."

"Maybe there was a witness who caught the license number."

"If there was one, he or she certainly didn't come forward. I just assumed I'd had a close call with a freak accident and left it at that."

He nodded. "Okay. What next?"

"Next was the dog. My run-in with him was . . . I don't know, maybe two days after the incident with the car." She described what had happened. "As soon as I was down on the ground and thoroughly frightened, he took off. Like he'd simply lost interest."

"You said it was a Doberman?"

"I said it *might* have been a Doberman. It's the same

with the car. You're so stunned when it happens that the details slip by you. And anyway, it was dark."

"Was the dog wearing a collar?"

"That's the last detail I'd have noticed."

"Not if your hand had hit something when you tried to push him away."

"My hands were busy protecting my face. I kicked out with my legs—pretty ineffectively, I'd guess. If that dog hadn't wanted to leave, he wouldn't have."

Matt seemed about to say something, then stopped and took a breath. "Did you call the police?"

Lauren shook her head. "The dog was gone. It hasn't been back since."

Even in the fading light, the tension on Matt's face was marked. "Then what?"

She took a drink of wine for fortification. On the one hand, Matt's grim concern was reassuring. On the other, it seemed to make the situation all the more real and, therefore, ominous. "Then the garage door crashed down. It's an old garage, an old door. I'd simply assumed it would hold."

"I checked it out. There's no apparent reason why it didn't. The chains are strong. So are the coils."

"Then what could explain it?"

He looked off toward the shadowed trees and didn't speak for several minutes. "There are ways to rig a door like that."

"But it worked perfectly the next day, and every day since!"

"There's rigging—and unrigging."

Apprehension made her gray eyes larger. "You're

suggesting that whoever might have tampered with it before it crashed down went back and fixed it again? But why would anyone *do* that?"

"What happened next?"

Lauren stared at him. He hadn't attempted to answer her question. Not that he ought to have an answer when she didn't, but at least he could have tried to soothe her. Brows lowered, she looked away. What had happened next? "I'm not sure about the next thing. It wasn't as obvious as the others . . . I mean, it could have been me."

"What was it, Lauren?"

She took a short breath. "After we'd gone on the cruise that night, I came home and noticed that some things were out of place in my bedroom. At least, they seemed out of place to me, but it might have been my own carelessness." When his silence demanded further explanation, she told him about the perfume, the shoes and the underwear.

"Nothing was taken? Money? Jewelry?"

"I don't have much of either lying around, but no, nothing was taken."

"And it was only the bedroom that was touched?"

"As far as I could tell."

"Did you go through the other rooms?"

"Of course I did! And nothing was touched—*as far as I could tell*. Honestly, Matt! I mean, it's possible that the spoons in the kitchen drawer were rearranged, but I don't set them up in any special pattern, so how would I know?"

He held up a hand. "Okay, okay. Take it easy."

Even the softening of his tone did little to calm her. "How can I take it easy? I feel like I'm at an inquisition, and the implication is that you think I've been irresponsible. Well, I haven't! Taken separately, not one of these incidents is particularly unusual. People on the streets have close calls with cars all the time. Wild dogs get loose; they attack innocent victims. Garage doors malfunction. And as for my personal effects, that could just as well have been my own fault. I'm not perfect! I might have been distracted! And *don't* ask me if I called the police, because I didn't!"

"I didn't ask," he said. His words were gently spoken; his gaze was solicitous. "And I'm sorry if I sounded critical. It's just that I'm concerned . . . and I'm a stickler for details. I like to know exactly what I'm facing." He slanted her a lopsided smile. "You were supposed to know that already."

Immediately ashamed of her outburst, Lauren sent him a look of apology. "I forgot."

"Well, don't," Matt went on in the same soft voice. "I'm looking for any possible detail that would give us some clue to whether the things that have happened are unrelated or not."

She shivered at the latter thought. "I know. And I appreciate your listening to all this. But I don't know in which direction to turn at this point."

"Which is why you should tell me everything." He paused. "All set?" When she nodded, he released a breath. "Okay. Some things were amiss in your bedroom. Possibly your own fault. What was the next thing that happened?"

"The car followed me home."

"Did you see where it picked you up?"

She shook her head. "It could have been anywhere. I was on Storrow Drive when I first noticed the head-lights in my rearview mirror."

"Make of the car?"

She shrugged and shook her head.

"Color?"

"Dark. At the time I thought it was maroon or brown, but it was hard to tell." Her eyes widened. "Do you think it could have been the same car that nearly hit me on Newbury Street?"

"I don't know. There are a hell of a lot of maroon and brown cars on the road. Without a make and model, we're clutching at straws."

"I'm sorry," she murmured. "Cars aren't my thing. I'm no good at identifying them."

"That's okay, Lauren. Do you remember when it finally dropped away?"

"It didn't, in a sense." She explained how she'd headed straight for the police station, where the car had nonchalantly pulled into a parking space. When Matt remained silent, she feared that he would chide her for not entering the station and complaining; she still wondered if she should have done that. "Well?"

"It's odd," he said at last. "Could have been a policeman having a little fun on his way to work, but all the way from Boston? And he stopped, then picked you up again."

"But he had to be harmless if he was a policeman."

"If, and that's a big if."

"Matt, he pulled into that space as if he knew just where he was going!"

"He may have pulled out just as smoothly once you drove on."

"And if I'd gone in to file a complaint?"

"He could have driven off anyway. You would have led the officer on duty to the parking lot, only to find that there wasn't any car there."

"Mmm. And the officer would have thought I'd dreamed the whole thing up."

"Possibly. Okay, the only thing left, then, is the matter of strange noises last night. Tell me exactly what you heard."

She did. "By the time I came out of the shower, there was nothing. Maybe I imagined it all."

"Maybe."

Then again, maybe not. "If someone had gotten *in* the house, wouldn't he have had to get *out*? I was so spooked that even the tiniest creak in the floorboards would have sounded like thunder to me. But there was nothing. I'm sure of it."

"And when you got up in the morning, there was no sign of an intruder?"

"Nothing."

"No window partway open? No dirt tracked onto the floor?"

"Nothing."

"And is that it? No other suspicious incidents in the past few weeks? Anything that, with a twist of the imagination, might seem odd?"

She thought about it, going back over the days with a fine-tooth comb. Eventually she shook her head. "Nothing."

Matt sat back on the bench, deep in thought. Sandy brows shaded his eyes. His mouth was drawn into a tight line. Lauren studied him, waiting to hear what he had to say. When he stood up abruptly and began to walk back toward the house, she was mystified.

"Matt?" She bolted to her feet, jogging to catch up. He looked at her almost in surprise, and she wondered where his thoughts had been.

"Oh. Sorry. I thought I'd put the bread in the oven now."

"But the timer—"

"We wouldn't have heard it." Sure enough, as they mounted the back steps they caught the insistent buzz.

Biding her time with some effort, she watched him open the oven door, flip over each piece of chicken, then slip the pre-buttered loaf onto the lower shelf. Without missing a beat, he carefully dropped the husked ears of corn into the now-boiling water.

Finally she couldn't wait any longer. "Well? What do you think?"

"Mmm. Chicken smells good."

"Not the chicken. My *predicament. Is* someone after me?"

Straightening, he leaned back against the chipped counter and studied her. "Is there a *reason* that someone should be after you?"

She couldn't believe the question. "Of course not! I haven't done anything. I haven't hurt anyone. To my knowledge, I don't have any enemies. I'm amazed you'd even ask that!"

"Just ruling it out. It's as good a place as any to start."

"Well, we've started. A more probable possibility is that these incidents have something to do with the farmhouse. Everything began after I moved in."

"When, exactly, did you move in?"

"The first week in June."

"And the car incident took place, what, at the end of the month?" He thrust out his jaw. "The delay doesn't make sense. If someone legitimately didn't want you living here, the incidents would have started while you were first looking over the place, or certainly as soon as you'd moved in. Besides, not all of the things have happened here. Nah, I don't think they have anything to do with the farmhouse."

"That'd be the most plausible explanation," she pointed out. "And it'd be the easiest one to follow up. I've considered the possibility that one of the neighbors doesn't want me here, but the few I've met have been pleasant enough, and I can't think of any reason that my presence would be objectionable. I know nothing about the former owners, though. I could speak with the realtor and go through the records of who has lived here in the past. If necessary, I could call in a private investigator, or even the police—"

"Don't do that," Matt interrupted, then quickly gentled his voice. "Not yet, at least."

Though Lauren herself hadn't been anxious to call the police, she was surprised by his vehemence. It occurred to her that he might be indulging her in her fancy while not quite taking it to heart. "What do you suggest?" she asked more cautiously.

"Let's consider the possibilities." He squinted with one eye. "Are you sure you can't think of someone who might get his jollies by scaring you?"

"Like who?"

He shrugged. "An old boyfriend?"

"An old boyfriend who'd come all the way from Bennington in search of a little mischief?"

"Then maybe someone you might have met since you've been here. Someone who asked you out. Or followed you around. Or just . . . looked at you for hours on end."

"You're the only one who's done that," she replied with a smirk. "Maybe you've got a Jekyll and Hyde thing going."

The twitch of his nose told her what he thought of that idea.

"Well," she went on, thinking aloud, "it could always be a random lunatic."

He shook his head. "Too persistent. Your average random lunatic may hit once, even twice, but not six times. Your average random lunatic wouldn't have access to a trained attack dog—"

Horrified, Lauren interrupted him. "Trained? Do you think that dog was trained?"

Matt gnawed on his lower lip, as though regretting what he'd said, but the damage had been done. "It's possible. If it was trained to respond to a high-pitched whistle that our ears can't detect, that would explain why it retreated so abruptly."

"Just enough to frighten me . . . not enough to harm me. What kind of insanity are we dealing with?" Her voice had reached its own high pitch.

He gave her shoulder a reassuring squeeze. "We don't know anything for sure, except that so far you haven't been hurt."

"But I *could* have been. If I'd been a little slower in leaving my garage that night . . . if there'd been no Good Samaritan near me on Newbury Street that day . . ."

Responding to the sudden pallor of her skin, Matt drew her against him and slowly rubbed her back. "Don't think about what might have been," he murmured. "Nothing's happened, and if I have any say in the matter, nothing will."

With her head pressed to his heart, Lauren believed every word he said. She didn't stop to ask him how he intended to protect her. She didn't stop to ask herself why she, who valued her independence highly, welcomed the protection. She only knew that Matthew Kruger filled a spot that, at this particular point in her life, was open and waiting for him.

He drew back from her to ask, "Think that chicken's almost ready?"

"The chicken!" Pushing herself away from him, Lauren flung open the oven door, reached for a pair of mitts and pulled out first the chicken, then the bread. "Thank goodness it's not burned! I'd forgotten all about it!" She teased him with a punishing glance. "And it's *your* fault."

"My fault?" He was the image of innocence. "You said *you* were the cook around here."

"But you've kept me preoccupied. I haven't even set the table!" The item in question was of the card-table variety, albeit inlaid with cane, and there were folding chairs to match. She'd picked them up to use until she bought regular furniture.

"Then you do that while I toss the salad," Matt suggested. He was already draining the sweet corn. "I picked up a creamy cucumber dressing—unless you've got a super dressing of your own."

The twinkle in his eye brought fresh color to her cheeks and a momentary curl of warmth to the pit of her stomach. "Creamy cucumber's fine. Super sauce I can handle; super dressing is still a way down the road." As she reached for the dishes, she said, "It's amazing . . ."

"What is?" Matt asked, removing the salad from the refrigerator.

"That you can take my mind off things. Not only dinner, but everything else. One minute I can be worried sick about what's been happening; the next, I forget all about it."

"Maybe you've been worrying for nothing," he ventured quietly. "Maybe all that's happened really *is* a coincidence."

"Maybe . . . but it's crazy. Everything's been so wonderful. I left Bennington. I have a new job, new home, new look—" The last had slipped out. She rushed on. "Maybe it's all too good to be true."

Matt poured dressing on the salad and began to toss

it. "I'm sure that whatever's been going on can be taken care of."

"But how can it be taken care of if I don't know what it is?"

"In time, Lauren. In time. Let's get back to the random-lunatic theory. Lunatic, perhaps. Random, unlikely." He held the salad tongs in the air for a minute before resuming his tossing. "Are you absolutely sure you can't think of anyone who might be behind it?"

Lauren set the silverware on the table with far greater force than necessary. "Yes, I'm sure. I've told you that, Matt. I don't know anyone who'd be capable of doing what has been done. Why do you keep harping on it?"

He hesitated. "Because the only other possibility is that we're facing someone who is neither lunatic nor random, but who has a very specific ax to grind. Maybe someone who has a grudge against your family."

Her jaw fell open, then snapped back into place. "If you knew my parents, you'd never even suggest that. They are utterly harmless. They live in an insulated little world. There may be competition within the academic community, but my parents have been so well accepted for so long that I can't begin to imagine anyone's acting out of jealousy, much less trying to seek revenge. And if someone did, he or she sure as hell wouldn't do it through me. I've declared my independence in ways that have my parents climbing those ivy-covered walls of theirs—" Her voice broke abruptly, and for a minute she wished she could retract what she'd said. Then she realized that there was no point in being coy. Matt, more than anyone, would understand.

He brooded for a minute as he placed the salad on the table, then reached for the wine. "What do you mean?"

Lauren opened the foil-wrapped bread with care. It was hot. "What I'm doing with my life isn't exactly what my parents had wanted me to do."

"In what sense?"

"Oh," she began, juggling the steaming loaf into a bread basket, "they would have preferred that I stay in Bennington and work at the museum. I'd be sur-rounded by culture, attend plays and lectures, take part in a weekly reading-and-discussion group. Then I'd marry some nice, pale-faced fellow whose interests lay in Babylonian astronomy or medieval art or com-parative linguistics. I'd go on to have sweet little chil-dren who would take up the cello at age four, read Dostoyevsky at age eight, write a novel at age twelve and beg for college admittance at age fourteen."

"And you? What would you prefer?"

"Me?" She set the bread basket on the table and looked up at him pleadingly. "I want to be happy. I want to do well at whatever I choose to do. I want to feel good about myself."

"And a husband and children?"

Shrugging, she brought the plates to the stove. "I haven't thought that far yet."

"Sure you have. Every woman dreams."

"Every man does, too," she countered.

"But I asked you first. What do you want in a husband? What do you want for your children?"

She put two pieces of chicken on Matt's plate, a single piece on her own. "The same thing I want for myself, I suppose. If a person is happy, and feels good about himself, everything else falls into place." She added an ear of corn to each plate before bringing both to the table.

"How can your parents argue with that?"

"They believe that certain things make a person happy. We just disagree on what those things are."

Matt was standing with one hand on his hip as he watched her. Straightening suddenly, he tilted a chair out and gestured for her to sit. "Brad's philosophy was similar. It's amazing how alike you are in so many ways. Then again, there are differences."

"Tell me more about him, Matt. Did he really feel the same way I do?"

Matt slowly seated himself and didn't speak until he'd pulled his chair in and spread a napkin on his lap. His expression was pensive. "He felt that what your parents wanted was different from what he wanted. But you already know that. I think he would have been surprised that you agree with him. He saw himself as the black sheep of the family."

"So much so that, regardless of what he did, it didn't seem to measure up?" she asked.

Matt frowned, then shifted in his seat. He drew the salad bowl toward him and prodded the lettuce with the tongs. In a sudden spurt of movement, he began to pile salad on Lauren's plate. "Is that the way *you* feel? That nothing you do can measure up?"

"Hey." She put her hand on his and pushed the tongs toward his own plate. "That's enough."

He served himself. "Do you feel that way, Lauren?"

"No. I'm pleased with what I'm doing. Brad tried to meet my parents' expectations, failed, then took off. I went along with their wishes and was fairly successful at it before realizing that it wasn't what I wanted. I left because I chose to. Brad left because he had to. I could have gone on forever up there, I suppose. Brad couldn't have survived." She took a breath. Her fork dangled over the chicken. "It wasn't that he didn't have the brains for it, but his temperament was totally different. He was more impulsive, more restless. Hyperactive, my parents always said, but I think they were wrong. He just wanted to use his brains for things other than scholarly pursuits."

"He did that," Matt drawled under his breath, but there was no humor in his expression. When he saw Lauren staring at him, puzzled, he spoke quickly. "Designing houses, interesting houses, takes brains, although it's not considered a scholarly occupation. It's too bad your parents couldn't have seen some of the work Brad did."

"They never even knew about it" was her sad reply. "They didn't know who he worked for or what he did. They were shocked at the amount of money that came to me when he died." She rolled her eyes. "For that matter, so was I."

Matt's hesitation was a weighty one. "They didn't

begrudge it to you, did they?"

"No." She snorted. "The only thing they begrudged was what I *did* with it." Spearing a tomato wedge, she waved it for an instant. "Family interrelationships are weird things. Expectations are often so unrealistic. It's as if we have blinkers on. I suppose I'm not that much more understanding of my parents than they are of me, but it's a shame. I'm an adult now. They're adults. Wouldn't it be nice if we *liked* one another?"

"It's not that simple. You're right. Unrealistic expectations can stand in the way. Or ego needs. It must be difficult in a situation like yours, where it would be impossible for you to rise above what your parents have done. They've been so successful in their fields. Maybe that's why both you and Brad felt the need to strike out on your own."

"Maybe. I hadn't thought about it that way." Lauren mulled over the prospect for several minutes, but what lingered with her was how insightful Matt was. "What about you? Are you close to your family?"

"Very."

"Are they in San Francisco, too?"

He shook his head. "L.A. I guess I needed a little distance, just as you do. The pressure coming from my parents was a more traditional one. They're retired now, but for years they both worked in a factory. They wanted my sister and me to rise higher, to advance socially. Unfortunately, there wasn't much money for college. I suppose I could have tried for a scholarship, but I wanted to work. Once I got going, I discovered that I could get the education I needed on the job. I've taken business courses here and there, and I've advanced, so I can't complain."

"How about your sister?"

Matt warmed Lauren with a grin. "Maggie's a speech therapist. She *did* go for a scholarship, won it and wowed 'em all at UCLA. I'm really proud of her. We all are."

"I can see that," Lauren said. His grin was contagious, or was it the way his cheeks bunched up and his eyes crinkled? Whatever, she was grinning back at him, wondering how a man could be so gentle and giving, yet so wickedly attractive. "Tell me more," she urged. "About when you were a kid, what you were like, what you did."

He made a face and tilted his head to the side. "It's really not all that exciting."

"Tell me anyway." She perched her chin in her palm and waited expectantly.

"Only if you eat while I talk. You haven't had more than a bite, and the chicken is fantastic."

Listening to Matt and watching him drove all thought of food from her mind. But if eating was his precondition, well . . .

He talked and she ate. She made observations and asked questions while he ate, then resumed her own meal when he talked more. By the time they'd had seconds of just about everything, including wine, she'd learned that, though a mischievous Matt had received his share of spankings as a boy, he'd grown up in a house filled with love. She'd also learned, but between the lines, that what Matt craved most was his own house filled with love.

When he offered to help her clean up, she accepted. It wasn't that she needed the help or that she was liberated enough to demand it. She'd thoroughly enjoyed the way they'd worked together getting the dinner ready, and she wanted to draw out the evening as long as possible.

Apparently Matt had the same idea. When the kitchen was as spotless as one that age could be, he suggested they relax for a few minutes before he left. They settled in the living room, which, aside from Lauren's bedroom, was the only room with furnishings. There was one sofa and two side chairs. They shared the sofa.

Lauren felt peaceful and happy and tremendously drawn to the man beside her. His arm was slung across the back of the sofa, his fingers tangling in her hair. The clean, manly scent that clung to his skin heightened her senses, while his warmth bridged the small space between them with its invisible touch.

"This has been nice," she told him, slanting a shy glance his way. "I'm glad you came."

His voice was like a velvet mist. "So am I." Sliding his arm around her shoulders, he drew her closer even as he met her halfway. His lips touched one corner of her mouth, then the other, then her cupid's bow, then her lower lip. He'd opened his mouth to kiss her fully when, unable to help herself, she laughed.

He drew back and stared at her for a minute, then cried in mock dismay, "Lauren! What kind of behavior is that? Didn't anyone ever tell you not to laugh in a man's face when he's about to kiss you?"

"I'm sorry . . . It's just that . . . you were tasting me one little bit at a time. . . . You really *are* cautious!"

His eyes danced mischievously. "Caution's gone" was all he said before he covered her mouth with his and proceeded to deliver the most thorough kiss she'd ever received. No part of her mouth was left untouched by any part of his, and by the time he buried his face in her hair, she felt totally devoured. She might have told him so had she been able to speak, but her breath was caught somewhere between her lungs and her throat, for his hand was sliding over her waist, over and up, ever higher, and anticipation had become as tangible as those long, bronzed fingers. When at last they reached her breast, she let out a soft moan and succumbed to the exquisite sensations shooting through her.

Lauren had never been touched this way, yet there was nothing demure in her response. Both mind and body said that what she was experiencing was right and natural; instinct, goaded by desire, set her fingers to combing through his thick hair, running over his broad shoulders, splaying eagerly across his sinewed back.

"Lauren." His voice was hoarse. "Lauren . . . I have to . . . we have to stop. . . ."

"No," she whispered. She held his head with one hand, pressing it to her neck. Her other hand covered his at her breast. "Don't stop."

A groan came from deep in his chest. "Do you know what you're saying, sweetheart? What it does to me?"

His voice was thicker now, foreign to her ears yet exciting. She held her breath when he transferred her hand to his own chest and slowly slid it lower.

Lauren could feel the strength beneath her palm, the tautness of his stomach, then the stunning rigidity beneath the fly of his jeans. She wanted to hold him, explore him, let him satisfy the ache that had taken hold deep in her belly, but the newness of it all brought a measure of sanity. With a shuddering breath, she sagged against him.

"Yes. Do stop," she whispered. She was shocked by her own abandon, not quite sure what to make of it. "Everything . . . everything's happened so fast . . . and there's still the other matter." Of her own accord, she retreated from him, taking refuge in her corner of the sofa and clasping her hands tightly in her lap. The aura of arousal, a telltale quiver, lingered in her body, but thought of that "other matter" gradually put it to rest.

Matt, too, retreated to his corner of the sofa. He shifted in an attempt to get comfortable, finally hunching forward with his elbows on his knees. His fingers were interlaced, not quite at ease. He cleared his throat. "Yes . . . that other matter."

"We didn't reach any conclusions."

A pause. "No."

"What do you think?"

Another pause. "I don't know."

"Should I call the police?"

"No." Emphatically.

"Why not?"

He didn't answer, but studied his hands and

frowned. "I have to ask you this, Lauren. I know it may sound terrible . . . but you did mention that your parents were against your coming here—"

"My parents? You think my *parents* could have been behind what's happened?" Vehemently she shook her head. "No. Absolutely not. They may disagree with me, but they'd never try to harm me."

"Maybe just scare you into going back—"

"No." She was still shaking her head. "Not possible! They wouldn't be capable of conceiving of violence."

"Maybe not violence, but if they've already lost one of their children—"

"Forget it, Matt. It's simply not possible. . . . I think I should call the police."

"No."

"You've been very firm about that. Why, Matt?"

He offered the longest pause yet. "Maybe it's . . . premature."

"Premature? Then you don't think there's a connection between the things that have happened?"

"I didn't say that. I just think we ought to give it a little time. Let me see what I can do."

"What can you possibly do? Neither of us knows where to begin!"

He didn't argue with her; neither did he agree. Instead, he scowled at his hands.

"Matt, I'm frightened." As much by the strangeness of his response as by everything else, she told herself. "I haven't been hurt so far, but maybe I've just been lucky. What if the next time—"

"You won't be hurt," he gritted out, raising his dark

brown eyes to hers. She tried to read his feelings, but they were shuttered. "I'll stay here. If something happens, I can take care of it."

Lauren stared at him. "You can't stay here! My bed's the only one—and—and anyway, you can't be with me every single minute of the day. You have to work. So do I. How can you anticipate when something will happen?"

"*If* something happens."

She bolted from the sofa and began to prowl the room. She was confused and upset. "You think I'm paranoid. I know you do. You think I'm making something out of nothing." Whirling to face him, she stuck her fists on her hips and glared. "The little lady with the rampant imagination. The fanciful little woman to be indulged—that's the macho attitude isn't it? That's where *you're* coming from!"

Matt's face paled. He sat up straight, then rose and began to walk stiffly toward the front door. His voice was flat. "I think I'd better leave. If that's the way you feel . . ."

Lauren watched him open the door, then close it behind him. What had she said? Had *she* put that look of hurt in his eyes? Had she been responsible for draining the emotion from his voice, that very same voice that had always been so wonderfully expressive?

Her gaze flew to the window. It was dark outside. Once Matt left, she'd be alone. Unable to take back the ugly words she'd said. Open prey to her own impulsiveness and . . .

The growl of his engine hit her ears as she wrenched open the front door. "Wait!" she cried, arms waving as she tore down the walk. "Matt, wait!" The car was halfway down the drive. Thinking only that she needed him with her, she flew in pursuit. "Don't go, Matt! I'm sorry! Please . . . don't . . . go!"

The taillights went on at the end of the drive, and the car slowed, about to turn onto the street. Lauren's steps faltered. She came to a tapering halt. She'd lost him. He was gone.

The car began to turn, then stopped.

She held her breath, then started running again. "Matt! Please! Wait!"

His tall figure emerged from the car but didn't move farther. Again she faltered and stopped. But the hesitation was only momentary. She knew what she wanted, knew what she needed. With a tiny cry of thanks that she'd been given a second chance, she raced forward.

CHAPTER SIX

Flinging her arms around him, Lauren hung on for dear life. "I'm sorry—so sorry, Matt!" She pressed her cheek to the warm column of his neck. "I didn't mean what I said. I was nervous and frustrated. I took it out on you." Slowly she eased her grip on him and met his gaze. Her voice grew softer. "Don't go. Please?"

"I don't disbelieve you, Lauren," he stated quietly.

"I know that. I accused you unfairly. I expected you to have answers where I didn't. It was wrong of me."

"Nothing's changed. I still don't have answers."

"I know that."

"And you still have only one bed." His hands came to rest lightly on her hips, fingers splayed. "If I were a saint, I'd offer to sleep on the couch, but I'm not a saint."

His words and the look in his eyes sent ripples of excitement through her. "I know that," she whispered.

"Then you know what I want?" he asked as softly.

Unable to speak, she nodded.

His gaze held hers captive for a minute longer; then he grabbed her hand. "Get into the car."

"What—?"

He was urging her into the driver's seat, his hands on her shoulders. "Slide in. Over a little. That's it." He was mere inches behind her, then flush to her side. "I'm not taking the chance that you'll change your mind." Tucking her arm through his, he put the car in reverse and sped backward up the drive. Then he all but swung her from the car, fitted one strong arm over her shoulder and half ran to the house.

"Matt?" She was laughing, breathless.

"Shhh."

Once inside, he continued up the stairs, straight to her bedroom. The light was off. He made no attempt to alter the darkness, and Lauren was relieved. She knew that she wanted what was about to happen. She also knew that the darkness added to its dreamlike quality. That a man like Matt wanted *her* was mind-boggling. Surely if he turned on the light, he'd have second thoughts; she'd have second thoughts. . . .

He took her in his arms and kissed her until the only thoughts she had were how wonderful he was, how unbelievably desirable he made her feel, how lucky she was to have found him. She gave herself up to his kiss, to his hands as they unbuttoned her shirt and unclasped her bra, to his fingers as they charted her flesh, branding her woman with fire and grace.

A soft moan came from deep in her throat, and she arched her back to offer herself more fully. Acceding to her wordless plea, he stroked her with gentle expertise. His fingers made firm swells of her breasts; his thumbs, tight buds of her nipples. And all the while his tongue correspondingly familiarized itself with every nook and cranny of her mouth.

His hands left her only to free himself of his shirt, and then he was back, crushing her close. His chest was warm and lightly furred. Its texture exhilarated her, though she wondered if it was simply the closeness, male to female, that pleased her so. There was something very, very right about what she felt. There was something very, very right about Matt. At that moment she didn't know how she'd ever doubted him.

While he held her lips captive, he reached for the snap of her jeans, released it, lowered the zipper. She gasped for breath when he knelt and eased the denim from her legs, then did the same with her panties. She clutched his shoulders for support and shivered, though her blood was hot, her body aching for completion. Modesty was nonexistent; she wanted him too badly.

"Please," she whispered shakily, "I need you, Matt."

For an instant, he buried his face in her stomach while he caressed the backs of her legs and her bottom. His breath was ragged, his hair damp against her hot flesh. She drove her fingers into the thick, sun-streaked pelt and held him closer, then urged him upward.

He didn't need much urging. Standing, he shed the rest of his clothes, then came to her naked, pressing her to him, graphically showing her that the need wasn't hers alone. She thrilled to the knowledge, unable to be afraid when Matt was all she'd ever wanted, all she'd ever dreamed about. The fact that she could arouse him to the state he was in was as heady as the state of arousal he'd himself brought her to.

He moved from her only to tug back the spread before lowering her gently to the sheets. "Lauren . . . God, Lauren . . ." he murmured, then kissed her again. He caressed and teased with his hands, his lips, his tongue, but the play took its toll. His body seemed on fire, trembling under the strain of the heat, finally unable to withstand it. Threading his fingers through hers, he anchored them by her shoulders and positioned himself between her thighs. With one powerful thrust, he surged forward.

Lauren arched her back against the sudden invasion, and a tiny cry escaped her lips. When he stiffened, she wrapped her arms around him to draw him close to her. He resisted.

"Lauren?" His voice was little more than a throaty whisper.

"It's okay . . . don't stop . . . don't stop."

His breathing grew all the more labored and he pressed his forehead to her shoulder. "I couldn't if . . . I wanted to," he finally managed, "but I can be more . . . gentle."

"Don't be!" she cried, for the instant of pain was gone, leaving only that swelling knot of need low in her belly.

But he was gentle and caring, moving slowly at first, letting her body adjust to his presence before he adopted the rhythm designed to drive her insane. What he didn't realize was that even his initial, cautious movements were delicious. His fullness inside her gave Lauren an incredible sense of satisfaction; the idea of receiving a man, of receiving Matt in this way, was the sweetest delight.

By the time he moved faster, Lauren was right with him. She adored the way his thighs brushed hers, the way their stomachs rubbed. When he bent his head, she strained higher. His mouth closed over her breast and began a sucking that pulled at her womb from one direction while the smooth stroking of his manhood pulled at it from another. Her hands roamed over and around his firm body, but even had she not touched him, she would have been intimately aware of every hard plane and sinewed swell he possessed. Their bodies were that close, working in tandem.

He murmured soft words of encouragement and praise. "That's it, sweetheart . . . ahhh . . . your legs . . . yes, there . . . so good . . ."

They moved as one then, each complementing and

completing the other. Lauren experienced a beauty she'd never imagined. She was drawn beyond herself into Matt, sharing, collaborating, merging with him into a greater being for those precious moments of emotional and physical bliss.

After the climax had passed, it was a long time before either of them could speak. They gasped for air, alternately panting and moaning, laughing from time to time at their inability to do anything more. At last Matt slid slowly to her side, leaving one leg and an arm over her in a statement of possession she had no wish to deny. His head was beside hers on the pillow, his cheek cushioned in her hair.

"How do you feel?" he asked in a thick whisper.

"Stunned," she whispered back. "I never imagined . . ."

"*You* never imagined . . ."

She forced her lids open and looked at him. "Then . . . it was okay?"

"It was more than okay," he teased in throaty chiding, "but you had to know that."

"No. I didn't."

His grin faded, replaced by a look of tender concern. He brought a shaky hand up to smooth damp strands of hair from her brow. "I'm sorry if I hurt you, Lauren. If I'd known, I might have been able to make it easier."

"It couldn't have been easier. I've never felt so wonderful in my life."

"Even at the start?" His arched brow dared her to deny the moment of pain she'd felt.

"Even then. If I hadn't felt a thing, something would have been lost. I wanted the pain. Does that make any sense?"

He didn't answer. Instead, he traced her eyebrow with his finger. "Why didn't you tell me, sweetheart?"

"I didn't think it mattered." She paused, experiencing a frisson of apprehension. "Did it? I mean, we're both adults. I knew what I was doing."

"Did you?"

"Yes!" She didn't understand what he was getting at.

"Lauren, I didn't do anything to protect you. It's possible I've just made you pregnant."

Her jaw slackened only slightly. Then, unable to control herself, she burst into a smile. "What an exciting thought!"

Matt closed his eyes for a minute. "You're supposed to be worried, sweetheart." He propped himself up on an elbow and looked down at her. "You're supposed to be thinking about this new life you have, the shop, your independence."

"But a baby!" Her eyes were wide. "I could adjust to that. It would be marvelous!"

"I didn't know you wanted a baby so badly."

"Neither did I." She scrunched up her nose. "But it probably won't happen. Just once, Matt. And it's the wrong time of the month." She brushed the strands of hair from his forehead and left her fingers to tangle in the wet thatch. "Are *you* worried?"

"Of course I'm worried. Babies should be planned, the logistics worked out. Everything should be clear from the start."

"There you go again. So cautious." She tugged playfully at his hair. "If I were to become pregnant, I'd manage. One way or another I would, because I'd want the baby enough to make everything fall into place."

"Such a romantic," Matt murmured, but there was a sadness in his eyes.

Her smile faded. "You're thinking that you'll be leaving soon."

"Sooner or later I will."

"It's okay, Matt. There are no strings attached to what happened tonight. I won't ask any more of you than you want to give."

He snorted and flopped back on the pillow. "That's cavalier of you."

"Would you rather I demand marriage?" she asked, confused. "Times have changed. Just because we made love doesn't mean you have to make an 'honest woman' of me. I don't feel dishonest. I feel . . . lucky."

He turned his head on the pillow so that he faced her again. "Explain."

"I never expected what happened tonight. What I felt, what I experienced, were so much more than I've ever dared to dream."

"Why not? That's what I don't understand. I don't understand why you were a virgin. You're beautiful, charming and intelligent. And you're right. Times have changed. Women your age are rarely inexperienced."

"Would you have had me throw myself at just any old man for the sake of experience?"

At the sound of hurt in her voice, he rolled over to cover her body. With his large hands cupping her face, he spoke gently. "No, sweetheart. Of course not. I'm the one who's been lucky tonight. To know that you've given me what you've given no other man . . . that was one of the reasons I couldn't stop when I realized what was happening."

"One of the reasons?"

Even in the dark she caught his sheepish grin. "The others are right here." He dropped a hand to her knee and lifted his body only enough to permit that hand a slow rise. He touched each and every erogenous zone before tapping his finger against her temple. "All of you—mind, body, soul. You turn me on, Lauren."

"Oh, God" was all she could whisper, because his tactile answer had set her body to aching again, and she hadn't believed it could be possible. She didn't know whether to be pleased or embarrassed, but that was her mind talking. Of its own accord, her body shifted beneath his with a story of its own.

As she'd already learned, Matthew Kruger was a good reader.

When the last page of this second chapter had been turned, she fell asleep. Her body was exhausted yet replete, her mind at peace. She was totally unaware that Matt lay awake beside her for long hours before curving his body protectively around hers and at last allowing himself the luxury of escape.

Lauren awoke the next morning to a strange sensation of heat running the entire length of the back of her body. Her lids flew open and she held her breath. Only her eyeballs moved, questioning, seeking, finally alighting on the large, tanned hand flattened on the sheet by her stomach.

Matt.

Shifting her head, she followed a line from that hand, up a lean but powerful arm to an even stronger shoulder.

Matt.

Quietly, almost stealthily, she turned until she faced him, and her heart melted. He was sound asleep, tawny lashes resting above his cheekbones, his mouth slightly parted, lips relaxed. Unable to help herself, she let her gaze fall along his body. Last night she'd savored him with her hands; this morning it was her eyes' turn to feast.

He was magnificent. Soft hair swirled over his chest, tapering toward his navel, below which the sheet was casually bunched. His hips were lean, as she'd known they'd be; the sheet was nearly as erotic a covering as the air alone might have been.

A self-satisfied smile spread over her face. She felt good. Complete. All woman. Giving in to temptation, she leaned forward and kissed his chest. He smelled of man, earthy but wonderful. Eyes closed, she drank in that essence as she continued to press the lightest of kisses into the warmest of skin.

When a hand suddenly tightened around her waist, her head flew up. Matt's eyes were still closed, but he wore the roguish shadow of a beard on his cheeks and a faint smile on his lips. "Am I dreaming?" he whispered.

In answer, Lauren shimmied higher, slid her arms around his neck and kissed his smile wider. She was further rewarded when he rolled onto his back and hauled her over him. Only then did he open his eyes.

For long minutes, they simply looked at each other. She wasn't sure what her own eyes were saying, but Matt's quite clearly spoke of pleasure. And affection. They made her feel special.

"Hi," he whispered at last.

She swallowed the lump of emotion in her throat. "Hi."

"How'd you sleep?"

"Fine."

"No ghosts?"

She shook her head.

"No strange noises?"

She shook her head. "Beth was right. She said I needed a bodyguard."

He closed his hands around her bottom and gave her a punishing squeeze. "So that's why you did it? Because you wanted a bodyguard?"

"You know better than that." She sucked in a breath when his hands pressed her intimately closer. "Matt?"

He was grinning. "It's your fault. You started it. In case you didn't know, a man's at his peak in the morning."

"I thought a man was at his peak in his twenties, and you're a mite beyond. You're shocking me."

"You're the one with the bag of surprises. A virgin is supposed to be shy and demure."

She grinned. "I'm not a virgin anymore, so my

behavior is excusable."

Rolling over, he set her on her back, then held himself up so that he could look at her. Just as hers had done moments earlier, his eyes touched her body as only his hands had done the night before. "You are beautiful, Lauren. God, I can't believe it." He met her gaze. "No regrets?"

Still basking in his approval, which both stunned and thrilled her, she shook her head. "How about you?"

One long forefinger drew a bisecting line from the hollow of her throat to the apex of her thighs. "No," he answered, but gruffly. "Not about this. About not having the answer to your problem, yes, I have regrets."

"Don't think about that," she whispered, feeling a strange urgency not to let anything intrude on this precious time with Matt. "Not now."

His grin was lopsided, slightly forced, and his eyes lingered on the soft curves of her body. "I think I'd better. It's either that or ravish you again, and I imagine you're going to be a little sore."

"Me? Sore?"

"Yes. You, sore."

"Oh."

With a deep growl, he gathered her into his arms and held her tightly. When his grip loosened, it was with reluctance. "I could use a shower and some breakfast. It's a workday, or had you forgotten?"

"Oh, my god!" She twisted toward the clock on the dresser, then pushed herself from his arms and bolted out of bed. "I'll take the shower first," she called over her shoulder. Remembering her sadly deficient water heater, she added, "Real quick."

Lauren was true to her word, but by the time she had returned to the bedroom, Matt was nowhere in sight. For a split second she panicked. Then she caught sight of his clothes on the floor. "Matt?" Wrapped in her towel, she headed for the stairs. "Matt?"

The aroma of fresh coffee filled the air, but he didn't answer. She was halfway down the staircase when the front door opened and Matt strode through, carrying a large leather suitcase. He was stark naked.

"Matthew Kruger! Where is your sense of decency? If one of my neighbors saw you—"

He'd taken the stairs by twos, and the smack of his lips on hers cut off her teasing tirade. He continued upward. "The trees were my cover. It's a gorgeous day outside."

Lauren couldn't think to argue. He was spectacular. Tall and straight. Broad back, narrow hips, tight buttocks. If it hadn't been for the time, she'd have followed him into the shower just to touch him again. The mere sight of him took her breath away.

But time was of the essence. She blow-dried her hair and put on makeup while Matt showered and shaved; then she dressed quickly and hurried to the kitchen. They were seated side by side, finishing off the last of the scrambled eggs and toast, when Matt laid out his plans for the day.

"I've got meetings set for ten and two. We can take my car into Boston, meet for lunch, then grab something on the way home tonight. Sound okay?"

His words were offered gently, not at all imperiously, yet they brought back to Lauren the crux of Matt's present mission. He intended to protect her as he'd promised, which meant that he was going to stick as close to her side as possible. On one level, she was thrilled with that prospect. On another . . .

"About my problem, Matt. Are we just going to . . . wait?"

"Pretty much. It'll be interesting to see if my presence here makes any difference."

"But if nothing happens, we won't know if you've scared someone off for good or simply put him off for a while. And you can't stay here forever."

"I know." He looked away. "I'm going to make some calls today."

"What kind of calls? To whom?"

"People who may have more insight than we do." There was an edge to his voice, but his gaze was soft when he glanced back at her. "Let me do the worrying for now, Lauren. You've done your share."

"But it's my problem! I can't just dump it on your shoulders and wipe my hands of it. That's not fair to you. You don't owe me anything."

For a minute he looked as if he would argue. He gnawed on the inside of his cheek, then lifted his mug and drained the last of his coffee. "Let's just say I owe it to Brad, then. He was my friend and you're his sister. The least I can do is to help you out when you need it."

That wasn't quite the answer she wanted, but she

knew she'd have to settle for it.

"Anyway," he added with an endearing grin, "I've got broad shoulders. I can handle it. Maybe it's the Spenser in me coming out, after all."

"Better you than Robert Urich. But are you sure?"

"Very sure. Hey, as far as work on the house goes, are you going to call those names I gave you or would you like me to do it?"

She winced. "Got a cold shower, did you?"

"Well . . ."

"I'll do it. You're doing enough. I'd love it if you were here when I meet with them, though. I have a feeling some of those guys show more respect when a man's around." The last had been offered on a dry note. She paused, then asked cautiously, "How long will you be here?" She envisioned two or three days, and the thought left her feeling empty.

He rubbed the back of his neck. "I was thinking about that last night. I have to be in Leominster on Thursday and Friday, but I could almost commute from here." He took a fast breath. "Unless you'd rather have the house to yourself again. I'll understand, Lauren. It's okay, really it is—Hey, crumpled napkins in the face I can do without first thing in the morning!"

"Then don't give me that little-boy pout," she chided as she carried their plates to the sink. But when she returned to the table, she gave him a hug from behind. "Of course I want you here," she murmured with her cheek pressed to his. "For as long as you can stay. Besides, you *do* owe it to me."

His hands clasped hers at the open collar of his shirt. "I do?"

"Uh-huh. You've awakened me to some of the finer points in life. Seems to me there's got to be an awful lot I still don't know."

"Then you *are* after my body! I knew it all along!"

"Could be," she answered with a grin. "Could be."

During the next few days, Lauren and Matt spent every possible minute with each other. They drove to and from Boston together. They met for lunch each day. When Matt wasn't working but Lauren was, he was parked so frequently on the bench outside the shop that Beth suggested they charge him rent.

"Either that, or hire him part-time."

Lauren wrinkled her nose. "After all we went through to convince Jamie to start full-time next week? No way. Besides, what does Matt know about art?"

"What does he know about *other* things?" Beth drawled suggestively. "That's what *I* want to know."

"Oh, quite a bit" was all Lauren would admit. She knew Beth was fishing. She hadn't made a secret of the fact that Matt was staying with her in Lincoln. But some things were sacred, not to be discussed with even the closest of friends, and for more than the obvious reasons. Lauren felt she was living a fairy tale. By her own admission, Beth was envious. The last thing Lauren wanted to do was to rub it in.

"Well," Beth said with a sigh, "at least he's managed to keep you safe."

"That he has."

Since Matt had been with her, there'd been no accidents, no close calls, no questionable occurrences. Indeed, Lauren felt safe enough almost to forget there was a problem.

Almost, but not quite.

Tuesday evening she asked Matt if he'd made any calls to those "people who may have more insight than we do." He said he had and that the ball was rolling. His tone was light. She hadn't dared ask more.

Wednesday evening, though, she couldn't help herself. As gently as she could, she inquired about it again.

"Have you heard anything yet?"

"No. It takes time."

"Time to do what? I don't understand."

"Questions can be asked, people consulted. Trust me, Lauren. Please?" Put that way, with an eruption of tension dissolving abruptly into beseechfulness, she'd surrendered.

But much as she tried, she couldn't shake the conviction that the things she'd experienced were linked and that, despite Matt's protective shield, they were bound to resume at some point. And she was frightened.

Thursday morning Matt crawled out of bed at dawn, showered, shaved and dressed, then woke Lauren to say goodbye. She was groggy. It had been another late night of sweet, prolonged loving. Only the realization that Matt was leaving brought her from her self-satisfied stupor.

"You should have wakened me sooner," she whispered, reaching up to touch his freshly shaved cheek. "I'd have made you breakfast."

"No time. They'll have coffee and doughnuts there."

"I wish you didn't have to go."

"I'll be back tonight."

"I know, but I've been spoiled. Leominster seems so far away."

He sighed. "I agree." He pressed his lips together, then forced a smile. "You take care of yourself, sweetheart, you hear? Drive carefully, and be sure to lock the doors."

"I will."

Lifting her in his arms, he hugged her before setting her back with a kiss on the tip of her nose. She knew not to ask for more. Where temptation was concerned, they were both decidedly weak.

"Good luck, Matt. I hope everything goes well."

He waved as he left the room. Climbing from the bed, she crossed to the window and watched him slide into his car, start the engine and drive off. In an attempt to parry the unease that settled over her, she took a shower and dressed, then forced herself to make breakfast for one and eat every last bit.

Only when she'd finished did she permit herself to sit back and think. She missed Matt. Already. After only two full days together, she'd gotten used to his presence. More than used to it. Addicted to it. Breakfast wasn't the same without him. Neither would lunch be. For that matter, she'd miss being able to look up at odd times and find him on the bench out-side the shop.

She wished he could stay forever, but that was an unrealistically romantic thought if ever there was one. Today he was off to Leominster. Next week, or soon after, he'd be back in California. What then? Would they talk on the phone? Visit each other from time to time?

She knew it wouldn't be enough for her. She wanted him in Lincoln with her. Whatever initial reservations she'd had about his background, his occupation or his character were nonexistent now. His background was blue-collar and strong, his occupation solid, his char-acter sterling. She'd never once glimpsed anything coarse in him. Rather, he'd proved to be unfailingly gentle and giving. Even his reticence about discussing Brad had ceased to matter. He was simply protective, skirting around what he knew to be a sensitive subject.

And he'd brought out a new side of her. Since she'd met him, she'd matured as a woman. He made her believe in both her looks and her sexuality. Whereas her confidence had come from looking in the mirror when she'd first returned from the Bahamas, now it came from the reflection of admiration in Matt's eyes. She didn't care what anyone else thought of her. Only Matt mattered.

So where was she to go from here? Sighing, she rose from the table. She'd clean up the kitchen, go to work and come home. Soon after that, Matt would return. She wasn't even going to think about tomorrow.

One day at a time. All she could do was take one

day at a time.

Cleaning up the kitchen was no problem at all. Going to work was another matter. When she tried to start her car, the engine refused to turn over. Not one to beat a dead horse, she returned to the house, called AAA, then sat waiting for half an hour until the tow truck arrived.

"Battery's dead" was the mechanic's laconic diagnosis.

"But that's impossible. This battery's barely four months old!"

"It's dead."

"How can a four-month-old battery die?"

Taking jumper cables from his truck, the man set to work recharging the battery. "Maybe you left the headlights on."

"I never do that."

"Anyone else drive this car? A kid? Maybe he forgot and left 'em on."

"There's no kid, and I'm the only one who drives the car. It's been sitting in the garage since Tuesday morning—" that was when Matt, in fact, had put it away, but he wouldn't have left the lights on "—but it's sat for longer than that without any trouble."

"No sweat, lady. The battery looks okay otherwise. I'll have it working in no time."

He did, and Lauren was only fifteen minutes late for work, but she was bothered by the incident. It occurred to her that the same person who'd sabotaged her garage door might have entered the garage during those days when the car was idle, switched the lights on for a good, long time, then switched them off without her being any the wiser. She decided to discuss it with Matt that night, but the sense of solace in that resolution wasn't enough to prevent a certain nervousness when she returned to the car after work. She found herself glancing around the large parking garage and into the back seat of the car before she dared climb into the front.

She held her breath. The car started. She drove to Lincoln without any trouble.

Matt wasn't due back until nine at the earliest, so she took the time to stop for groceries before arriving at the farmhouse. It was still light out, and she was grateful. She imagined herself being watched and knew that, had it been dark, she would have been terrified.

Relief came in small measure after she was locked safely inside the house. Focusing determinedly on Matt's return, she stowed the groceries, prepared all the fixings for dinner, then poured herself a glass of wine and took refuge in the living room. While lights were burning in the rest of the house, she chose to sit in the dark. Hiding. Brooding. Wondering. Worrying. She knew that her imagination was getting the best of her, but that didn't stop it from happening.

Minutes seemed to stretch into an eternity, though it was barely after nine when finally she heard a car whip up the drive. Hurrying to the window, she peered cautiously out. Her relief was immediate and considerable when Matt climbed from the car. Even before he'd stepped over the threshold, her arms were around his neck.

"Matt, it's wonderful to have you back!"

He had one hand at the back of her head, the other arm around her waist. "Mmm. You're good for my ego. Such a welcome, and I haven't even been gone fourteen hours."

"Close. Thirteen and a half." She lifted her face for a kiss that was instantly comforting and thoroughly satisfying. "How did it go?"

"Very well. I think we've finally worked out the last of the bugs with the locals, so we can get the permit we need, which is great, since we've got everyone else lined up and ready to go."

"Good deal!"

"And I spoke with Thomas." Thomas Gehling was the general contractor whom Lauren had called on Tuesday. "He's looking forward to meeting with us Sunday morning."

"But if he's going to be involved with your project, will he have time to do mine?"

Matt threw an arm around her shoulder and drew her into the house with him. "You have to understand construction lingo. When I say that everyone is lined up and ready to go, it means that if we're lucky, we'll have broken ground within six weeks. And then there's the heavy work that has to be done first—blasting, digging, pouring foundations. The plumbers and electricians and carpenters you'll need won't be required at our site for three months minimum. Thomas will have more than enough time to oversee work here—that is, if you find that you like him and

144

what he has to say. You're under no obligation to use him. There are other names on that list."

"Of the ones I spoke with, I liked him the best. Call it instinct, or whatever, but something meshed even on the phone." She was well aware of the fact that Matt's using Thomas Gehling for his own work might have slanted her view. She trusted Matt's judgment. But she had liked Thomas. He spoke intelligently and seemed perfectly comfortable dealing with a woman.

"I think you'll be impressed when you meet him." Having reached the kitchen, Matt went directly to the sink, turned on the water and squirted a liberal amount of liquid soap on his hands. "So how was your day, sweetheart?"

"Fine—I mean, okay. God, I can't believe it happened again."

"What?"

"I've been a nervous wreck all day, counting the minutes until you got back so I could tell you what happened. Then you walk in here, bringing a sense of security, and I forget all about it."

He stared at her over his shoulder. "What happened?"

"My car wouldn't start this morning. The battery was dead. I had to get a truck here to jump-start it."

"The battery was dead? Didn't you say you'd gotten a new one just before you left Bennington?"

"I did. That's what's so weird. The man from the garage suggested that I'd left my lights on by mistake. I'm sure I'd never do that."

A thick cloud of suds coated Matt's hands, but he

paid it little heed. His brows knitted low over his eyes. "I was the last one to drive your car. I put it in the garage Tuesday morning before we left for Boston in mine. I'm sure the lights were off. There'd have been no reason for me to turn them on to begin with, and the car started perfectly, so they couldn't have been left on the night before."

"That's what I figured." She was standing close by the sink. "The only logical explanation is that someone's been tampering in the garage again."

He shot her a sharp glance. "Was anything else wrong with the car?"

"No, and it started perfectly when I left work tonight."

Bending over the sink, Matt splashed soapy water on his face. Lauren reached into a drawer and had a clean towel waiting by the time he'd rinsed and straightened up. No amount of wiping, though, could remove the concern from his features.

"It may have been a fluke," he suggested quietly.

"Do you believe that?"

He hesitated. "No."

"Matt, don't you think it's time we called the police? I mean, when it was only a couple of incidents, they might have thought I was crazy, but at this stage the situation has to be considered suspicious. At least if the police were aware of the possibilities, they could patrol the area more closely."

Matt's expression grew more troubled than ever. "The police might scare him off, and then he'd only wait for things to die down before starting again. What we need to do is to catch him."

"Come on, Matt," she chided, "I was only kidding about playing Spenser."

"It wouldn't be too hard to rig up some booby traps." His eyes were growing animated; he was obviously warming up to the idea. "I think I could manage it, with a little help from a friend."

"From what friend?"

"One of the guys I met in Leominster. He works at a nearby lumberyard." Matt gave a mock grimace and scratched the back of his head. "Seems to me that he mentioned something about having done time."

"A convict? You're going to enlist a *convict* to save me?"

"An ex-convict. And he's been straight for ten years."

"Matt, what *is* this?"

"His specialty was breaking and entering, and he was a genius at it."

Lauren narrowed her eyes. "How long did you spend with this guy?"

"Not long. Can I help it if he's proud of what he's done?"

"Not only after, but before." She grunted, then muttered under her breath, "I can't believe I'm standing here listening when I should be on the phone talking to the police."

Matt put his hands on her arms and stroked her coaxingly. "Come on, Lauren. It's worth a try. You know how the police are—"

"I don't know how the police are. I've never had

dealings with them before, contrary to *some* of your friends."

He kissed her forehead. "The police ask millions of questions and then get their minds set on an answer that isn't the one you've given or the one you want to hear. These local departments just aren't geared to taking the offensive, and they sure as hell wouldn't call in the state police or the FBI in a situation like this." His voice softened, taking on a hint of teasing that was reflected in his eyes. "If you were worried about contractors being chauvinists, just wait until you've met the police. They'll treat you like a sweet little thing who's slightly soft in the head." He cupped said item in his hand and gently massaged her scalp. "And even if they decided that you just might be on to something, there's the matter of red tape. They could step up their patrols, but that'd be all. They'd have trouble getting authorization for much else. More than anything, they'd be reluctant to do something that might backfire in court."

Lauren was having trouble fighting him when he was so close and touching her so gently. "You're not reluctant," she stated, but the accusation she'd intended came out sounding more like admiration.

"Not one bit." His thumbs traced the delicate curves of her ears. "I want whoever's been harassing you to be caught. I have to believe that once we find out who it is, we'll find a motive as well."

"You're seducing me," she breathed.

"Me?"

"Don't look so innocent. You're seducing me."

"I am not. I'm simply trying to convince you to let me have a go at it."

"At what? That's the issue." Her voice was whisper-soft, not seductive in itself, simply . . . taken. "Do you want a go at playing cops and robbers, or at making love with me?"

"I'll make you forget, Lauren," he murmured, lowering his head until his lips feathered hers. "I'll make you forget everything else."

She caught her breath when he nipped at her lower lip. He was already making her forget, damn him—bless him. At this moment, she wanted to forget.

"I'll make you forget everything else," he repeated hotly against her neck. "And that's a promise. Word of honor."

Matt made good on his promise. Right there, propping Lauren against the kitchen counter, he made love to her with such daring that she forgot everything else but what she felt for him, with him.

He also made good on the promise to call his friend, the breaking-and-entering expert, who showed up at the farmhouse bright and early the very next morning with a carload full of booby-trap makings the likes of which Lauren had never imagined. She had to leave for work before the last of the snares were set, and remarked only half in jest that she'd never make it back into the house alive.

Matt called her from Leominster in the middle of the afternoon to say that he was going to have to attend a dinner meeting and that he wouldn't be back until late.

Disappointed but fully appreciative of the demands of his work, she decided to stay in the city after the shop closed to have dinner with Beth and then see a movie.

"Nervous about going home?" Beth teased.

Lauren chuckled—yes, nervously. "It'll be dark, and they've hooked up so many gadgets that it's very possible I'll be the first one caught. You wouldn't believe it, Beth. There's a gizmo on the garage door that has to be deactivated, or else a huge black net descends on an intruder. And once the net falls, *it* sets off a god-awful clanging. The doors to the house have hidden latches that are attached to electrical devices that deliver a shock powerful enough to stun, and the shock in turn sets off an alarm."

"You're right in the middle of a spy novel. I love it!"

"You wouldn't if you had to negotiate everything yourself. There are even hidden snares along the edge of the woods. You'd think we were trapping mink."

"I'm telling you, you've got all the makings of a best-seller. Just think, when this is over, you can write it up. Before you know it, you'll be signing autographs and doing the talk-show circuit."

"Thank you, Beth. I'll settle for catching one man and turning him over to the police."

"But what if it isn't *one* man?" Beth tossed out with imaginative anticipation. "What if there's a whole syndicate that's got some kind of grudge against you? What if you catch one man and another takes over where the first leaves off, so you catch the second? Meanwhile, the first dies mysteriously in jail, so the second decides to sing, and before you know it, there's enough evidence to convict the *entire* syndicate. You'll be a hero!"

"Heroine," Lauren correct dryly. "And I don't believe we're dealing with any syndicate. What would a syndicate have against me?"

"Maybe it was using your vacant farmhouse as its headquarters, and then you came along and, boom, moved in lickety-split, and there's still some very valuable and potentially condemning material stored in the cellar—"

Lauren scowled at her. "What happened to your theory about the ghost of inhabitants past?"

"Too passé. I think I like the syndicate idea better."

"I don't like *either* of them, and if we're going to have dinner together, you'll have to swear you won't go on like this. You're making me nervous."

"I thought you were already nervous."

"You're making me *more* nervous."

Beth patted her arm, then squeezed it. "I'm just teasing, Lauren. You know that. Just teasing."

That was what Lauren told herself when, later that night, after the movie had let out and she and Beth had gone their separate ways on the streets of Boston, she had the uncanny sensation of being followed.

CHAPTER SEVEN

The sensation was vague at first, and Lauren wondered if her imagination was simply working overtime. She glanced over her shoulder, then faced forward again. There were people around—she wished there were even more—but none appeared to be suspicious. At least, no one had ducked into a doorway when she'd looked back.

She had walked a bit farther and turned a corner when the sensation intensified. A prickling arose at the back of her neck, accompanied by a frisson of fear. Instinctively she quickened her step, mentally charting the course she'd have to take to reach the garage. It consisted of main streets for the most part, with a single alleyway at the end.

She darted another glance behind her and saw the same outwardly innocuous people—several couples, a handful of singles, all staggered at intervals. If someone grabbed her, she'd yell. There were plenty of bodies to help.

She walked on. Fewer people were ahead of her now; some had turned off toward the subway stop. She assumed the same was true for those behind her, and the thought added to her unease.

She turned another corner. There was no one ahead of her now, and she didn't dare look back. Unbidden, she recalled her childhood. There'd been a dog in the neighborhood, a large German shepherd of which she'd been terrified. Her mother had always instructed her to walk calmly past it on the theory that dogs could smell fear. Could people smell fear? Lauren wondered now. She was sure she reeked of it.

Imagination. That was all it was. Imagination getting a little out of hand. The sounds she heard not far behind weren't footsteps. They were the knocking of the air-conditioning unit in the building she passed . . . or the creaking of heat as it escaped from the engine of a newly parked car alongside the curb . . . or . . .

Eyes wide, she shot a frightened glance over her shoulder and gasped. There was a man. He was very tall, large-set, dressed in black, and he was not twenty feet behind and gaining steadily on her.

Uncaring if she was jumping to conclusions, she began to run. She turned another corner and ran even faster. Her heels beat a rapid tattoo on the pavement, merging with the thundering of her heart to drown out all other night sounds of the city.

She passed another long—agonizingly long— building, then reached the alley, in actuality a single-lane driveway. At its end stood her salvation, a guard booth.

She was breathless and shaking, terrified of looking back and losing time, tripping or slamming into the wall. She cursed her side, which ached; cursed the shoes she wore and the heat that seemed to buffet her and slow her progress. By the time she reached the booth, she felt as though she'd run a marathon.

"Thank God," she whispered, panting as she sagged against the thick plastic enclosure. Then, with a burst of energy, she scrambled to the booth's opening. The guard, a young man with a punk hairstyle at odds with his uniform, sat balanced on the back legs of his chair. A dog-eared magazine lay open on his lap. The heavy beat of rock music thrummed from the stereo box by his side. He was chewing gum; the vigorous action of his jaw only enhanced the indolence of his stare.

"Someone was following me," Lauren gasped and darted a frantic glance toward the alley through which she'd run.

Looking thoroughly bored, the guard followed her gaze. There was no one in sight.

"He must have turned away when he saw me heading toward you," she explained, trying to calm herself enough to think clearly. "Listen, I need a big favor."

The young man blew a bubble, popped it and licked the gum back into his mouth. "Depends what it is."

"Could you walk me to my car?"

He gave a one-shouldered shrug. "I'm on duty."

"I know, but there aren't many cars leaving the garage now. With the gate down, they'll wait. It won't take you long—two, maybe three minutes. Just until I lock myself in."

He fingered his earlobe, which sported a crescent of multiple studs. "I'm not supposed to leave this booth."

"But I'm in danger!"

Slowly, his head nodding in time with the music, he looked back toward the street. "Don't see anyone."

"He may have taken the stairs. Please! I need your help!"

After what seemed forever, the front legs of the chair hit the floor. "So. Chivalry calls." The guard stood up, yawned, then pushed his shoulders back.

The show was wasted on Lauren, who saw right through it to the scrawniness of his physique. Not much to protect her with. But he wore a uniform. There was safety in a uniform.

"I'm the new guy on the block," he drawled. "I was given specific instructions—"

She felt sweat trickling down her back. "Look, I'll argue on your behalf if you get into trouble. It seems to me your boss would reward you for helping a regular tenant."

"You're a regular tenant?" His gaze drifted down her body.

"Yes." She sighed in exasperation, feeling suddenly tired. Instinctively she knew she was safe standing at the booth with even as unlikely a guard as this, but there was still the threat of the inner garage to overcome. She wanted nothing more than to be locked in her car and on the road, headed for home. "Please. Just walk me upstairs. You could have been up and back in the time you've spent talking with me."

He grinned. "Yeah, but talking with you beats sitting here by myself." He cocked his head to one side. "Sure. I'll walk you upstairs."

Lauren jerked her eyes toward the thick pipes overhead. "Thank you," she breathed. By the time she looked down, the guard had let himself out of his cage and was swaggering toward her.

She glanced worriedly back toward the exit, but it remained empty.

"Come on, love. Up we go." He took her elbow and she jumped, wondering for an instant if she'd leaped from the frying pan into the fire. Unfortunately, she was the proverbial beggar who couldn't be choosy. So she clamped her mouth shut and let her cocky gallant lead the way to the stairs.

He dropped her elbow to open the door. Her apprehensive gaze examined every nook of the stairwell as they started up.

"Floor?"

"Third." Had the stairwell always been this narrow? He chewed away at his gum. "Work around here?"

"Yes." Had the stairwell always been this confining?

"Kind of late leaving, aren't you?"

"Yes." He wouldn't try anything. He wouldn't dare. She knew where and for whom he worked.

"Hot date?"

"Yes . . . he'll be waiting for me on the corner as soon as I leave here."

They climbed the last set of stairs in silence. Though Lauren didn't look, she could feel the smirk on her companion's face. He hadn't believed her. She'd hesitated too long, then spoken too quickly. Damn, but she wasn't good at this.

He swung open the door, then stood aside to let her through. "Always park on the third floor?"

She was looking nervously from side to side, trying to see into corners where a tall, large, dark form might be lurking. "It depends," she offered distractedly. With no assailant in sight, she blindly fumbled in her bag for the keys.

"Where's your car?"

She pointed. They reached it half a minute later.

"There," he announced as she unlocked the door, checked the back seat, then all but threw herself behind the wheel. "Safe and sound."

She locked the door and rolled her window down,

just enough to murmur a heartfelt "Thank you. I do appreciate what you've done."

"How about a ride down?"

"Uh . . ." Dumbly, she looked at the passenger seat, then leaned over and tugged up the button on the opposite door. Already striding around the front of the car, the guard let himself in.

She had her window up tight and the car started before he'd closed the door, and she took the ramps at breakneck speed. Her passenger didn't seem to mind. She suspected he enjoyed the daring ride.

She brought the car to an abrupt halt by the booth, let the guard out and quickly relocked the door. By the time she'd straightened up, he was at her window and making a rolling gesture with his hand. Again she lowered the window several inches.

"Your card?" he asked with an impudent grin.

"Oh." She rummaged in her purse, drew out the card and handed it over. While he studied it, her gaze alternated between the rearview mirror and the windows on either side.

"Looks okay . . . Lauren." Chomping briskly on his gum, he returned the card, then winked. "Drive carefully now." The last word was muted through her reclosed window. He twisted backward in a move she was sure he practiced regularly on the dance floor, pressed a button and released the gate.

Without another word, Lauren stepped on the gas. She held her breath and didn't expel it until she'd reached the relative safety of Government Center.

With great effort, she forced her rigid fingers to

relax on the steering wheel. She took long, deep breaths, feeling safer with each block she put between herself and the parking garage. No one appeared to be following her. To double-check, she swung from one lane to the other, then, a block later to the first lane. She annoyed several drivers, but she didn't care. All that mattered was that the headlights in her rearview mirror were ever varied.

During the drive home, her emotions ran the gamut from fear to confusion to anger. It was the latter that was dominant by the time she pulled up in front of her own garage. She left the engine running and the headlights on; she had a death grip on the wheel again, and her teeth were clenched. She barely had time to debate whether she should sit this way until Matt returned— she didn't expect him for a while yet—when a pair of headlights pierced the darkness behind her.

She sucked in a breath. It was *him!* He'd followed her after all! Frantic, she struggled to decide on the best course of action. The other car neared. She had to think quickly. She could make a mad dash for the safety of the house, but it would take time for her to work around the booby traps.

Too late.

She could run from the car and head for the woods in an attempt to make it to a neighbor's before being overtaken, but the woods, too, were booby-trapped, and that man had been large and ominously physical-looking.

Too risky.

She could lean on the horn in the hope that the noise

would either scare him off or arouse someone's attention.

That seemed her only option.

Her hand was on the horn, about to exert force, when the car behind her sounded its own horn in short, repetitive blasts. Her fear-filled gaze snapped to the rearview mirror.

Matt! It was *Matt!*

Lauren had never felt so relieved, or so foolish, or so furious in her entire life. Storming from her car, she met him halfway between the two. "I cannot *take* any more of this!" she screamed, hands clenched by her sides.

"Lauren, what—"

"It's gone on too long! Why *me?* What have *I* ever done to deserve this—this torture?"

"Take it easy, sweetheart—"

"I've *had* it, Matt!" She took a step back, eluding the hands he would have put on her shoulders. "This isn't fair! I'm a nervous wreck. I'm getting a permanent crick in my neck from looking over my shoulder. Someone's following me. Someone isn't. Someone's been in the house. Someone hasn't. Someone's sicced a dog on me. Someone hasn't. I don't know who to trust and who not to. For all I know, *you* were the one who stalked me in Boston!"

"*Me?* I just this minute got back from Leominster!"

"But how do I know that?" she fired at him. She was visibly shaking; the emotional strain was taking its toll. "How do I know *anything?* It's always in the dark. *I'm* always in the dark. I'm afraid to pull into my garage for fear I'll become a sitting duck in a big black net. I'm afraid to go into my house for fear I'll be electrocuted at the front door." Her voice grew as wobbly as her knees. "I can't live this way." She ducked her head and withered into herself, whispering, "Damn it, I can't live this way."

She didn't have the strength to elude Matt this time. He put his arms around her and held her while she cried softly.

"It's okay, sweetheart," he murmured. "Let it out. You'll feel better, and then we'll talk."

"I won't feel . . . better. . . ."

His arms tightened, hands gently kneading her back. "Sure you will. You're upset now. Sounds like you had a bad day."

"Bad night. . . ."

"Come on. Let's go inside."

A short time later, Lauren was huddled in a corner of the living room sofa, holding the glass of brandy Matt had pressed into her hand. He drew one of the side chairs close and propped his elbows on his knees. "Okay. From the top. What happened tonight?"

"It's not just what happened tonight. It's *everything*."

"But tell me about tonight. I need to know, Lauren."

She studied the rim of the brandy snifter and shrugged. "I panicked." Painstakingly, she explained how she'd walked back to the garage. "Then there was that awful last stretch when only one man was behind me."

"Did you see what he looked like?"

She tipped the snifter until the brandy came perilously close to its rim. "Not really. I glanced back once and got the impression of someone big and tall and dark. Then I started running and didn't look back again."

"He didn't follow you once you ran?"

"I don't know. I didn't look. By the time I reached the garage, I couldn't see him. I conned the guard into walking me up to my car."

"Smart girl."

She snorted. "Fine for you to say. You didn't see the guard."

"It was still smart. A paid guard wouldn't try anything. He'd never get away with it."

"That was what I figured, not that I had much choice at the time."

"But you made it to your car safely. Did you see anyone when you were driving away from the garage?"

"I wasn't looking." She paused to take a healthy swallow of brandy, made a face, recovered, then went on. "I just locked the doors and drove. No one followed me home, at least no one I could see. I was checking for that." Her voice rose. "But when I got here, I didn't know what to do. Everything was dark, and I was sure that if I tried to get into the house, I'd get caught in one of your snares. Then you drove up, and I thought it was *him*—but I really don't know if there *was* a him. The man I saw could have been after me. Then again, he could have been minding his own business."

Matt closed his hand over hers and urged the snifter to her lips again. The brandy was doing its thing; at least she'd stopped shaking.

"I'm sorry I frightened you," he said.

"I thought you'd be later."

"I left Leominster as soon as I could. I was worried."

The eyes Lauren raised brimmed with discouragement. "What am I going to do, Matt?" she whispered. "I can't go on this way."

"I know, sweetheart. I know." His expression was grim. "Do you think someone's keeping tabs on you during the day?"

"While I'm at work, you mean?"

He nodded. "Have you ever gotten the feeling that you're being followed in broad daylight?"

She thought for a minute. "No."

"Ever remember seeing anyone who might fit the description of the man you saw tonight?"

Again she pondered his question, then shrugged in frustration. "There have to be dozens of tall, large-set men who wander through the Marketplace each day. I've never noticed anyone special . . . other than you." When he glowered at her, she added a sad "That was a compliment," and his glower promptly faded.

"Oh. Thank you."

"What *am* I going to do?"

"I'm thinking. I'm thinking." It was a while before he spoke again, and then it was almost to himself. "You haven't gotten any strange phone calls, heavy-breathing type of thing? And there hasn't been any direct contact, like a note or anything?"

She shook her head, but Matt's attention was on the floor. His brows were knitted together, his lips clamped into a thin line.

"I think," he said at last, "that you should finish your brandy and get to bed. You've had a frightening—"

"Finish my brandy and get to bed? That won't solve anything!"

"There's nothing to be solved tonight. You're safely locked in, and I'm here."

"But tomorrow! I have to go to work tomorrow! You can't be with me every minute, and I don't even want that. I've never been helpless or clinging before, but it seems that lately I'm throwing myself at you the instant you get here."

"I don't mind," he volunteered with a half grin, only to be cut off.

"Well, I do! I don't like what I've become, Matt. I can't continue living this way. I won't!"

What had existed of a grin was wiped clean from his face. "I agree, Lauren. Something has to be done. It's simply a matter of deciding what. Just . . . just let me sleep on it, okay?"

"I know what should be done. The police should be called in."

He took her hand. "Do you trust me?"

"Of course I trust you. I just think that—"

"Do you *trust* me?"

She knew he was testing her. There was nothing of the little boy about him now. He was all man. Eyes locked with his, she nodded.

"Then let me sleep on it. Give me until morning to

figure out what the next step should be."

At that moment, Lauren came out of herself enough to see the lines of fatigue that shadowed Matt's face. He was tired. And worried. "But it's not your responsibility—"

"Till morning?"

She clamped her lower lip between her teeth, then let it slide out. Her nod was slower in coming this time, but when it did, it conveyed the trust he sought.

Morning arrived, and Lauren awoke to find that Matt was no longer in bed. Tossing her robe on, she hurried off in search of him. He was just replacing the telephone receiver when she entered the kitchen.

"Matt?" She halted abruptly and stood suspended on the threshold. There was something about the tired slump of his shoulders that filled her with dread.

He covered the distance between them and took her in his arms. His words came out in a rush. "I have to go back to California for a couple of days, Lauren. I've just spoken with the airline and made a reservation."

For a minute she couldn't say anything. She'd known that sooner or later he'd be leaving, but . . . "Now?" she whispered through a tight throat. "Why *now?*"

"It's important. You know I wouldn't leave if it weren't."

"But . . . what should I do?" The instant she said the words, she hated them, hated herself, hated the situation.

"I think you should consider visiting your parents."

"No."

"What about Beth? You could sleep over at her place."

"No."

"Then take a room at a hotel. Maybe the Bostonian, or the Marriott. Something close to work."

"No!" She freed herself from his grasp and wrapped her arms around her waist. "I'm not running away. I won't be forced out of my own home!"

Matt ran a hand through his hair, which looked as if he'd done that more than once. For that matter, between the creases on his brow and the weary look in his eyes, she wondered if he'd slept at all. He seemed to be exerting a taut control over himself, but then, so was she. She refused to fall apart, to be reduced to a simpering weakling. No strings, she'd told Matt, and no strings there would be.

"It's very important that I go, Lauren."

Her chin was firm. "It's all right. You can go."

"I don't want to."

"But it's all right. I'll be fine." Hadn't she always been before?

"It's just for two or three days."

"I understand."

"No, you don't. You think I'm running out on you."

"I think just what you told me, that it's important for you to fly back." She was feeling distinctly numb. "When does your plane leave?"

He glanced at his watch. "In two hours."

"I can drop you at the airport on my way—"

"You'll be late. I'll drive myself and leave the car at the airport."

She nodded. Without another word, she turned and retraced her steps to the bedroom. She thought of nothing but getting ready for a regular day's work.

Matt showered while she dressed. They said little to each other during breakfast. Only when she had swung her pocketbook to her shoulder did she look at him. Even her self-imposed anesthetization couldn't fully immunize her against the swell of emotion that hit her.

"Have a safe flight," she whispered.

He walked her to the door. "You know how to work the latch for this thing?"

"Yes." He'd reviewed the process in detail when they'd entered the house last night.

"Be sure to reset it once you've let yourself in or out."

"I will."

They passed through and headed for the garage. "And this one?"

"Yes. I've got it now."

"Lauren, I really wish—"

"Shh. Please, Matt. You have to do your thing, and I have to do mine." She pressed the hidden switch that allowed her access to the garage without mishap, but before she could enter the car, Matt stopped her. He put both hands on her shoulders and looked her straight in the eye.

"I know you're angry, Lauren, and hurt. Believe me, I'd never be leaving if I didn't think it was absolutely necessary."

She stared up at him, saying nothing because there was nothing she would permit herself to say. Only when he tugged her close and wrapped his arms tightly around her did she allow herself a moment's softening. Closing her eyes, she leaned into his strength. By the time he'd released her, though, she was on her own again.

"Be cautious, Lauren," he said. His voice was thick, his gaze clouded. "When in doubt, go with your instincts. They're good. Trust them."

For a split second, she wavered. Her instincts told her that Matt shouldn't go, that she needed him here, that whatever it was that drew him back to California wasn't as important as what was happening between them in Massachusetts. Her instincts told her that his trip would bring no good where they were concerned.

But reason ruled. Matt's home and job were in San Francisco. She had no claim on either. She was right in what she'd told him; he had to do his thing and she had to do hers. And hers was to carry on with her life, just as it had been before Matthew Kruger had entered it.

"Take care," she whispered, then slipped into her car. She didn't look back to see Matt by the garage door after she'd backed out and around, or to see him still standing there when she drove down the drive and turned into the street. If she was aware that she'd left part of herself with him, she put that particular ache down to the general upheaval her life had gone through in the past few weeks. Doggedly she kept her sights ahead.

As the day passed, Lauren had less control over her emotional state than she might have liked. Much as she tried not to, she thought of Matt. *He's arriving at the airport now. His plane is taking off now. He's over Pennsylvania, Illinois, Kansas, Utah.* Out of the blue, she'd feel tears in her eyes, and though she cursed her preoccupation, she knew that it was diverting her mind from other thoughts.

Beth, who'd been quick to sense something amiss, tried to get her to talk, but all Lauren would say was that Matt had been called back to his home office for a few days.

"But I thought he was here for another week at least."

"Things come up."

"And he didn't elaborate?" There was an undercurrent of accusation in Beth's words.

Lauren, who was carelessly flipping through the morning's mail, ignored it. "Other than to say it was important that he go." She frowned. "I don't believe it. Another letter for Susan Miles."

"Who's Susan Miles?"

"Beats me. But it's addressed to her, care of this shop. There was one yesterday, too."

"Mark it 'return to sender, addressee unknown' and stick it back in the mail."

"I would if I could, but I can't. There's no return address."

"Postmark?"

"Boston. If whoever sent it doesn't get an answer, he'll just have to show up here to see what's wrong."

"He? How do you know it's a he?"

Lauren held out the letter. "Look at the handwriting. It's heavy. And messy. Has to be a he."

Beth donned her imagination-at-work look. "A he. Hmm, I smell possibilities in this one. You've already got a guy, so forget you. Let's concentrate on me. Suppose, just suppose, some fellow was given the name of a girl he was told worked here. A blind-date kind of thing. Only either he got the girl's name screwed up or the friend who set him up was playing a joke."

"Why would a guy *write* to set up a blind date?"

"Maybe he's too shy to call. Or he's simply taking a new approach. A new approach—that's it." She eyed Lauren through a playful squint. "Not all that different from sitting on a bench for two days, or sitting on it for hours a third day just reading."

"Point taken," Lauren admitted dryly. "I suppose this guy's gorgeous and witty and bright."

"Naturally."

"Then why does his handwriting look like a thug's?"

"It's not like a thug's. It's . . . creative."

"Ahh. Then whatever is inside this envelope," Lauren said, waving it, "must be equally as creative."

"I'm sure it is." Beth's voice dropped conspiratorially. "Let's open it."

"We can't do that, Beth. It's not addressed to us."

"It's addressed to our shop."

"And what if your gorgeous guy comes in to collect the letters he's incorrectly addressed? He'll be mortified."

"He'll be so taken with me that he won't have time to be mortified. Besides, we can say we threw the letters out. So what harm is there in opening them first? Do you have the other one?"

"Yes, but, Beth, I don't think this is a great idea."

"Don't think." Snatching the gray envelope from Lauren's hand, Beth quickly opened it. She removed a sheet of matching stationery, unfolded it, then turned it over, puzzled. "Blank. There's nothing on it."

Lauren, too, stared at the blank sheet. "Maybe he lost his nerve the second time around."

"Where's the first?"

Lauren fished the envelope from a drawer in the desk and, her own curiosity piqued, opened it. "The same. The paper is blank. What's going on here, Beth?"

"Who knows?" Beth continued the game, but her enthusiasm was waning. "Maybe his tactic is to be mysterious for a while."

"So we have to wait for the next installment to find out who the mad letter writer is?"

Beth shrugged. "Looks that way." She headed for the front of the store, leaving Lauren to dispose of the blank love letters as she saw fit. For some reason Lauren herself didn't understand, she folded both sheets back into their envelopes and tucked the envelopes into the drawer.

This activity had provided only a temporary respite for Lauren, as did most of work that day. Unfortunately, by the time she knew that Matt had landed and been swallowed up in his own life again, she could no longer free herself of those other, more ominous thoughts.

"How'd you like a roommate for a night or two?" she asked Beth when they were getting ready to close the shop. She'd tried to sound nonchalant, but the gesture was lost on Beth, who knew better.

"I'd love it, Lauren. You know that. You're welcome to stay at my place whenever you want."

"I know you have a date—"

"No, I don't."

"Listen, it's okay. I just don't feel like driving back to Lincoln. You can go out. I'll make myself at home—"

"I don't have a date, Lauren."

"But that fellow Joe—"

"Asked me out and I refused. He wanted to go camping. Overnight. I didn't have equipment, and I'm not keen on camping, and I'm even less keen on Joe."

"How do you know? You've just met the guy."

"Exactly. Have you ever heard of camping overnight for a first date?"

Lauren shrugged. "Might have been interesting."

"Maybe for you and Matt. No, chalk that." Beth grunted. "Matt might have left you stranded in the woods while he raced off to scale some nearby peak. How could he simply abandon you this way, Lauren? I still can't believe it."

Lauren kept her voice calm. "He has his own life."

"But he's barged his way into yours—"

"He didn't barge his way in anywhere."

"Okay, then he wormed his way in. He's made himself nearly indispensable—"

"He has *not*. I can do just fine without him."

"Mmm. That's why you can't bear the thought of going home."

Lauren's gaze lowered to the scrap of fabric she was fraying. "It's not that. But after last night I feel . . . uncomfortable." She'd told Beth earlier about the episode near the garage. "It's still too fresh in my mind."

"Matt wasn't around then, either. Why do men do this, Lauren? Why aren't they around when you need them?"

"It's not a question of need," Lauren rationalized. "I'm independent. I can take care of myself."

"You should go to the police. I think what you're facing is more than even Matt can handle. Why is he so vehement against it?"

"He has good reasons. He may be right."

"Maybe his reasons aren't so noble."

Lauren tensed. "What do you mean?"

"It's occurred to me that much of what's happened to you has been since Matt showed up."

"That's not true! Three of those incidents happened before he ever got here!"

"No," Beth returned, determined to make her point. "If my memory's correct, three of those incidents happened within mere days of his first introducing himself to you. He said he was here in Boston on business. For all you know, he was here in the city that very first time, when the car just missed you on Newbury Street."

"I'm not sure I like what you're implying."

"I'm not sure I do, either, but it may be worth considering."

"Absolutely not! What could Matt possibly have to do with those incidents? What reason could he have to wish me harm?"

"Maybe something to do with Brad?"

"That's impossible. Don't even think it, Beth. It's out of the question."

No more was said about it, but Beth had accomplished her objective. Lauren fought it. She told herself that Beth was either playing the game she played so well or simply jealous. Lauren closed her mind to it while she and Beth walked over Beacon Hill to Beth's apartment, where they shared a congenial dinner and evening. Later that night, though, while Lauren lay quietly on the sofa bed trying to fall asleep, unwanted thoughts flitted in fragments through her mind.

Ironically, Matt's phone call didn't help. It came at two in the morning, shortly after Lauren had fallen into a restless sleep. The phone was on the table by her head. She nearly jumped out of her skin when it rang.

"Hello?"

"Lauren! I've been worried sick! When there was no answer at the farmhouse, I started calling hotels. You said you *weren't* going to Beth's!" He sounded angry. That was all Lauren needed.

"Why, Matt, how good of you to call in the middle of the night. I'm fine, thank you. How are you?"

"Lauren, you said you weren't going anywhere!"

"I changed my mind."

"Damn it, you could have let me know. I was sure something had happened!"

"How could I have let you know? I don't know where you are, much less at what phone number."

"I'm at home, and I'm the only Matthew Kruger in the San Francisco book!"

"How did I know you'd be trying me? You didn't say anything about calling."

She heard a deep sigh at the other end of the line. "Right. I'm sorry. It was my fault. Are you okay?"

"I'm tired, Matt." *And confused. Very confused.* The sound of Matt's voice, imperious, then gentle, only added to her confusion.

"I'm sorry to be calling so late. I started trying the house an hour and a half ago. When there was no answer, I figured maybe you'd gone to another movie or something, but when you didn't return, I started imagining things and it all began to spiral. You are okay?"

"Yes, I'm okay."

"Nothing happened today?"

"No, nothing happened."

"Thank goodness."

His voice clearly held relief. For that matter, Lauren mused, everything about his voice was clear. He could just as well be calling her from around the corner. . . .

"Well," he went on, less sure of himself now, "I just wanted to hear your voice. And to tell you that I'm going to try to catch an afternoon flight out of here tomorrow. By the time I get into Logan and on the road, it's apt to be pretty late. It may be easier if I go to a hotel—"

"No!" she interrupted. She could hear the fatigue in his voice, and it pulled a string somewhere deep inside her. This was Matt, the man she missed, the man she wanted to see, to be with. "No. Meet me in Lincoln. I'll be there."

"But you may be sleeping. I'll frighten you."

"Just give a honk like you did the other night and I'll know it's you."

"Are you sure?"

"I'm sure."

"Okay, sweetheart." His voice lowered. "I miss you."

"Me, too, Matt."

"See you tomorrow night, then?"

"Uh-huh."

"Take care, sweetheart."

"You, too. Bye-bye, Matt."

She replaced the receiver and sank back to the bed, only then realizing that she hadn't even asked how he was doing. Maybe she hadn't wanted to. Maybe she'd been afraid he'd give her an evasive answer. He hadn't spelled out the reason for his abrupt return to San Francisco—if indeed he was there. Was his business on the West Coast shrouded in mystery, or was her imagination at work again?

After tossing and turning for better than an hour, she finally fell back to sleep. When she awoke on Sunday morning, she felt weary and tense. Even Beth's light-hearted chatter didn't lighten her mood; irrationally, perhaps, she blamed Beth for having planted the seeds of doubt in her mind.

Driving to Lincoln in broad daylight was accomplished comfortably. Lauren arrived there moments before Thomas Gehling pulled up. She liked him instantly, finding him easygoing, intelligent and polite. As they walked through the house, they discussed a wide range of possibilities. She hired him on the spot.

That was the high point of her day. The tension, the confusion, the worry, were back in full swing by the time she'd returned to Boston. Work at the shop was a blessing, but a short-lived one. All too soon she was headed back to Lincoln. This time around, she was a bundle of raw nerves.

A confrontation was imminent. She felt it in every fiber of her being. By nature she was a peaceful, accommodating sort, but the events of the past few weeks had upset her equilibrium. It was one thing to suspect that an unknown lunatic was after her, yet quite another to suspect that it was Matt. He was either with her or against her. She had to know one way or the other.

Arriving home at dusk, she was assailed by every one of the fears she'd been free of that morning. Glancing anxiously from side to side, she inched her way up the drive. Her first thought was to leave the car outside, but she knew that its protection, and hence her own, came from the trap that was set inside. Dashing quickly from the car to the garage, she fumbled to disengage the alarm and raise the door. That done, she quickly brought the car inside, lowered the door and reengaged the snare, then tackled the front door of the house. Beads of sweat were dotting her upper lip by the time she'd finally closed the door behind her and reset the alarm.

Then she made dinner, ate practically none of it and waited. She picked up a book, turned page after page without absorbing a word and waited. She dozed on the living room sofa, awakening with a jolt at the slightest sound—though most were in her dreams—and waited.

Midnight came and went. Then one o'clock. It was nearly one-thirty when she finally heard a car approach. This time she didn't rush to the window. She didn't so much as shift on the sofa. She sat quietly in the dark, waiting.

CHAPTER EIGHT

Lauren held her breath when she identified the click and scrape at the front door as the disengagement of the makeshift electrical alarm. Her eyes pierced the darkness, never once leaving the broad oak expanse as, with an aged creak, the door slowly opened. The man who came quietly through was tall, very tall, and large-set. Though he could have doubled for the man she'd seen behind her in Boston on the previous Friday night, there was no doubt in her mind that this time it was Matt.

"You didn't honk," she accused in a voice that shook.

His head twisted. "Lauren!" Setting his suitcase on the floor, he groped for the light switch. The weak glow that subsequently filtered into the living room from the hall was enough to reveal her position on the sofa. "What are you doing up, sweetheart? I thought for sure you'd be in bed."

"You didn't honk."

He paused, turning his head slightly. "The thought of it seemed jarring at this hour. I really didn't want to wake you up." He stood back-lighted in the archway of the living room, his face in shadows. "But you weren't sleeping, were you?" Crossing the room, he hunkered down and curled his fingers lightly around her arms. Her skin was cold. "Why aren't you in bed?" he asked softly.

"We have to talk."

"You sound strange. What's wrong?"

She didn't move. "I'm not sure. That's one of the things we have to discuss."

He frowned at his hands, dropped them to the sofa on either side of her hips, then met her gaze. "What is it, Lauren?"

"I've been sitting here thinking. I've spent most of the day thinking. And last night, too."

He sank back on his heels, hands falling to his sides. "About what?"

"You. I want the truth, Matt." It was a struggle to keep her voice steady when so much was at stake, but she managed commendably. "I want all of it. No evasion. No seduction. I want to ask questions and have them answered."

178

"I don't understand. I've always given you answers—"

"They were never enough, but that may be my fault. Maybe I haven't *asked* enough."

"I don't know what you're getting at."

She tucked her legs more tightly beneath her. "Three weeks ago I was happy. My life was shaping up so beautifully that I had to pinch myself to make sure it was real. Then certain things started happening, and I'm suddenly stuck in the middle of a nightmare. Someone is after me. I don't know who or why."

"What's this got to do with *me?*"

"You showed up right after it all began, Matt. By some coincidence, you appeared out of nowhere. You claim to be a friend of my brother's, but my brother has been dead for a year, so I can't ask him about it. You have biographical facts about Brad, any of which you could have picked up by reading a standard job résumé. You have insight into his character, most of which you could have gained in one night of heavy drinking with him, even if he'd been a total stranger up until then."

"I don't believe this," Matt muttered, but Lauren was just beginning.

"That first night when you introduced yourself to me, you said you'd been in Boston for a week. It was during that very week that I was nearly run down by a car on Newbury Street. Nothing about the car registered with me. It could very easily have been a nondescript rental, just like the one you've been driving."

"Lauren—"

"Then a dog attacked me. You were the one who suggested it might have been trained to pull away when a special whistle was blown. That thought wouldn't even have occurred to me, yet it did to you. Why?"

"It's common knowledge—"

"And then my garage door crashed down." Despite the warmth of the night, her hands were freezing. She tucked them more deeply in the folds of her shirt. "You're a builder. You seemed familiar enough with the workings of that door to be able to rig, and unrig, a malfunction."

"This is absurd, Lauren! Do you know what you're saying?"

"I'm not done," she declared. "Let me finish."

He was on his feet, prowling the room. "I can't wait to hear the rest."

She ignored his sarcasm, knowing only that the time for silence had passed. "There was the matter of an intruder in my house. You found the problem immediately. A lock on one of the windows was broken. In fact, you used that very window to get into the house, supposedly to scout around. How can I be sure it was the first time you'd entered the house that way?" When Matt took a sharp breath to defend himself, she rushed on. "The car that followed me all the way home from Boston was compatible in both size and shade to your rental. And the timing was perfect. You could have left me at my garage, picked up your own car—even on another floor of the same garage—and tailed me out. Then there was the night when I heard strange noises. You said you were in Leominster. It was a convenient alibi, but I have no proof, do I?"

"I'll give you names and numbers—"

"My car battery went dead; you were the last one to drive the car. Someone followed me late at night in Boston; you conveniently arrived here within minutes after I did."

"I was in *Leominster*—but I told you that once before, didn't I? I thought we agreed on it."

"That was what you wanted, for me to agree on it."

"I wanted you to trust me."

"So you told me. Many times. And I've been completely taken in, because I thought you were one of the most sincere, straightforward men I've ever met. Maybe I was wrong, Matt. Maybe I've been playing into your hands all along."

He stood before her then, hands on his hips, his face a mask of steel. The oblique light from the hall did nothing to blunt his obvious irritation. "What brought all this on? That's what I'd like to know. You did trust me. At least, I thought you did. Where did I go wrong?"

Lauren's composure was beginning to slip. If Matt was innocent—and his reaction was far from conclusive on that score—she was going to hate herself for the accusations she'd made. On the other hand, if he was guilty as charged, she was in a lot of trouble.

"You went wrong," she began with a shaky breath, "when you took off for California on Saturday morning."

"You *were* angry."

"No. But I was puzzled and maybe a little hurt, because the trip was so sudden and you were so tight-lipped about it. And that got me to thinking, and suddenly there were more questions than ever. I'm an intelligent person, Matt. 'Together,' to quote you. You could have told me anything and I'd have understood. Okay, what happens with your work is your business. But you've shared other things with me, which I realize in hindsight you've been very selective about. Why discuss some things and not others? Unless you're hiding something. Unless there's something you don't want me to know."

He threw a hand in the air. "It's Beth. You've been listening to Beth. This sounds like one of her hare-brained plots."

Lauren stared him out. "Days ago I wanted to go to the police. Any person in his right mind would do that in a situation like mine. But I didn't go to the police, because you told me not to. You've been adamant about it! *Why?*"

"You want to know why?" Matt raged suddenly. His eyes were narrowed, his head thrust forward. "I'll tell you why! Because your brother, Brad, was up to no good during the last few years of his life, and if I'd gone to the police when I suspected that Brad's boss was behind what was happening to you, it would have all come out. *You'd* have been hurt. I was trying to protect *you!*"

Lauren sat in stunned silence as the warm summer night crowded in on her. One minute she felt smothered, the next chilled. In the third, she was stifling again and began to sweat. Dropping her gaze to the floor, she pressed a finger to her moist upper lip, frowned, then looked back at Matt. "What did you say about Brad?' she asked in a timid whisper.

Matt stood with his feet braced apart, one hand massaging the taut muscles at the back of his neck. At her question, he lowered his head, put two fingers to his forehead and rubbed. "Brad was in trouble." His voice held a blend of sadness and defeat. Lauren knew he'd have to be a consummate actor to produce such a heart-wrenching tone on cue.

"What kind of trouble?" Her stomach had begun to jump. She pressed a hand to it.

"Please. Lauren, you don't want—"

"What kind of trouble?" When he didn't answer, she repeated the question a third time. *"What kind of trouble?"*

Matt sighed in resignation. "He'd been padding invoices and expense vouchers, then pocketing the difference."

"I don't believe you."

"Maybe that's just as well. Brad's dead. Nothing will ever be proved one way or another. Just rumors. Lousy rumors."

"You believe them."

"I knew Brad." He took a quick breath. "Please, don't misunderstand me. Brad and I were close. He was a loyal friend. I respected him in many, many ways."

"But?"

"But all along I knew there was one part of him that

was unsettled. It was as if he was looking for an opening, and his boss unwittingly gave him one. Chester Hawkins was a crook. We both knew it. We discussed it many times. Bribes, kickbacks—you name it, Hawkins did it."

"But padding expense vouchers—that's small-time stuff. What could Brad have hoped to gain?"

"It's not small-time when it's done over and over again."

"For how long?"

"Two years, maybe three. It adds up."

"But *why?* Why would he have done it?"

Matt dropped into a side chair. "Maybe he felt it was poetic justice, stealing from a thief. More likely he felt that an accumulation of wealth was the only way he could prove his worth."

Lauren moaned softly. Her head fell back against the sofa and she closed her eyes. When she spoke, her voice was wobbly. "I knew there was too much money. It didn't make sense. Right from the start I wondered, but I took it. I took it and I used it."

"Which was exactly what you *should* have done!" Matt sat forward and spoke with renewed force. "Brad earned every cent of that money. He was overworked and underpaid for years. What he did might have been punishable in a court of law, but there was still a certain justice to it. He gave Hawkins his life, for God's sake, and there was only a piddling insurance policy on it! Hawkins wasn't big on employee benefits. He gave the bare minimum. Brad earned that money, Lauren. And he wanted you to have it."

Lauren swallowed hard, trying to ingest all that Matt had told her. "Did he really? Or did you tell me that just to make me feel better?"

"He said it. Believe me—ah, hell." Matt flopped back in the chair. "Believe what you want. The fact is that you've put the money to good use. No one can ever take it away from you."

They were back to square one. "Someone's trying. Is it this fellow, Hawkins?" she asked nervously.

"He claims not."

"You *spoke* to him?"

Matt was out of his seat, pacing again. "What did you think I went to San Francisco for?"

"I didn't know! I assumed it had something to do with your own work. You didn't volunteer any details!"

"I went to confront Hawkins."

"And?"

"He says he's innocent."

"Do you believe him?"

"I'm not sure." Matt stopped his pacing and stared at her. "On the one hand, he wouldn't dare try anything. I wasn't the only friend Brad had. If Hawkins tries to pin something on Brad, even posthumously, any number of us will cry foul. Hawkins can't risk that. There's too much that can be pinned right back on him."

"On the other hand . . ."

He took a deep breath. "On the other hand, I wouldn't put it past him to try something on the sly. He and Brad had reached a stalemate. Each knew what the other was doing, so it was a form of mutual blackmail. Hawkins didn't dare fire Brad for fear he'd squeal. But Brad's gone now. It's possible that Hawkins thought he'd go after some of that money—"

"By terrorizing *me?*"

"Sick minds work in sick ways. Besides, Hawkins wouldn't do it himself. He'd hire someone. If he's discovered that you've invested the money between the shop and this place, he may be out for his own private form of revenge."

"So we're back where we started."

"Not . . . quite," Matt stated with such quiet thunder that Lauren's pulse skipped a beat before racing on. "There are still certain allegations you've made that have to be resolved. Y'know, you're right." He cocked his head and eyed her insolently. "I may well be the man Hawkins hired, playing you now just as I've played you all along—orchestrating events, then showing up and explaining them away."

"But why *would* you?" she cried.

"You're the one with the answers." He flung himself back into the chair. "You tell me."

"I don't *have* the answers. That's what this—this is all about! I don't have *any* answers. My mind is running in circles!"

"Could be I'm getting paid a pretty penny for this."

"You don't want the money," she protested. "You're not ambitious that way! You told me so the first time we met!"

"Could be I was lying. Could be it was all an act." He jacked forward in the chair. "And since you're hurling accusations, I've got a few of my own. You were a virgin for twenty-nine years. Then you met me, and within a week we became lovers. Strange things were happening to you. You were frightened. You needed protection." He snorted. "Pretty high price to pay for it, I'd say."

She felt as though she'd been slapped. "No! I didn't—"

"Then again, maybe you were truly infatuated. I was different from the men you'd known. More physical. Brawny. But now that you've gotten what you wanted, you're scrabbling for reasons to put me off."

"No, Matt! How can you—"

"I don't meet your high standards. Is that it, Lauren?" His eyes bore into hers. "You're prepared to believe the worst because you just don't think I'm good enough for you?"

Unable to bear another word, Lauren sprang up from the sofa and rounded on him. "That's not true!" she screamed, grabbing his shoulders and shaking him. It was a pitiful gesture, since he was so much larger than she, but her fury was beyond reason. "It's not true! And I wasn't *prepared* to believe the worst!" His face blurred before her eyes. "But I had to know—had to know. I'd never been with another man, because no man had meant anything to me until you came along!" Tears trickled unheeded down her cheeks, and her hands stilled, impotent fingers clutching fistfuls of his shirt. "I've been dying, slowly dying for the past two days, grasping at straws, wondering if it was possible that—that I'd made a big mistake and given you everything and that you were really on the other side."

Her knees gave out then, and she sank to the floor between his legs. Her head was bowed. She wept softly. "It hurt so to . . . to think that, and I knew I had to get . . . get it out in the open, but that hurt, too . . . and . . . and . . ." Her fingers curved around his knee, gently kneading in a silent bid for forgiveness.

Matt put a tentative hand on her hair. "And what, Lauren?" he asked softly.

Her head remained down, her muffled voice punctuated by sniffles. "I love you . . . and I've hurt you . . . and somehow this new life that was supposed . . . supposed to be so wonderful is all messed up!"

With a low groan, he slid to the floor. His thighs flanked hers as he took her into the circle of his arms. "Oh, baby. Sweetheart, shhh." He rocked her tenderly. "You've just said the magic words. Nothing's messed up. Everything's suddenly clear."

She shook her head against his chest, too upset to comprehend.

He spread a large hand over the back of her head, buried his face in her hair and pressed her closer. "It's all right," he whispered between soft kisses. "Everything's going to be all right."

Lauren let her tears flow. They were a purging of sorts. It wasn't that she agreed with Matt or understood things as he seemed to, but being held in his arms this way, absorbing his strength and incredible tenderness, she felt herself slowly emerging from the hell she'd been living for the past few days.

He rubbed her back, caressing her gently. He whispered soft words of endearment and encouragement; with each one the darkness receded and she moved closer to the light. The warmth of his body thawed her inner chill. She fed on his strength like a creature starved for it.

Then he tipped her chin up and kissed her, and the last of her anguish broke and dissipated like a fever at the end of a long illness. She felt suddenly free, light-headed and very much in love. Shaping her hands to his cheeks, she gave herself up to his kiss; but because she offered as much as she received, Matt was as aroused as she by the time they finally parted, panting.

While she strung slow kisses along the line of his jaw and his chin, she worked at the buttons of first her shirt, then his. His hands were already in full possession of her breasts before she'd finished the latter, and when she came to her knees to press closer, the squeeze of her thighs against the mounting ache between them was a necessity.

From numbness such a short time before to this rich blossoming of the senses, Lauren reeled. Everything about Matt turned her on, from the vitality of the thick, sun-burnished hair through which her fingers wound to the musky scent of the rough, sweat-dampened skin beneath her lips to the virile cords of muscle straining against the rest of her body.

"I love you," she whispered against his mouth. "I love you, Matt." Her hands slid from his head down his chest, savoring the journey. But urgency was quickly mounting. She released the snap of his jeans, then the zipper, and worked her way beneath the waistband of his shorts until her fingers found what they sought. He was thick and hard, needing her in the same way that she needed him.

He gave an openmouthed moan and whispered her name, then set her back and shoved his jeans lower. "Hurry," he rasped as Lauren rocked back on her bottom and tore her own jeans off in jerky movements. He reached for her with urgent fingers, bringing her close until she straddled his thighs.

"Love me, Matt. Please, love me . . ."

"God, yes . . ."

His hands covered her buttocks, urging her downward even as she guided him inside her, and there was nothing then but paradise. His hands on her body, stroking . . . inflaming . . . lifting. His tongue wet and greedy on her throat, her collarbone, her breasts. Her own hands clutching his bronzed flesh, molding . . . straining . . . her mouth rapacious, her hips meeting his every thrust with matching ferocity.

They brought each other to near-peak after near-peak of exquisite sensation, and when the final climax hit, their cries were simultaneous, prolonged and distinctly triumphant.

For long moments, Lauren was aware of nothing but the state of heavenly bliss in which she floated. Then came Matt's ragged breathing. It took her a minute longer to realize that her own throat was contributing to the rasping sound.

Very gradually the gasping eased, then ended, yet neither of them made a move to leave the other's arms. Their bodies remained joined, and Matt defied the limpness of his limbs to hold her even closer.

"I love you, Lauren," he murmured hoarsely. "Please, please don't doubt me again. I think it would—" His voice broke. "It would destroy me."

Her face buried in the warm crook of his neck, she whispered his name over and over again. Her arms, too, had taken on a strength that denied passion's drain, and she held him with no intention of ever letting go. "I'm sorry" came her muffled cry. "I shouldn't have suggested those awful things."

"No, it's good you did. You were right. They had to come out in the open." He tipped her head back and looked into her eyes. "We need the truth, sweetheart. Both of us. There are so many things we can't figure out, but the situation becomes only more complicated if we can't be honest about ourselves and our feelings." With one arm supporting her back, he gently smoothed damp tendrils of hair from her cheeks. "I have insecurities. Lots of them. They hit me like a ton of bricks when I first met you, and they've kept me a little off balance ever since."

"You didn't need to worry about *anything!*"

"But I did. At the start I worried that you'd associate me only with Brad and that you'd transfer the rift between you and him to me. I worried that you'd turn down your nose at my occupation, that you'd categorize me and put me in a slot and wouldn't like the things I suggested we do. Then, when I began to realize how I felt about you, I was afraid you wouldn't feel the same." He slid his cheek against her temple. "And all the time I was worried about what was happening to you. I imagined Hawkins might be behind it, and I was reluctant to tell you the truth. Maybe I wouldn't be able to protect you or catch the bastard before he really hurt you."

"You'll be dead long before I will if you keep up that worrying," Lauren quipped softly, "and *then* where will I be?"

"Do you love me?"

"I do love you."

"And you're not bothered by who I am and where I come from?"

"Only that you come from the opposite coast, and that's much too far away."

A tremor shot through his body and he gave her a bone-crushing squeeze. "God, you're wonderful. You're beautiful and bright and warm and giving. What did I ever do to deserve you?"

Lauren was thinking the very same thing, but with the pronouns reversed. "I love you," she whispered. She'd never tire of telling him so, and with that knowledge and the intimate closeness of his body, her insides began to quiver. She tightened her lower muscles and was rewarded by the faint catch in Matt's breath; then, as he grew inside her, she began to move.

It was much, much later, after they'd finally sought out her bed, that she turned in his arms. "Matt?"

His eyes were closed. She was wondering if he was asleep when she heard his low "Hmm?"

"Do you realize what we did?"

He shifted his hips and smiled smugly. "Mmm-hmm."

"But without anything." After that first night, Matt had taken the responsibility of protecting her. "Aren't you worried?"

"You told me to stop worrying."

"But if we make a baby . . ."

His eyes opened slowly, but the smugness remained on his face. "If we make a baby, we'll have it. It'll be beautiful and bright and healthy."

"But the planning, the logistics . . ."

The light in his eyes grew brighter. "I love you, Lauren. If a baby comes out of that love, I think I'd be the happiest man alive."

With a soft sigh of elation, she nestled more snugly against him. "Oh, Matt, I love you so." Basking in a special glow, lulled by the strong and steady beat of his heart, she fell into a deep and untroubled sleep.

Come morning, Lauren and Matt awoke together, showered together, dressed together, cooked and ate breakfast together. Neither seemed to tire of touching the other, or smiling, or whispering those three precious words.

It was only when they were getting ready to drive into Boston that Lauren permitted herself to think beyond the fact of their newly shared love. Matt sat sideways on the sofa, sorting through papers in his briefcase. Curling an arm around his neck, she slid onto his lap.

"We can't go to the police," she began quietly. "You're right. If they start looking into things and somehow come upon Brad's dealings, his memory will be sullied. I'm not sure my parents would care, but I would. So that leaves us back where we began. What should we do?"

Matt finished straightening a pile of letters, set them in the briefcase and snapped it shut. "I think maybe it's time to call in some help. Not the police—someone private." He slipped an arm around her waist. "That way we can control what comes out. Hawkins may be behind this, or it may be someone totally unrelated to him."

"In which case the motive is still a mystery."

"We need a fresh ear, someone who might ask questions we haven't thought of or see things from a new angle." He paused. "Should I get a name and make a call?'

"Yes. We have to do something. I don't want to live with a shadow hanging over me, especially not now."

Matt was in total agreement. Through one of the corporate powers he'd been dealing with in Boston, he contacted a reputable private investigator by the name of Phillip Huber and set up a meeting for the following morning. In the meantime, he stayed as close to Lauren as he could, returning to the shop between business meetings of his own, taking her to lunch, then dinner. When they finally arrived back in Lincoln, it was late. Given the minimum of sleep each had had—not to mention the strain of jet travel on Matt, about which Lauren teased him unmercifully—they were both tired.

Absently she picked up the mail and flipped through it. Gas bill. MasterCard bill. Advertisements. She lifted the next piece of mail, a disconcertingly familiar gray envelope, and stared at it.

Susan Miles. Addressed directly to the farmhouse.

Fingers trembling, she tore open the flap, pulled out the stationery and unfolded it. A separate piece of paper floated to the floor, but once again, the stationery itself was blank. Stooping, she lifted the paper that had been enclosed. Roughly cut at the edges, it was a picture of a gleaming fox fur coat, apparently taken from a magazine. The model had been unceremoniously decapitated.

"Matt?" she called faintly, then louder: "Matt!"

He appeared at the top of the stairs, his shirt unbuttoned, its tails loose. Lauren's anxious expression brought him trotting down immediately.

She spoke quickly. "Last Friday and again on Saturday we received a letter at the shop addressed to a Susan Miles. Neither Beth nor I know anyone by that name. We assumed it was simply a mistake. Now there's a letter addressed to Susan Miles *here*." She held out the piece of stationery and watched him turn it from front to back.

"It's blank."

"So were the other two. The only difference is that this one came with a magazine clipping." She offered it as well. "Just a picture of a fur coat. Nothing else."

Matt studied the clipping, frowned back at the blank sheet of stationery, then took the envelope from her hand and examined the raggedly scrawled address. "There's got to be a message here," he said at last. "We may not be understanding it, but there's got to be one. You say the other two letters were exactly like this one, but without the clipping?"

"That's right. Same gray stationery."

"Same handwriting on the envelope?"

"Yes. And the same Boston postmark. I didn't think much of the first two. They were addressed to the shop. It could have been a simple mistake. Taken with this last one, though, there has to be something more personal in it. Whoever sent them knows my home address. He's got the name wrong, but he knows where I work *and* where I live."

Much as Lauren's stomach was doing, Matt's jaw clenched. "Right." He rubbed his forehead with his finger. "Is it possible that you've been mistaken for someone else? For this Susan Miles, perhaps?"

Lauren didn't say anything. Her heart was hammering, and the knots in her stomach had tightened painfully.

Matt's focus remained on the pieces of paper he held. "Mistaken identity . . . that would make sense. All along you've had no idea who would have a reason to threaten you. We know there's a chance it could be Hawkins, but if it's not, this might be something to go on. If we could identify and locate this Susan Miles . . ." He looked up and caught Lauren's stricken expression. "Sweetheart?" When she swayed, he held her arms to steady her. "What is it?'

"I don't believe this is happening," she whispered. Her eyes were wide, dry but filled with the horror of conviction. "I don't believe it. I knew it was too good to be true."

Matt ducked his head, bringing his face level with hers. Every one of his features broadcast love and tenderness, and his voice was filled with hope. "It's okay, sweetheart. It's good, in fact. At least it's another lead to follow, and now that we've contacted an investigator—"

She covered her face with her hands. "My parents were right. I shouldn't have done it. I played with what fate had decreed, and now I'm paying for it."

"Lauren, what—"

"My face, Matt!" she cried. "It didn't always look this way. When I was a very little girl, my bones developed improperly. I was ugly. You saw a picture! You know!"

"My God," he whispered, finally putting the last piece of the puzzle into place. "I thought it was just a bad picture. I never dreamed . . ." Seizing her wrists, he drew her hands from her face and clutched them to his chest. His eyes slowly toured her features. "You had surgery," he said in amazement.

She nodded. "My chin was practically nonexistent, and my jaw was so badly misaligned that I had trouble eating. That's why I was so skinny."

"And you're so beautiful now. It's incredible!" He took her chin and turned her face first to one side, then the other. "No scars," he announced excitedly. "It must have been done from the inside. When, sweetheart?"

"This past spring, right before I came to Boston. I went to a clinic in the Bahamas. The recuperative period was ten weeks. Part of that time I stayed in a rented apartment and returned to the clinic on an out-patient basis."

"Unbelievable." Done with its journey, his gaze coupled with hers. "Just this past spring. So if I'd come six months before, I'd have found you in Bennington looking exactly as I'd expected. It all makes sense now—your inexperience with men, your talk of a new life, a new look . . ." His eyes lit with pleasure at a new thought. "Part of Brad's money went toward this, didn't it?"

"Some. Insurance paid for most of the surgery, since it had become a legitimate medical problem."

"And you feel better?"

"Physically *and* emotionally." She hesitated. "What about you, Matt? How do you feel?"

"How do I feel?" he echoed, puzzled.

"About what I did. Having plastic surgery and all."

"I think it's marvelous! If you'd looked this gorgeous much earlier, you'd have been snapped up before I could have found you."

"But what do you think about the surgery itself? Does it . . . bother you?"

"Of course not! Why would it bother me?"

"It bothers my parents. They were against my doing it."

"Hell, it's no different from a kid wearing braces on his teeth to correct a bite problem that would become troublesome in time. Or someone having his nose fixed to correct a deviated septum."

Lauren blushed. "I had that done, too."

"You did!" He grinned. "What did it look like

before? The picture I saw was a head-on shot."

"It was crooked," she admitted sheepishly. "And lousy for breathing. I used to snore something awful."

"You sure don't now. I love your nose." He ran a finger down its smooth slope. "It looks so—so natural. The whole thing looks so natural! I'd honestly decided that the picture was just a bad one. Either that, or you'd simply come into your own as you'd grown older."

"Then Brad didn't say anything specific?"

Matt's voice mellowed. "No. It wasn't often that Brad spoke of home, but when he mentioned you, there was always a certain tenderness in his voice. In spite of the rift, you had a special place in his heart. He worried about you. Wow, if he could only see you now!"

"Yeah," Lauren drawled wryly. "I've got a new face that apparently looks so much like someone else's that an enemy of that someone else is out for blood."

"Hey, we don't know that!"

"Well, maybe not blood, but something, that's for sure." She sent a pleading look to the ceiling. "I don't believe this. I just don't believe it. It's like something only Beth could have dreamed up, but she didn't." She arched a brow at Matt. "You do agree that the mistaken-identity theory is the strongest one we've had?"

"Mmm. Not that I'm ruling out Hawkins. But, given the letters for Susan Miles, this theory is more plausible."

"What could the newspaper clipping mean?"

"I don't know. If the letters were real letters with

writing and all, it wouldn't be so bad. But three blank sheets of stationery—that's odd."

Lauren sighed. "So, we look for Susan Miles."

"It's the way to go. Seems to me that'd be right down our investigator's alley."

It should have been. Lauren and Matt met with the detective at a small coffee shop in Boston early the next morning. They told him everything, from a detailed account of each of Lauren's mysterious incidents to their theories involving, alternately, Brad's boss and Lauren's new face.

Phillip Huber went off in search of Susan Miles. Unfortunately, after a full day of poring through State House and registry records, he could find no evidence of anyone by that name living in the area.

The next day he went through the records of the local and state police, and the day after that he made use of his considerable network of contacts to broaden the search to include the rest of New England and New York.

By Thursday night, Lauren and Matt were no closer to finding Susan Miles than they'd been at the start, and by Friday afternoon, the search was temporarily abandoned.

Lauren left the shop shortly before four, intent on getting to the bank and back before Matt came for her. He'd been her shadow for most of the week, and she'd loved it. But that day he'd had business to attend to, so she set out on the errand alone.

With the luxury of Jamie's working full-time, Lauren was taking off early. It was a beautiful day. She and Matt planned to return to Lincoln to change, then drive one town over, rent a canoe and explore the Concord River.

She walked at a confident pace, buoyed by the anticipation of the outing, lulled into security by the peaceful week it had been. Since Monday, when the letter for Susan Miles had arrived at the farmhouse, there had been no incidents. Of course, Matt had been close at hand, a visible deterrent to mischief, and Phillip Huber had taken his turn when Matt had been busy.

Lauren had barely turned down the side street on which the bank was located when a car slid smoothly to the curb. Its door opened, and she was jostled inside by a burly hulk that had come from nowhere on her opposite side. Before she knew what had happened, she was seated in the back seat of a car that would have been roomy except for the two giants who crowded her between them.

She tried to squirm, but she was solidly pinned. "What—what is this?" she cried between attempts to free herself.

"Sit still, pretty lady," the man on her left said. "You know what it is."

"I—do—not." She was trying to elbow herself out of the human vise, only to find that the vise had tightened. "Let me out of this car!" she gritted. She began to pound at the thighs flanking hers but succeeded only in having her wrists immobilized by a single beefy paw on either side. "You can't do this!"

"We've just done it," the same man pointed out. His voice was calm, matter-of-fact, infuriating.

"Well—" she kicked out "—I'm not—" she writhed lower in the seat "—having it!" She managed to hike herself forward but was pitched back by the arm of steel that crossed her collarbone and tightened. She bit at the arm and heard a low grunt. Before she could struggle free, she was slapped viciously across the side of her head. Sharp pain radiated through her entire skull, rendering her utterly dazed. She sagged limply against the seat and fought to catch her breath.

"That's better," the man on her left said. "Now sit there and *don't move*."

She couldn't have moved if she'd tried, and she couldn't even try. The blow had robbed her of what little strength had remained after her futile attempt to escape. Her head lolled against the upholstered seat, and for long moments she could do nothing but hope to regain her equilibrium. Her jaw hurt something fierce, and she felt a momentary flash of hysteria. If they'd broken her jaw after all she'd gone through to set it right, after all she was going through because she *had* set it right . . .

"You've got the wrong girl," she managed to mumble through stiff lips.

"Mmm" came a hum from her left. "Somehow we knew you'd say that."

"You do." Gingerly she worked her jaw. It was sore, but at least it functioned. "I don't really look like this . . . I had repair work done to correct a problem . . ."

"We know the problem."

The one on the left was apparently the designated speaker. She dared a glance at him. He was dark-haired, dark-eyed, dark-looking in every respect. His eyes were focused straight ahead, following the course the driver was taking.

"If you know the problem," Lauren ventured, "then you know this is all a mistake."

"The problem is that you didn't want to be found." He looked at her then, and she cringed under his scrutiny. "It's subtle, I have to say that much. You're clever. Didn't do anything drastic, thought we'd be off looking for someone *completely* different. Or maybe you just thought what you had was too beautiful to tamper much with. You always were a haughty bitch."

"You've got the wrong woman," Lauren pleaded in a shaky voice. "As God is my witness, I'm telling the truth. The surgery I had was to correct a problem I've had from childhood. You can contact the clinic. My doctor will tell you."

The man was looking forward again, a smug look on his face. "We've already been to the clinic. That was a fancy job you did with the records, and if we were stupid we might have been put off. But we're not stupid, Susan. I think it's about time you realize that."

"I'm not Susan! I know you think I'm Susan Miles, because that's the name on those envelopes, but *my* name is Lauren Stevenson! Lauren Stevenson, from Bennington, Vermont. I have family and friends still there—you can check."

"Lauren Stevenson." He rolled the name around on

his tongue in a way that made her want to vomit. "It's as good an alias as any."

"It's *not* an alias!"

Dark eyes glittered dangerously back at her. "Keep your voice down. I have a headache."

"I'll talk as loud as I want—" she fairly shouted, only to have her words cut off by the human mitt that clamped over her mouth. It had come from the right, but the voice, as always, came from the left.

"I'll gag you. Is that what you want?"

"No," Lauren answered the instant the mitt had left her mouth. She had to be able to communicate if she was to get anywhere.

"Then keep your voice down. And talk with respect." The last had been tacked on almost as an afterthought, but the man appeared to find immense satisfaction in it.

She wasn't about to argue. Physically, she was out-sized and outnumbered. All three men—one on either side of her, plus the driver—were huge. Their sedate business suits did nothing to disguise the bulk of their physiques. Intellectually, though, she had to believe she was at least on a par with them, if not above. Yes, she was terrified, and terror had a way of fudging the workings of the mind. But if she could stay cool and somehow control her fear, she had a chance.

In keeping with that, she considered her captor's command. If it was a respectful tone he wanted, a respectful tone he'd get. Far more could be accomplished with sugar than with vinegar.

"Who are you?" she asked quietly, directing her

efforts solely to the man on the left.

"Now, that is an insult if I ever heard one. You know who I am."

"I don't."

"I sure know you." He tilted his head to the side and studied her lazily. "You're looking good, Susan. Hair's a little shorter. Face looks good. Makeup's different. Easing up on it, are you?"

"Where are you taking me?"

He gave a careless shrug. "I'm not sure."

"What are you going to do with me?"

"I'm not sure."

"You must have a plan."

"Oh, yes."

She waited, but he said nothing more, so she dropped her gaze to her lap. "The plan is to make me nervous. Just as you've been doing for the past two weeks."

He puckered his lips, then relaxed them in acknowledgement of her perception. "Very good."

"But you do have the wrong person," she argued, albeit in a respectful tone. "The first few things you did didn't even make me nervous, because I had no reason to suspect there was anything to them."

"You wised up."

"Not really. It was the mail for Susan Miles that pulled it all together. Up until then I couldn't imagine what anyone would have against me." The issue of Chester Hawkins was irrelevant. "That's when I realized it had to be a case of mistaken identity."

"Sure," he drawled.

Lauren felt a movement in the arm that was pressed against her right side, and she looked sharply toward the hulk connected to it. The man was laughing. Silently, but laughing nonetheless. On the one hand, she was livid; on the other, she was more frightened than ever. They were obviously prepared for her denials, which practically defeated her efforts before they'd begun, but she wouldn't give up. There had to be *some* way out of this mess—if only she could find it!

CHAPTER NINE

For the first time since her abduction, Lauren looked beyond the confines of the car to the outside world. If she'd expected to see narrow, unfamiliar streets, she was mistaken. The car was on Storrow Drive, taking the very same route out of the city that she traveled every day.

She wished she knew what her wardens were up to, but she hadn't gotten that far yet, so she thought of Matt. Surely he'd have arrived at the shop. Surely he and Beth would be getting nervous when she didn't return from the bank. The bank!

"I have money," she exclaimed in a burst of hope. "If it's money you want, I'll give you all I've got." She fumbled in her purse for the envelope containing the cash and checks she'd been on her way to deposit, but her offer was immediately denied.

"We don't want money. The boss pays us plenty."

"Who's the boss?"

"Come on, Susan. We're not really as dumb as you'd like to think."

"I don't think you're dumb at all," Lauren declared quietly. "You've just made an innocent mistake. I'm not Susan, and I don't know who 'the boss' is. And *because* you're not stupid, you'll realize that I'm telling you the truth before you do anything drastic. If you go ahead with whatever you're planning, sooner or later someone *will* call you stupid—because you'll have done whatever you're planning to do to the wrong person."

He shot her a sidelong glance. "You've gotten quick with words. You never used to talk this much."

"Maybe Susan Miles didn't, but I always have. Look, there are any number of people—people who've known me for years—who can vouch for my identity."

"Like the medical records in that clinic did?" His question dripped of sarcasm.

"If you don't believe the records, that's not my problem."

"But it is. Seems to me it's very much your problem."

He was right. She had to take a different tack. "Okay. So you don't believe the records and you won't believe my friends. You tell me. Who am I supposed to be? Just who *is* this Susan Miles?"

"You want to play games? I'll play games. Susan Miles was the boss's best girl. He gave her everything any woman could want—" his eyes pierced Lauren's and his voice grew emphatic "—like a safe full of jewels and a closet full of furs. Where are they, Susan? We haven't been able to find them yet. Did you sell everything to bankroll that little shop you've got, or the house?"

"Jewels?"

"And furs."

"That clipping," she murmured, horrified. "Matt was right. There was a message in the clipping, but we just didn't get it."

The man on her left said nothing.

"I don't have jewels *or* furs. I bought the shop and the house with a legacy from my brother, who died a year ago." In other circumstances she'd never have volunteered that information, but these were unusual circumstances, to say the least.

"A legacy from your brother. Touching, but not terribly original, although I suppose it is different from the dead-uncle or maiden-aunt story, or that of the parents who were tragically killed in an automobile accident."

"My parents are alive and well and living in Bennington, Vermont. Check it out in a phone book. Colin and Nadine Stevenson."

The man on her left was silent.

"How *else* would I get money to open that shop? I've never had anything of my own like that before."

"Oh, please."

"I did?"

"How quickly you forget."

"What was it? What did I own?"

"A charming little boutique in Westwood Village.

Actually, you were running it into the ground. After you died, the boss put one of his own men in charge, and it's begun to turn a pretty profit."

"I *died?*" Lauren felt as if she were in the middle of a slapstick comedy, only nothing was funny. She was totally bewildered. "But if I died, what am I doing here and why are you after me?"

The man on her left seemed to weary of her questions. "You didn't die," he growled. "You just made it look like you'd died. You took off with the jewels and furs, changed your face, bought your shop and your house and thought you could get away scot-free." His expression grew even darker. "Well, let me tell you, no one does that to the boss and gets away with it. And no one does it to *me!*"

"What did I do to you?" she whispered fearfully.

"You made a fool of me. I was the one who reported that you burned to death in that car."

"Oh."

"Yes, 'oh.' It's been a sweet pleasure putting you through hell these past couple of weeks. What was it like, Susan, knowing someone was on to you?"

"I *didn't*. I told you—"

"I'll bet you didn't believe it at first. You always were arrogant, with your pretty little nose stuck up in the air."

"It's not my nose—"

"When you finally admitted to yourself that you'd been found out, did you think of running? It wouldn't have done you any good. We'd have been right on your heels." He sniffed loudly. Lauren decided he had a deviated septum of his own. "I've enjoyed it. And the best is yet to come. What I've got planned for today will singe your hair. I mean *really,* this time. Think about *that* while we take our little drive."

Their "little drive" had already taken them to the outskirts of Lincoln. Lauren stared out the window and swallowed hard. *Singe?* She began to shake. What was he planning? Did he intend to kill her? She had to escape. And soon. But how?

They turned off Route 2 and began the drive down the street she took each night. She would have stiffened in her seat, or sat straighter, but she had precious little room to move in and barely more strength. Her arms and legs were beginning to ache from a combination of tension and the steady pressure applied from both sides. Her face hurt. Her stomach was knotting.

"Where are we going?" she asked in a small voice.

"Don't you recognize the streets?"

At that moment they turned down the very road that would lead to her house.

"Thought you might want to take a last look."

"A . . . last look?"

The man on her left said nothing.

"This is a mistake. It's all a mistake. I really am Lauren Stevenson. *Really.*"

"Sure."

She took a quick breath. "Look, you can come inside the house and I'll show you everything. I have identification—a birth certificate, college diplomas, even pictures of my family." Her captor's snort told her what he thought of the validity of that identification. She barely had time to wonder how one could possibly forge family pictures when another thought hit her. "I have a passport! Picture and all!" It didn't take a snort from her left for her to realize she'd struck out again. The passport would do her no good. If there'd been various point-of-entry stamps recorded over a period of time, she might have proved that Lauren Stevenson had existed long before Susan Miles had supposedly died. But Lauren's passport had been issued shortly before her trip to the Bahamas. Ironically, she hadn't needed it; it had never even been stamped. And yes, the picture was of her "before" face, but the files in the clinic had contained a similar picture, which these men had written off.

"So much for identification," she muttered under her breath. Then her head shot up. "My car! The registration!" Her face dropped again. "I reregistered it when I came to Massachusetts."

The man on her left seemed to be enjoying himself. "Keep thinking, pretty lady. See if you can come up with something we haven't already looked over. Don't forget, we've been through most of your belongings."

Lauren's nostrils flared, and for a minute she forgot herself. "You know, it wasn't so bad that you sampled my perfume and fiddled with my shoes. If that's what turns you on, okay. But my *underwear?* I mean, there's kinky and then there's—ahh!" Her arm had been wrenched up sharply against her back. She twisted to ease the pain. "Please," she gasped out in a whisper. "Please—that hurts!"

"I don't have to take your smart mouth. You're not

calling the shots around here—*I am!*"

"Please," she begged, then gasped again when her arm was released. She hugged it close and alternately rubbed her elbow and her shoulder.

By this time the car was approaching the farmhouse. Lauren held her breath as she peered out the window, praying that Matt might be there, though she knew he wouldn't be. He was in Boston, waiting for her, maybe out looking for her by now.

The driver slowed in front of the garage, shifted into reverse, backed the car around and headed for the street again.

"Weird place," the man on her left said. "Pretty run-down. I really thought you had more class."

Lauren bit her lip and said nothing. She gazed longingly out of the window, hoping to see a neighbor walking along the side of the road, in which case she'd force some sort of ruckus inside the car that would attract attention. But she saw no one. The road was as quiet and peaceful as it had always been.

To her amazement, they drove on into the center of town. She marveled at the gall of her keepers, until she realized that she couldn't have made a stir if she'd tried. Large hands suddenly manacled both of her arms, just as burly legs had gripped her calves. She might have bucked in the middle, but no one outside the car would have noticed. And if she yelled—

"Don't even think it," the man on her left advised. "Mouse here has a mean right hook. It'll be even meaner the second time around."

"But if you're going to kill me anyway, why

would it matter?"

He grinned. "The pain, Susan. The suffering. It'll be bad enough for you as it is. If you want it worse, well, then, go ahead and scream."

Lauren didn't scream. But she did decide that this man's grin had to be the ugliest thing she'd ever seen. And she vowed that if she ever escaped, she'd take great pleasure in personally wiping it from his smug face!

They passed the police station, and she stifled a cry. They passed the market, and she bit her lip. "You won't get away with this. There are two good men who are probably on our trail right now."

"Two good men? Well, I know about the dick you hired. I suppose he's a good man, but he won't find a thing. As for Kruger, haven't you figured that out yet?"

"Figured what out?"

"He's one of ours."

She didn't even blink. "You're lying."

The man on her left shrugged. "Suit yourself. Cling to romantic illusion if you want."

"You can say anything else and it might make me nervous. But Matt—one of *yours?* Not by a long shot."

"What do you think his quickie trip to the coast last weekend was for, if not to check in with the boss?"

"I know what his trip was for, and it wasn't your boss he was checking in with."

"You're awfully sure of yourself."

"Where Matt's concerned, yes."

"Why? What proof do you have that he's not with us?"

She knew she'd be wasting her breath to mention things like love and trust. "He has the proof. Or, if you want to be crude, it was on my sheets the morning after we first made love. I was a virgin. If Matt had been with you, he'd have known something was strange. Unless, of course, your boss is some kind of eunuch."

"A virgin," the man on her left mused. "Kruger didn't mention that to us."

"Of course not. He doesn't know you from Adam."

When he shrugged again and simply repeated, "Suit yourself," Lauren knew she'd scored a point.

That was the last bit of satisfaction she was to have in a while. They left Lincoln behind and drove along backcountry roads with no obvious destination, at least none obvious to Lauren. Her mind jumped ahead, touching on possible stopping places and possible forms of punishment in store for her, then recoiled in fear, seeking refuge in more purposeful thoughts.

"Did she have any birthmarks?" Lauren asked suddenly.

The man on her left frowned at her.

"Susan Miles. Did she have any distinctive birthmarks? There had to be *some* way I can prove I'm not her."

"Birthmarks. That's an interesting thought. I could ask the boss about it. Do *you* have any distinctive birthmarks?"

"No."

"Are you sure?"

"Yes."

"Maybe we should pull over to the side of the road. If you strip, I can check you out."

He was goading her. She looked away. "I don't have any birthmarks," she muttered half to herself as she shriveled into the seat. Her arms and legs had been released once they'd left Lincoln proper, but she might as well have been shackled for the little freedom she'd gained. Shoulders hunched, she tried to minimize contact with the bodies on either side by making herself more narrow. It was a token gesture; the more she narrowed, the more the two men spread.

They drove on and on. She lost track of their direction, and much of the scenery was unfamiliar. With each mile, though, she grew more edgy. They couldn't drive forever. Sooner or later they'd have to stop. And what then?

"Y'know," the man on her left offered, "you really blew it. You had it all. The boss adored you—"

"Who is he?"

"Oh, Lord."

"What's his name? If he's the one who's behind all this, don't I have a right to know his name?"

"You don't have *any* rights, pretty lady. You gave them up when you double-crossed him."

"I didn't double-cross anyone!"

His nonchalance faded. "I'd watch my tone if I were you. It's getting uppity, and if there's one thing Mouse can't stand, it's uppity women. Right, Mouse?"

Mouse grunted.

"I'm sorry," Lauren said as conciliatorily as she could. "I didn't mean to sound uppity. It's just that you assume I know everything, but I don't, and I feel as if this whole thing has to be an awful joke, except no one's laughing, and I'm sitting here trying to figure out a way to prove to you who I am, but my mind is getting all foggy and . . . and . . ." She'd begun to shake. Tucking in her chin, she closed her eyes. "I don't feel very well."

"Throw up in this car, lady, and I'll make you lick it up."

She swallowed hard against the rising bile and took several deep breaths through her nose. The strain was getting to her. Her insides continued to shake; she wrapped her arms around her middle as though to hold them still, but it didn't work. She was hot and tired and positively terrified.

"It's amazing," the man on her left said. "You're quite an actress, after all. Funny, you should be such a flop in Hollywood."

"I thought you said Susan had a boutique," Lauren murmured weakly.

"Yeah. But she was like everyone else in that town. Between running the boutique and pleasing the boss, she read for every bit part she could. Had a couple of walk-ons." He sent her a look of ridicule. "She wasn't much of an actress, at least not on the silver screen. What she's doing now is remarkable."

"I have never been, nor had the slightest desire to be, an actress."

"Sure."

Lauren didn't have the strength to argue further, and they didn't stop driving. Dusk fell over the landscape. She thought she'd explode if something didn't happen soon. Once she cast a glance over her shoulder. The man on her left picked up on it instantly.

"Sorry. No one's following."

She grew defensive. "Aren't we stopping for dinner or something?"

He simply laughed.

"Or the bathroom? Don't any of you need one?"

"We're like camels. You'd better be, too. No, we're not stopping. Sorry, but you'll have to think of some other way to escape."

She tried. Oh, Lord, she tried. But, imprisoned in the car between two dark-suited sides of beef, she was hamstrung. There was no hope for escape unless they stopped, and it terrified her to think of where that would be and what they had planned for her then.

Just as she was beginning to bemoan the darkness, she noticed that the car was heading back toward the city. Of course. It made sense. Psychological torture. The purpose of the long ride had been to set her further on edge.

"Look, you've accomplished what you've wanted," she confessed without pride. "I'm thoroughly frightened. You can drop me off anywhere. I'll even take my chances and thumb a ride home."

"Is that what you thought, that we'd just let you go? Susan, Susan, how naive you are."

"What are you planning?"

The man on her left made a ceremony of debating whether or not to tell her. He moistened his lips, scratched the back of his head, then shrugged. "I guess it's time you knew. We're gonna do what we thought had been done months ago."

Lauren's heart was slamming against her breast. "What was that?"

"Your car plunged off the road and burst into flames. There was nothing left but ashes. The ashes were supposed to be you, so the boss gave you a fine burial." He sighed. "In this case, the burial came before the death, so we're kinda doing things ass-backward. But you will burn, Susan. Take that as a promise. You will burn."

Where Lauren got the breath to speak was a mystery. Perhaps the source was her desperation. "It's a threat, and you won't get away with it."

"Oh, we'll get away with it, all right. We're not novices at this type of thing."

"You're killers, then. Hit men. Is your boss connected with the mob? Well, let me tell you, if the mob kills its own, that's one thing. But I've got nothing to do with the mob or your boss or Susan Miles or you, and that makes me an innocent victim. I swear, you won't get away with it!"

The man on her left laughed. "Ah, pretty lady, that's priceless. Tell me, what do you intend to do once you're dead? Haunt us?" He laughed again.

Lauren gritted her teeth, no mean feat since they were chattering. "You'll get yours. So help me, you'll get yours."

When his laugh only came louder, she lapsed into silence. She'd save her strength, she decided. At some place, at some time, she'd glimpse a chance to escape. She'd need every resource she had when that time came.

Unfortunately, she couldn't seem to glimpse that chance to escape. After they had arrived back in Boston, the car drove down Atlantic Avenue, parallel to the harbor. It turned into a darkened path, continued to the end and stopped.

"Let's go," the man on her left said.

Before he'd even left the car, the man on her right had seized her. His arms were like cords of steel around her legs and shoulders. She was literally crunched into a ball with her face smothered against his chest. As she was carried from the car, she called on those resources she'd saved to try to free herself, but her bonds only tightened. Her scream was a pathetic sound muffled against the man's shirt, and she grew dizzy from the lack of air.

Terror was a driving force, though. Frantically she fought against the arms that held her. Futilely she tried to turn her head and gasp for air. While the doomed battle waged, she was carted up a flight of stairs, then another and another. Her captors' footsteps hammered against the wood planks, each forceful beat driving another nail into her coffin.

Then she was released, dumped unceremoniously onto the floor of a cavernous room. Gasping and trembling, she pushed herself up and looked around. It was dark, but she knew she was in a warehouse—rank and decaying, abandoned warehouse.

The two men loomed over her. Their bodies were straight, their legs planted firmly apart. Their stance was aggressive, but it couldn't have intimidated her any more than she already was.

The man who'd been on her left abruptly hunkered down. She inched back on the floor, but she couldn't escape his hand when he took a strand of her hair between his fingers. He spoke with lethal quiet. "Your final resting place, pretty lady. Take a look around. Try to find a way out. It'll keep your mind busy."

"Where are you going?" she whispered.

"I've got a call to make."

"To whom?"

He let the strand of hair sift through his fingers. "Who do you think?"

"Your boss?" A sudden flare of fury gave her voice greater force. "You tell him for me that he's an idiot! You tell him that he's murdering the wrong woman and that he'll pay—"

When the man raised his hand, palm up, she ducked her head and shrank back. But he didn't hit her. Instead, he slowly lowered his hand until it gently brushed her cheek. "Such a pretty face," he murmured. "Such a shame—"

Her lips moved in a mere whisper. "You know I'm telling the truth. You do."

"I know you'd like to think that. It's okay. Hold on to the hope if you want. It won't be much longer. We'll be back soon."

"And then?" The devil made her ask that. Her eyes

were wide with pleading.

"Then," he answered quietly, ever calmly, "we will sprinkle you with gasoline and set you on fire." She gasped and began to shake her head, but he went on. Too late, she realized she'd played into his hands by asking what he planned to do. Clearly, he took pleasure in her horror. "We'll watch you burn, Susan. This time there will be no doubt that you've died."

"Someone . . . will find me."

"I think not. Y'see, there's a contract out on this building. The man who owns it wants to build condominiums here, like those others along the waterfront, only he's a little strapped for money." The man glanced at his watch. "Roughly two hours from now, one of Boston's best torches will set fire to this place. It'll go up so quick that by the time the fire department gets here, the floor you're on will have long since fallen through. Your ashes will be hopelessly scattered. There's no way anyone will know you've been here, much less be able to prove you died here."

"Please," she cried, feebly grasping the lapels of his jacket, "please don't do this."

"Are you sorry, Susan? Do you finally regret what you've done?"

Lauren was weeping softly. "I haven't done anything . . . you *have* to believe me . . . *I'm not Susan Miles!*"

The man threw back his head, took a deep breath and stood up. Together with his sidekick, he made the long walk across the rotting floor. At the door, he looked back.

"You can scream as much as you want. No one will hear you. And Mouse will be right outside this door in case you decide you want to take a walk." He glanced at his buddy. "I think he'd like to get his hands on you again. Right, Mouse?"

Lauren never heard Mouse's answer. She found herself alone, trembling wildly and feeling more frightened than ever. For long moments of mental paralysis, she remained where she was. Then the bottom line came to her. It was do or die. Life or death. Scrambling to her feet, she began to explore her prison, seeking any possible hole or loose plank or trapdoor that might offer escape.

The boss was lounging by the pool when his houseboy brought out the cordless phone. He took it, nodded at the boy in dismissal, then put the instrument to his ear. "Yes?"

"We have her. She's safely tucked away. And she's dying just thinking about dying."

"Good. When will you do it?"

"Soon. Uh—did you get the pictures I sent?"

"This morning."

"What do you think?"

"With her hair that way and the clothes, she looks a little younger, more innocent, but it's Susan, all right."

"Are you sure?"

There was a pause. "Aren't you?"

"I thought I was until we picked her up today. Somehow, close up, she seems different."

"That was her intent."

"No. Not just in looks, but in character. The woman we've got does seem more innocent. Susan would have tried a come-on. She'd have promised us all kinds of little favors if we let her go. This one hasn't done that—like it's never occurred to her that she's got a marketable commodity. She's terrified, but half of it seems to be that we won't believe her story. Either Susan has suddenly become one hell of an actress, or we've been tricked."

The boss lit a cigarette and took a long drag. "You think it's someone else?"

A pause. "I'm not sure."

"Is it possible that Susan could have set up someone else to smoke us out?"

"Possible, but not probable. This one claims she had her face fixed to repair a medical problem, just like the clinic records said. If she's telling the truth, it'd be just too convenient that Susan would have happened to find her, looking so similar and all. And if she knew about Susan, she'd have squealed by now. She's scared, really scared."

"So it wasn't a setup. It has to be Susan."

"Or someone who looks like her."

Silence dominated the next half minute. Then, "It's not like you to get cold feet."

"That's what I've been telling myself, but something just doesn't feel right. If we do have the wrong woman, we'll be in trouble."

"I thought you had it arranged so that no one would know."

"I do. It's foolproof."

"So what's the problem? If it's really Susan, she'll be getting her due. If it's not Susan, but someone she set up to take the fall for her, let her take the fall. That'll get Susan to shaking all the more."

"And if it's simply a case of mistaken identity?"

"I can't believe that. The resemblance is too strong."

"But we'll never know. That's the problem. Once this one's dead, we'll never know for sure whether we've taken care of Susan or not."

"Damn it, what do you suggest?"

"I suggest . . . that we let this one escape and then continue to follow her for a while. If she suddenly runs from Boston and tries to change her looks again and sets herself up somewhere else, we'll know for sure that she's Susan. She won't have a head start on us this time. We'll be watching her constantly."

"I don't like this. I want Susan dead."

"So do I. But I want to make sure it *is* Susan who's dead."

"I thought this was all clear-cut. You'd found her. You'd been tormenting her. You've got her set to fry. It's all very neat. I don't like waffling."

"It's your decision, Boss."

The silence this time was the lengthiest yet. It ended with a low growl of frustration. "Ah, hell. Let the girl go. Then follow her. Do you understand? *Follow her.* If you lose her, so help me, you'll die right along with her!"

"Right."

"And let me know what's happening."

"Right."

Lauren was amazed by the simplicity of her escape, although she assumed anything would have seemed simple in comparison to what she'd been through and the fate she'd so vividly been made to envision. After a lengthy search of the room, she'd found old planks sealing up a shaft. She'd pried them off—most had crumbled in her hands—and discovered a door leading to what was a cross between a dumbwaiter and a freight elevator. After climbing onto the platform, she'd pulled and tugged on a fraying cord of rope until she'd lowered the platform to its base. Then she'd shouldered her way through the rotting wood of the door and burst into a run along the street floor of the warehouse. Moments later, she was in the summer night's air.

Smelling vaguely of dead fish and other refuse, the air was the sweetest she'd ever breathed. But she didn't pause to savor it. She continued running out to Atlantic Avenue, veered left around the corner and didn't stop until she'd reached the first of the waterfront restaurants. She barged inside and made her way to the maître d's desk.

"I need a phone," she gasped, hunching her shoulders against the pain in her chest.

The maître d' smiled politely and gestured. "Right over there, in front of the rest rooms."

"No! I don't dare!" She shot a glance at the phone by his hand. "You've got one here. I'm being followed, and if I go back there, they're apt to catch . . .

me again and I can't risk it . . . because they want to kill me and I . . . have to make this call. Please?" Her breath was coming in agonizing gulps, but she was beyond caring.

"This phone is reserved for—"

"Please!" she whispered. "It's critical!"

"I could call the police for you."

"Let me . . . please?"

Whether he acquiesced because, in her disheveled state, she didn't look like a troublemaker, or because he had a hidden streak of protectiveness in him, Lauren would never know. As soon as he reached to turn the phone her way, she snatched up the receiver and began to punch out the number of the shop. It was the closest place Matt might be, unless he was out searching. She had to try three times before her shaking fingers hit the right buttons.

"Lauren! My God, where *are* you?" Beth exclaimed. "We've been looking all over for you! Matt's half out of his mind, and the police won't do anything about a missing person for at least twenty-four—"

"Where is he? I need him, Beth. Where is he?"

"You sound awful!"

"Where's Matt?"

"He's out looking for you. He calls in here every few minutes. We've got Jamie stationed at your house."

Lauren's fingers had a death grip on the ridge of wood running around the top of the maître d's desk. "I'm at Fathoms. The restaurant. On Atlantic Avenue. Tell him to come *right away*."

"Where have you been? Are you all right?"

"Just tell Matt. I have to go." Lauren set the receiver back in its cradle, looked up at the maître d' and said, "You can call the police now." Then her knees buckled and she sank to the floor in a dead faint.

By the time she came to, she was lying on a couch in the manager's office. It took her a minute to get her bearings; then she bolted up, only to be restrained by two firm but gentle pairs of hands.

"It's all right, miss. You're safe. The police are on their way."

She recognized the maître d' but looked warily at his companion.

"I'm the manager, and you're going to be just fine."

"Matt . . . Matthew Kruger . . . he'll be looking for me."

"It's all right," the manager assured her. "The police will be here any minute. We won't let him get to you—"

"No! He's my—my—he's okay. He's not one of them. I need him."

The two men exchanged a glance before the manager spoke again. "Then we should let him in?"

"Yes!"

He nodded toward the maître d' who turned and left. When the door opened several minutes later, two uniformed officers entered. By this time, Lauren was sitting upright, sipping shakily from a glass of water. One of the officers sat down beside her on the couch; the other knelt before her and began to ask questions. Lauren barely heard the questions, much less her answers. At the slightest movement or sound, her eyes flew toward the door.

After what seemed forever, but was probably no longer than fifteen minutes, Matt burst in. His eyes were wild, his tanned skin was pale and his entire body was trembling, but that didn't stop him from catching Lauren when she rocketed into his arms or from crushing her tightly to him.

Brokenly, he whispered her name. He took her weight when her legs seemed to dissolve from under her and melded her body to his. She was crying softly, clinging to his neck, unable to say anything for a very long time. At last he lifted her and carried her back to the couch, which the seated officer had vacated for that purpose. Taking her onto his lap, Matt began to stroke her hair, her back, her arms.

"It's all right, sweetheart. Everything's going to be all right. I'm here. Shh." His breath was warm on her forehead, her ear, her cheek.

"Oh, Matt . . . you have . . . no idea . . ."

Framing her head with his hands, Matt examined her closely. "Are you all right?" His gaze focused on the faintly discolored side of her face, and his voice came out in a croak. "What happened to your cheek?"

"He hit me. It was Mouse, but he wasn't the one in charge."

Matt looked up quickly at the manager. "Can we get some ice for this?"

The man nodded and hurried out, but Matt's attention was already back on Lauren. "Can you talk about it, sweetheart? From the beginning?" His thumbs stroked the tears from beneath her eyes. "The officers will listen. You'll have to go through it only once."

Nodding, Lauren slowly launched into her tale. It was interrupted from time to time—when the ice arrived; when she began to cry again; when Phillip, who'd been out searching for her, too, joined them—but she managed to get through it all before she collapsed, emotionally drained, against Matt.

It was Phillip, soft-spoken and dependable, who turned to the officers. "You'll look for the car?"

"You bet," the older of the two answered. "And if the warehouse hasn't already been torched, we'll search it." He grimaced and rubbed his neck. "I'm afraid we don't have much to go on. Dark blue Plymouths are pretty common. But we'll check out the local rental agencies and the hotels. Three oversize men might be remembered, particularly if they've been here for a while. Of course, they could be staying somewhere other than at a hotel."

Matt was cradling Lauren against his chest. "We'd be grateful for anything you can do. And we'd like to be kept informed."

"Can we reach you at—" The officer flipped back several pages in his notebook and read off Lauren's Lincoln address.

Matt caught Phillip's headshake. "No. They know the house. I can't take the chance they won't return. We'll be at the Long Wharf Marriott. You can either call us there or leave a message at the print shop."

With a nod, the policemen left, followed several minutes later by Phillip. Matt studied Lauren with tender concern. "Feel up to moving, sweetheart?"

When she nodded, he helped her to her feet, then wrapped an arm around her waist and guided her out. Less than half an hour later, they were in a spacious hotel room overlooking the harbor. Despite her exhaustion, Lauren insisted on taking a shower. She felt dirty all over. With her eyes closed or open, she could smell the men who'd abducted her.

She scrubbed herself until her skin was pink, while Matt stood immediately outside the shower. He helped her dry off, tucked her in bed, then sat down beside her. If she'd ever doubted his love, she doubted no more; it was indelibly etched on every one of his features.

"Want some aspirin?"

She shook her head and managed a wan smile. "We don't have any, anyway."

"I could call down for some."

"I'm okay." She reached for him and whispered, "Just hold me, Matt. Just hold me."

He did. After a time, he moved back to shed his own clothes, then climbed under the sheets with her and held her for the rest of the night.

Come morning, Lauren had recovered to the point where she could think more clearly. Matt had been at that stage from the moment she'd fallen asleep in his arms.

They were sitting cross-legged on the bed, dressed only in white terry velour robes. She'd begun to gnaw on a strip of bacon when she set it back down. "I've been thinking, Matt. Theoretically, those guys are still after me. But something's odd. I escaped too easily."

Matt wasn't eating, either. "I know."

"It took me a while to find that shaft, but the one who went to make a phone call hadn't returned. No one heard me tearing off the strips of wood. No one heard the elevator. No one chased me down the street. Considering the way they manhandled me earlier and spelled out exactly what they planned to do to me, it just doesn't make sense."

"Maybe the terror they put you through was the end point of the exercise."

She thought about that for a while as she leaned against the headboard and sipped her coffee. "I suggested that to him, and he denied it. Maybe I managed to convince him that I wasn't Susan Miles, or at least plant some doubts—"

"In which case he *let* you escape. If only we knew for sure whether your escape was deliberate or accidental. I have no intention of assuming that you're off the hook until I have proof of it, which means either finding those thugs or—"

"Finding Susan Miles."

"Right. If we could find her and convince her to go to the police, they could question this boss of hers. At least then he'd know he had the wrong woman in you, and we could breathe freely."

Lauren sat forward and reached for the bacon. Matt's presence, his commitment to her cause, the fact of the two of them working together to resolve the problem—all gave her a sense of optimism that, in turn, awakened her appetite. "So," she said between bites, "we have to find Susan Miles, which may be easier said than done. No doubt she's using a different name, and she's probably had plastic surgery to alter her looks, so that's where we'll begin."

He nodded. "The clinic in the Bahamas."

"Right. That's where the boss found out about me, though how he knew to check out that particular clinic is a mystery. I wonder if Susan had been there before, or if she'd mentioned it to him at some point."

"If that was the case," Matt reasoned, "I doubt she'd be stupid enough to go back there when she was trying to flee him. On the other hand, the boss may have had some information we don't. Airline tickets, hotel reservations, something. I think we should fly down and talk with your doctor. Can they spare you at the shop?"

"They'll have to. The shop means a lot to me, but my own health and safety mean more. Between Beth and Jamie, things will run smoothly."

Matt popped a cube of cantaloupe into his mouth. "That Beth is a character. You wouldn't believe some of the stories she came up with to explain your disappearance. She even dared to hint that Brad had come back from the dead and taken you off to some hideaway to heal old wounds!"

"Did she really say *that?*" Lauren grimaced, then sighed. "She's got an unbelievable imagination. I think she's incurable."

"I think she's also incredibly devoted and loyal. She refused to budge from that shop yesterday because she wanted to be there if you called, and when you finally did, she all but sent out the cavalry to find me. She called Jamie to pass on your message in case I contacted the farmhouse first. She got in touch with Phillip—he has a phone in his car—and sent him looking for me. She was ready to tell the police I'd stolen her car so they would go out in pursuit. You're lucky to have her for a friend, Lauren."

Lauren reached out and touched his cheek. There was warmth in her fingers and love in her eyes. "I'm lucky about a lot of things. Very, very lucky."

The police weren't so lucky. They had nothing to report to Matt except the fact that shortly before they'd arrived to search it the night before, the warehouse had gone up in flames. The fire marshal's office was investigating arson, but that case had little to do with Lauren's, and there was no sign whatsoever of either the dark blue Plymouth or the three oversize thugs.

Accompanied by a pair of officers from the Lincoln police department, Lauren and Matt returned to the farmhouse at noontime on Saturday, packed their bags and headed for the airport. Matt took a few minutes to phone Phillip to keep him abreast of their plans. Then he and Lauren were airborne, en route to the Bahamas.

To the best of their knowledge, they hadn't been followed.

CHAPTER TEN

Upon landing, Matt took Lauren directly to one of the plush hotels on the island. It had become clear to him in the course of the flight that she was suffering a delayed reaction to what had happened the day before. She'd been shaky and restless, unable to do more than pick at the meal that was served. She'd dozed off, then awakened with a start to a fit of uncontrollable trembling. He'd teased her, saying that *he* was the one who was supposed to be nervous, but his fear of flying took a back seat to her upset. He'd known that what she needed most was a peaceful restorative night.

First thing the next day, though, they went to the clinic. Purposely, they didn't call in advance. They knew that the boss's men had been there, and they weren't sure how they'd be received. Lauren was convinced that the doctor would not have willingly colluded with thugs, but Matt reserved his own judgment until their meeting.

Richard Bowen was in surgery. They insisted on waiting in the room just outside his office and caught him the minute he returned. Richard was surprised and pleased to see Lauren, doubly pleased to find her with Matt. After the brief introductions, he ushered them into his sanctuary. Neither Lauren nor Matt missed the subtle blanching of his face as she explained what had happened.

"They made it very clear that they'd seen your files," Matt concluded for her when he sensed that

Lauren wasn't sure exactly how to confront the doctor. She obviously liked and trusted him, and she was loath to toss accusations his way. Matt had no such qualm. "Did you show anyone those files, or know that they'd been seen?"

To Lauren's relief, Richard was not offended and deeply shared their concern. "My files are confidential. The only way I'd have shown them to anyone would have been if Lauren had specifically requested it."

"Then how—" Lauren began, only to be interrupted.

"About a month ago there was a break-in here. My file cabinets were forced open and the files rifled. Records of hundreds of patients were left scattered all over the office. Nothing was taken that I could tell. Until now I've had no idea what the burglars were after."

"And Susan Miles?" Matt prompted. "Have you treated a patient by that name?"

Richard widened his eyes for an exaggerated second. "Treated, no. Spoken with, yes. Oh, yes. She came by to see me last fall, maybe early winter. She wanted to discuss having some minor work done. It never got past the discussion stage, so I don't have a file on her, but I'll never forget her face. She was stunning. A real beauty." He cast an apologetic glance at Lauren. "Yes, Lauren, you do look a lot like her now."

"Did you do it intentionally?" Matt growled. It was obvious that Richard Bowen had been taken with Susan Miles's looks. For him to try to form another woman in her image might have been conceivable, if infuriating and possibly unethical.

Richard chuckled. "I'm a plastic surgeon, not a miracle worker. It's only in the movies that one face can be completely altered to look like another. No, in Lauren's case, it was pure coincidence. The hair's the same in texture and color, and the figure is complementary, now that Lauren's put on weight. The eyes were alike all along. But, if I remember correctly, and I'm sure I do, Susan Miles wore much more makeup. As for the rest—the nose, the cheekbones, the jaw— they all just came together. You have to understand that in cases like Lauren's, the end results are sometimes a mystery even to the doctor until everything's done. Reconstructive work can go this way or that in the healing process." He smiled ruefully at Lauren. "Yours went the way of Susan Miles."

"From what you say, I should be happy about that," Lauren mused, "but given all that's happened . . ."

"There are differences," Richard pointed out, "but mostly I think they come from within. The woman I spoke with had a harder edge to her. She was very much like so many of the others I treat, women whose inner tension does things to their faces that no amount of plastic surgery can correct."

"Then she didn't really need plastic surgery?" Lauren asked. She looked at Matt. "Maybe she was planning on disappearing even back then."

Richard spoke before Matt could comment on that supposition. "There were a few things that could have been touched up, but basically they could have gone another five or ten years without attention. People would have thought her beautiful if she'd done nothing."

"Did you tell her that?" Matt inquired. Richard gave him a wry, what-do-*you*-think look. "But she didn't come back."

"No. I never saw her again."

Lauren sat forward. "We have to find her. We know she came from the L.A. area and had a boutique there. Did she say anything to you—drop any names—that might give us a clue?"

Richard sat back in his chair and frowned, trying to absorb all that Lauren had told him. "I don't think so."

"She was probably with a man," Matt offered. "A very wealthy and powerful man."

"Wealthy and powerful men are a dime a dozen on the islands. She did say that she was here on a pleasure trip and had heard about the clinic from a friend."

"No name?" Matt asked.

Richard shook his head. "Fully one-third of my patients have been from the West Coast. They like coming here for the ambience, and for the distance. They can go on an extended vacation far from home, then return looking positively marvelous with no one the wiser." His frown deepened, and he chafed one eyebrow with the knuckle of his forefinger. "I can picture her sitting here talking with me. I'm sure I asked her where she way staying—it's standard small talk in a place like this—and I don't think it was one of the large hotels, because I would have formed a mental image of her there. Maybe a smaller—no—" He hesitated, concentrating. "A boat. I think she mentioned something about the marina."

Matt grunted. "There have to be dozens of marinas. She didn't say which one?"

"If she did, I don't remember."

"Then it'll be like finding a needle in a haystack, and we don't even know which haystack to search."

"How about other clinics on the islands?" Lauren asked.

"There are none I'd recommend, and I doubt a woman like that would go to a second-rate place." Richard held up a hand. "No conceit intended."

"None presumed," Matt offered in his first show of faith. "Can you tell us anything else about her—how she wore her hair, any distinctive jewelry or style of dress?"

Richard closed his eyes as he called back the full image from his memory bank. "Her hair was pulled away from her face in a chic kind of knot. She was wearing gold jewelry—large hoops at the ears, a chain around her neck. She had several rings, maybe one with a stone, and she was wearing white silk slacks and a blouse. Oh, and high-heeled sandals. I noticed that because her toenails were polished to match her fingernails, and the pink was the same color as the sash around her waist."

"You were very observant." was Matt's wry comment.

Richard laughed good-naturedly. "It's my business to be observant when it comes to women's looks, and this woman was well worth the look. I remember thinking how elegantly she'd coordinated everything.

She was stunning. Truly stunning."

Matt pushed himself from his chair. "The description may prove to be helpful somewhere along the line. I hope." It went without saying that they were still at the very start of that line. He held out a hand for Lauren. "Come on, sweetheart. We'll have to rethink our strategy."

Richard walked them to the door. "I'm really sorry I have no more information. If only—" His brow rippled. "Wait a minute. There is something. I mean, it'd still be a long shot, but—"

Matt and Lauren had turned hopeful faces his way. "What is it?" Lauren asked, holding her breath.

"She smoked. I remembered thinking that in time her face would show it. It does, you know."

"But where does that get us?" Matt prodded.

"She was using a little green box of matches. Not a matchbook, but a little green box. I remembered thinking, 'Ah, she's been to Terrance Cove.' It's one of the more showy restaurants around here. Just the place for the wealthy and powerful."

Matt and Lauren exchanged a look of excitement. "Let's try it, Matt," she said. "We've got nothing to lose."

It was Matt who turned to shake Richard's hand and thank him. Belatedly, and purely on impulse, Lauren gave the doctor a hug. "You've been great, Richard. How can we ever thank you?"

His grin was crooked. "You can find Susan Miles and get both of you out of danger. Her friends don't sound very charitable."

Lauren agreed, then slid her hand into Matt's.

A taxi took them to Terrance Cove, which, fortunately, had just opened for lunch.

"What are you going to say?" Lauren asked. "If Susan Miles was with the boss, who presumably made the reservations, the people at the restaurant would have no way of knowing, much less remembering, her name."

"But the face," Matt cooed. "Ah, the face. Susan Miles had a memorable face. And, sweetheart, you've got that face. *I* always knew it was memorable, but then, I'm slightly biased."

Lauren pinched him in the ribs, but she was buoyed. She held her head high when they entered the restaurant, and tried to look every bit the boss's woman while Matt did the talking. His story sounded conceivable enough.

"My fiancée is looking for her identical twin. They've been separated for two years, and we just got word that she was here last winter. Her name is Susan Miles." He looked at Lauren affectionately. "And this is her face. Does it look at all familiar? Ring any bells? Susan might have had her hair pulled back, and she was probably wearing more makeup and jewelry. But the similarities are marked." He paused. "She might have been with a rather impressive man, and if we can find him, we can get a lead on her."

The maître d' stared at Lauren long and hard. "I'm sorry," he said in crisply accented English. "I don't recognize her. But I only work afternoons. The man who was working evenings last winter was recently retired. He is living in Miami with his daughter and grandchildren."

"It's very important that we reach him," Lauren urged. "We have no other leads. Do you have an address or a phone number?"

The man seemed to waver. His indecision came to an end when Matt pressed a folded bill into his hand. "Wait here, please. I'll see what I can do."

As soon as he had disappeared, Lauren leaned close and whispered to Matt, "Why does that always work?"

He whispered back, "It doesn't, at least not always. I was prepared to give him another. He sold himself cheap."

"That was quite a story. *Identical twin?*"

"Beats the other explanation."

Neither of them commented on the fiancée part of the tale.

Within minutes the man returned with a small index card on which he'd printed the name of the former employee and his Miami address. Matt pocketed the card, and he and Lauren headed back to the hotel.

"To Miami?" Lauren asked.

"To Miami."

"When?"

Matt glanced at his watch. "As soon as we can get a flight."

They both knew that the personal visit was a must. They could easily get the man's phone number and call him, but Lauren's face was the key. So they put back the few things they'd taken out of their suitcases, returned to the airport they'd landed at less than twenty-four hours before, and caught the first plane to Miami.

The flight was short and uneventful. As always, they were watchful, alert to any face that would be familiar, or threatening, or in any way suggestive of a tail. As always, they saw none.

After the plane had landed, they took a taxi straight to the address printed on the index card—a modest house on the outskirts of the city. Various bicycles and toys littered its driveway. Instructing the driver to wait, they approached the door.

It was opened by a gentleman in his early seventies. The children crowding behind him called him "Papa," but his actual name was Henry Frolinette.

Matt repeated the story they'd given the maître d' at Terrance Cove, stressing simultaneously their regret at disturbing him and the urgency of their mission. The man nodded, looked closely at Lauren and nodded again.

"I don't know the name," he admitted, "but I do remember the face. They came to the restaurant more than once."

"They," Matt echoed. "Then she was with the man."

"Oh, yes. A dapper sort, and a generous spender. There were usually eight or ten in his party, though the individuals differed—except for the woman. Miss . . . Miles, you say?" When Lauren nodded quickly, he went on. "Miss Miles was always with him. And Mr. Prinz always picked up the check for the entire group. He paid in cash, too, I might add."

Lauren's gaze met Matt's. "Prinz," she breathed.

Matt was already looking back at Henry. "Do you know his first name?"

"Oh, yes. He's been quite a presence in the islands over the years. Theodore Prinz, from Los Angeles. Not that everyone speaks highly of him, mind you. There have been rumors about the nature of his work. I never believed them, personally. He is a good-looking man, very well behaved and dignified, and he was always more than gracious to me."

Unfortunately, Henry Frolinette was unable to give them any specific information on Susan Miles. Lauren and Matt discussed it that night over dinner at the beachfront hotel they'd checked into.

"At least we have the boss's name," Lauren mused, "but that's about all. I suppose we could show up on his doorstep and tell him he's made a mistake, but—"

"He wouldn't believe us, and we'd only be putting ourselves right back in his hands. No, if anything's going to stick, we have to find Susan Miles. If Henry had been able to pinpoint a marina, maybe we could have gone back and found someone who might give us a clue to where she went when she left Prinz. But to use Theodore Prinz's name alone would only be asking for trouble. Word is bound to get back to him, and if he's half as powerful as I suspect, we'd be playing with fire."

"So?"

"We call Phillip, who can use his contacts to get the lowdown on Prinz. If Prinz is involved enough with that boutique to have his own man running it, the name of the place will be sandwiched in there with the rest of the information. At least, it will be if Phillip is worth his salt, and from what I've seen, he is."

Lauren didn't understand. "But what good will it do to know the name of the boutique? We can't show up there, any more than we can show up at Prinz's home. If we start asking questions of nearby shopkeepers, they're apt to call Prinz. Besides, I'm sure he had his men question everyone in sight when he started looking for Susan himself."

"True. But what if we go further back? What if Phillip can get hold of the original papers for that shop?"

"What if Prinz bought it for her in the first place?"

"Maybe he did and maybe he didn't. If he didn't, there might just be some information—even data on loan applications—that could lead us to where she came from—or even to a friend or a family member whom she might have contacted when she relocated."

"But wouldn't Prinz have done that?"

Matt's eyes were filled with excitement, and his voice held a kind of restrained glee. "Prinz went forward. He obviously felt he knew Susan well enough to anticipate what she'd do. He must have known of her visit to the clinic when they were in the Bahamas. That's why his men went there right away. They found what they were looking for, so why look further?"

"But you'd go backward," Lauren stated with sudden comprehension. And admiration. "Cautious Matt. Wants to know the ingredients before he takes a taste."

"It makes sense, doesn't it?"

"Sure does. And in spite of the danger, you're enjoying yourself."

"Sure am. I read somewhere—maybe not in a Spenser novel, but somewhere—that private investigators often locate people who've been missing for years by staking out the graves of their parents. Unless this Susan Miles is truly made of ice, she's been in touch with someone from her past, and more likely than not, that someone is a family member." He straightened in his seat and sighed. It was as though he'd suddenly set down the mystery novel he'd been reading and returned to reality with a jolt. "All *we* have to do is find that family member."

"What's happening?"

"They flew back to Boston. Looks like she's not trying to disappear. Kruger's with her constantly. They're staying in a hotel in town, but that may be because workmen have started tearing up her farmhouse."

"Tearing it up?"

"Remodeling. At least, that's what it says on the side of the truck parked out front. I don't think she's planning to abandon the place, Boss."

"Then she's not Susan."

"Looks that way. She's still pretty nervous, y'know. Looks all around her whenever she goes out, and, like I said, she doesn't go anywhere alone. More than that, the police are in and out of her shop."

"Susan wouldn't have dared call the police."

"Right."

"So. She's not Susan. Do you think she's given up the search for Susan?"

"I don't know. Word has it that the detective's been doing some research."

"About what?"

"The boutique."

"You have to be kidding! How did they find out about that?"

"I told her."

"Not smart. Not smart at all."

"It was when I had her in the car. I thought she was Susan then."

"They'll get my name."

"They've already got it."

There was a pause, then an arrogant "No problem. The boutique's on the up-and-up. You'll just have to be doubly careful with Susan's demise."

"What about Lauren Stevenson? And Kruger? And the dick, for that matter? If they do manage to find Susan for us and then something happens to her, they'll know who to blame."

"But Susan's death won't be traceable to us. It could be an accident; it could be part of a larger scheme. If it looks like someone else kills her, that's not my worry. And if a whole bunch of people shoot each other to bits, so much the better. I don't care how you do it, but keep us clean. I pay you good money to handle things like this. Do what you have to. Don't bore me with the details. I want Susan dead!"

"We've hit pay dirt!" Matt exclaimed with a broad grin as he set down the telephone. He was seated at the desk in the back room of the shop, and Lauren was propped expectantly at its edge.

"What did he say?" The call had been from Phillip. She'd known that much, but had been unable to follow the conversation, which had been distinctly one-sided in favor of the detective.

"He said," Matt began slowly, savoring the suspense, "that Susan bought the boutique herself and she financed it with a loan from a local bank. The loan application listed two people as references, neither of whom are named Miles, but both of whom are from Kansas City."

"Kansas City. Where she grew up?"

"Either that, or where she was living before she hit L.A. It doesn't really matter. At least we have contacts." He patted the scrap of paper on which he'd jotted the two names.

"But what if these contacts are somehow related to Prinz? What if one or the other of them was the instrument of Susan's introduction to him?"

Matt was shaking his head. "According to Phillip, neither of the names has shown up in any of the information he's gathered on Prinz. There's still that possibility, but I think it's remote. And even if it's not, neither one has any direct association with Prinz now, which means that we'll be safe." He lifted the receiver again and called the airport. Within hours, he and Lauren were headed for Kansas City.

"Poor Matt," Lauren mused when they were airborne again. "For someone who hates flying, you've done your share in the past few days."

He leaned close to her, denying the steel arm between them. "It's worth it. Every hateful minute."

Lauren smiled and whispered. "You are a wonderful man."

"Nah. I'm just along for the ride."

"That's one of the reasons I love you." She kissed his too-square chin. "You didn't ask for any of this."

"But I asked for you," he murmured deeply. "All my life I've been asking for you, and now that I've found you, I'll take any ride, as long as you're along." He sought and captured her lips, kissing her thoroughly. "And when this is all over," he whispered against her mouth, "we are going to take a vacation to beat all vacations. We'll fly somewhere and stay put for two weeks, just the two of us. Sun and sand and moonlit nights . . ."

"Sounds wonderful, but you'll have used up all your vacation time by then."

"So I'll take more."

"And if your boss objects?"

"I'll quit."

She grinned. "Mmm. I'd like that. San Francisco's too far away."

"My thoughts exactly." He kissed her again, softly, deeply. His mouth was just leaving hers when the flight attendant came by with lunch.

Beneath the lighthearted teasing, Lauren had been very serious. San Francisco *was* too far away. But she couldn't think about the future. Not yet. There was still too much to be done to ensure that she had a future at all.

Bright and early the next morning, Lauren and Matt showed up in the office of one Timothy Trennis. The office was done in obvious taste and at obvious cost; the man was in his early forties, neatly dressed and pleasant-looking. When he saw them, his mouth dropped open. His eyes were riveted to Lauren's face.

"Susan?" he asked uncertainly.

"Almost," Lauren said gently, "but not quite. I am looking for her, though. We thought maybe you could help us."

Timothy continued to stare at her, then slowly shook his head. "The resemblance is remarkable. It's been a long time since I've seen Susan. I could have sworn—" He seemed to catch himself, and his cheeks reddened. "But you'd know, wouldn't you?"

Lauren nodded. "It's very important that we reach her. Do you have any idea where she might be?"

"Is she in trouble?" he asked with genuine concern.

Lauren looked hesitantly at Matt, who took over. "She may be if we don't find her. Someone else is looking for her. It's critical that we find her first."

"It's that Prinz guy, isn't it?"

"Do you know about him?" Lauren asked.

Belatedly, Timothy gestured for them to sit. When they'd done so, he lowered himself into a chair near his desk. "Susan and I dated for a time. I always knew she had greater ambitions—ambitions that went beyond Kansas City, I mean. When she decided to move to Los Angeles, I wasn't surprised. We kept in touch for a while, so I knew she was seeing Prinz. I made it my business to find out about him, and when I tried to caution her subtly, she pretty much severed all contact between us."

"When was the last time you heard from her?" Matt asked.

Timothy thought about that for a minute, making rough calculations in his mind. "It had to have been more than three years ago."

"And there's been nothing since then?"

Timothy shook his head.

"Is there someone she *might* have contacted? Someone she's kept in touch with—family, maybe?"

"If there is, I don't know about it. Susan rarely talked about family. There was an older sister, and her mother. The father died when she was a child, and the mother remarried. Susan detested her stepfather. She left as soon as she could."

"Do you know where the mother lives?" Lauren asked.

"Susan grew up in a small town in Indiana. Whether the mother's still there is anyone's guess. I don't even know her married name."

"How about the sister?" Matt queried.

"The sister was older by five or six years, took off after high school and got married. Susan never mentioned her. I simply assumed they'd lost contact, too."

Matt looked at Lauren. "Another strikeout." He fished the scrap of paper from his pocket. "What about, uh, Alexander Fraun? Do you know him?"

Timothy nodded. "Susan worked for him. He owns a pair of dress shops in the area. Nice-enough fellow. You could try him. He may have information I don't." As Lauren and Matt stood up to leave, he added, "I hope you find her. I always wished her happiness."

Lauren smiled warmly. She liked this man and felt he'd given them the first positive picture of Susan Miles to date. "We'll tell her that when we find her," she said. *When,* not *if.* Pessimism had no place here; there was too much at stake for all of them.

"They're in Kansas City."

"Kansas City? Clever. Susan was from Kansas City. They *are* looking for her."

"Will they find her?"

"In Kansas City? No. She wouldn't go back there. It's too obvious." There was a pause. "It is possible, though, that she's contacted one of her old friends there." A smug smile. "And if that's the case, Kruger and the girl will find out. They're doing our legwork for us."

"Seems to me I'm doing it anyway, following them around like this."

"You're not stupid enough to let them see you, are you? After that little kidnapping stunt, the girl would recognize you instantly."

"Don't worry. We've got Jimbo tailing them close, and she never saw him, so we're safe."

"But you're not far."

"No, sir."

"Good. I don't trust Jimbo to do the heavy work."

"Neither do I, and I have a personal investment here, too. Susan's kept us running in circles. That kind of thing inspires revenge."

"Mmm. I like that. Very good."

Alexander Fraun was harder to reach. When Lauren and Matt arrived at the address Phillip had given them, they were told that Fraun was at the other store. When they arrived at that one, they were told that he'd gone to a luncheon meeting and would be back at the first store that afternoon.

They went to lunch themselves, then returned to the first store to await the elusive Mr. Fraun. Shortly before two o'clock, he entered the small outer office in which they sat. He had started to pass through into his own office, after glancing briefly their way, when he did a double take on Lauren and came to an abrupt halt.

"Susan?" he asked uncertainly.

"Almost," she said gently, "but not quite." She felt she was living a broken record and quickly moved to free the needle from its cracked groove. "My name is Lauren Stevenson. And this is Matt Kruger. We're looking for Susan and thought you might have some idea as to her whereabouts."

"Come into my office," the man said with a broad wave of his hand. He was as different from Timothy Trennis as night from day. Not only was his office a disaster area, but the man himself looked as though he'd seen better days. Lauren estimated that he was in his late fifties. His bald pate was scantily covered with strands of gray that had been called to the rescue from somewhere just above his ear. He had chipmunk cheeks and a multi-tiered chin, both of which coordinated perfectly with his girth. There was something about him, something strangely genuine, that made Lauren like him on the spot.

"Now," he said, scooping a pile of ancient magazines from the torn vinyl sofa so that Lauren and Matt could sit down, "what's this about Susan?" He propped himself on the edge of the desk. The wood groaned.

"We're trying to find her," Matt explained. "We were told she worked for you once."

"What do you want with her?" Fraun shot back with such suspicion that Lauren, for one, wondered if Prinz's men had reached him first.

Matt did the talking, apparently taking the man's suspicion for protectiveness. He explained just why he and Lauren were anxious to find Susan.

Fraun shifted his gaze back to Lauren. "You look just like her. For a minute when I walked in, I thought she'd come back."

"We know that she went to Los Angeles when she left here," Lauren offered, "but we were hoping that you might have heard from her."

"She's not still there?"

Lauren shook her head.

The wrinkles on Fraun's brow echoed higher on his bald head. "I thought she was. Last thing I heard from her, she had her own boutique." He smiled. "Susan was good. She had a way with color and style." He gave his head a little toss. "She was wasted here. I told her so. I mean, my goods are nice enough, but she needed high fashion to make the most of her talents."

"When was the last time you heard from her?" Matt asked.

Fraun suddenly scowled at him. "How do I know you're on the up-and-up? How do I know you two haven't come to do her harm?"

Lauren, too, saw protectiveness this time. As briefly but meaningfully as she could, she told him where she'd come from and where she worked, then did the same for Matt. "We don't wish Susan any harm. We have no reason to do her harm. If Matt and I can locate her, Susan and I stand to benefit—Susan, because she'll be aware of the danger and be able to do something about it; me, because if Susan does something about it, I'll be out of danger, too."

Fraun tugged a slightly warped pad of paper from beneath a haphazard pile of letters. "I'm going to write down your names and addresses. That way, if anything happens to Susan, I'll know who to call."

"Then you know where she is?" Lauren asked in excitement.

"Driver's licenses, please."

Lauren and Matt exchanged a glance and dug into their respective pockets for identification. Only when the man had taken notes to his satisfaction did he put down the pad and face them.

"No, I don't know where Susan is," he admitted. "The last time I heard from her was nearly two years ago. She sounded fine then. Why did she leave L.A.?"

"We're not sure," Matt answered. "But we do know she left. We'd hoped she'd contacted you, or someone else she knew before."

"You could try Tim—"

"We already have. He suggested we try you."

Fraun sighed and gave a shrug that made his belly shake. "I don't know what to tell you. I can't believe Susan's in trouble. She was always honest, and a hard worker."

"She probably still is," Lauren speculated. "It's just that she had the ill fortune to get mixed up with a man who's probably neither of those things. Can you think of anyone she may have contacted? Timothy said she wasn't close to her family, but there's always a chance she could be in touch with one of them."

Fraun shook his head. This time his jowls shimmied. "Tim was right. She wasn't big on her family. She did mention the sister from time to time."

"Do you know her married name," Matt asked, "or where she's living?"

"Nah— Wait just a minute." He bounced off the desk and tugged at the drawer of a file cabinet. It resisted his efforts, yielding at last, but with reluctance. Lauren understood why. The drawer was nearly as overstuffed as was the man rummaging through it.

"How can you find anything in there?" she asked on impulse.

"I find. I find. It just takes a little time."

It took a good fifteen minutes, during which Lauren and Matt sat by helplessly, glancing from each other's faces to the man at work to the calamity of his office.

"Here we go!" Fraun exclaimed at last. He held up a sheet of paper that had a permanent press running diagonally through it. "Susan's original employment application. You see," he cried victoriously, "it sometimes pays not to clean out drawers." Holding the paper at arm's length, he ran his eyes down the form. "Aha! Person to call in case of emergency: Mrs. Peter—Ann—Broszczynski. Relationship: sister." Proudly, he offered the form to Lauren. "St. Louis. Think you can get there?"

Lauren looked from the form to Matt and grinned. "You bet we can." When she returned her gaze to Alexander Fraun, she realized that, with a beard and a little more hair, he would have reminded her of Santa Claus.

Ann Broszczynski was not living at the address listed on the employment application, which was understandable, Lauren and Matt told each other, since the application had been filled out seven years before. The people presently living at that address didn't know what had become of the Broszczynskis, but the telephone company did.

A phone booth with its book miraculously attached and intact gave them the information they needed, and a taxi delivered them to the right address. It was another apartment, but a nicer one, more a garden complex. Lauren felt a certain pleasure that Susan's sister had moved up in the world.

The door was answered by a teenage girl who reminded Lauren of the guard at the garage where she parked. Definitely a music fan. If the net of lace banding her curly hair, the penciled mole just above her lip, or the abbreviated top and minuscule straight skirt hadn't given her away, the fingerless lace glove on her hand would have.

"Mmm?" the girl mumbled.

"We're looking for Ann Broszczynski," Lauren explained. "Is she in?"

The girl tilted her head back and hollered to the ceiling, "Mom!" A minute later she stepped aside to make room for the woman who approached.

Ann Broszczynski was a clean and attractive representative of middle America. She wore jeans, a sleeveless blouse and an apron, the latter serving at the moment as a towel for her wet hands. Her hair, a little lighter than Lauren's, was shoulder-length and swept behind her ears. Even devoid of makeup, her face was lovely.

It was also momentarily stricken. Her eyes were huge. She opened her mouth, then closed it and stared at Lauren in puzzlement.

Lauren smiled. "I look a lot like Susan, I know, but my name's Lauren Stevenson. This is Matt Kruger. We wonder if we could talk with you for a few minutes."

"Are you friends of Susan's?" the woman asked, more wary than curious, a fact that Lauren attributed to the distance between the sisters.

"Indirectly, yes," Lauren answered. "May we come in?"

Ann didn't budge. "Susan and I don't see each

other," she returned a little too quickly. "We go our own ways."

"I know that. But we need to talk with you. No one else has been able to help us."

"Why do you need help?" Ann shot back.

Matt, who'd been silent up to that point, suddenly understood the problem. "We don't wish Susan any harm, Mrs. Broszczynski. If anything, the contrary is true, which is why we're here. Susan is in danger. Apparently you know that, or at least you know she's living somewhere new under an assumed name and that there's a potential for danger if she is discovered. What you don't know is that Lauren was mistaken for Susan by Theodore Prinz's men. For weeks they've put her through hell, using one scare tactic after another. Last week they abducted her and came very close to killing her. It was during the time she was being held that she learned about Susan." He spoke with soft urgency. "We need to find your sister. She must be told that she's being hunted. We have to convince her to go to the police. Between her testimony and Lauren's, we know that something can be done about Prinz."

Ann was pale. She gnawed at her lower lip and clutched the folds of the apron in her fists.

"May we come in?" Lauren asked again, this time pleadingly.

After another moment's hesitation, the woman nodded. Shooing her daughter away, she led them into a small, modestly furnished living room. None of them sat; the air was too tense for that.

"I'm not sure if I know what you're talking about," Ann burst out. "I'm not involved in Susan's life."

"We realize that," Matt said quietly, intent on convincing her of the legitimacy of their mission. "We've just come from Kansas City, where we spoke with both Timothy Trennis and Alexander Fraun. Do those names ring a bell?"

After a pause, Ann nodded.

"Do you trust them?" he asked. When, after another pause, Ann nodded again, he went on. "Alexander Fraun was the one who found your name on Susan's old employment application. He was obviously fond of Susan and wouldn't have given us your name unless he trusted us." Though he raised a hand to emphasize his point, his voice remained soft. "We wouldn't be bothering you if we had anywhere else to turn, but no one seems to know where Susan is or what she's doing. Prinz doesn't seem to be aware that Susan had any family, which may explain why no one has reached you sooner. But it's simply a matter of time before he gets to you, and then to Susan, because it may well be that you're the only one who knows Susan's new name and address." He paused, gentling his voice all the more. "Will you tell us, Ann? We only want to help."

"I wish my husband were here," Ann wailed softly, hands tightly clenched before her. "I'm no good at things like this."

"You're Susan's sister. It's your decision, more so than your husband's."

"But things are so tenuous between Susan and me,"

she argued. "For years we had very little contact. She was in one world, I was in another. There was no middle ground between us. I don't want to do something that will anger her, or worse, put her in danger."

"Then you have to tell us where she is," Lauren urged. "*None* of us will be safe until we find her and convince her to go to the police with us. For all we know, Matt and I are just one step ahead of Prinz's men right now."

Ann pondered Lauren's words nervously, her gaze shifting from one spot in the room to another. Then she brightened. "Why don't you let *me* call Susan? I can tell her everything you've told me—"

"Do you think she'll believe you—or that we're legitimate?" Matt cut in. "She'll run, Ann. She's done it before, and she'll do it again if this isn't handled right. She needs to *see* Lauren and the physical similarity between them in order to believe what's happened."

Ann looked from one face to the other. "You're asking an awful lot."

Lauren nodded. "We know."

"If you turn out to be the bad guys—"

"We're not! You can call the police back home, either in Boston or Lincoln. They'll verify everything that's happened to me."

"And Fraun took precautions of his own," Matt added soberly. "He has our names and addresses. He knows where to send the police if anything happens to Susan."

"I'll never forgive myself if she's hurt because of me!"

Matt put every ounce of feeling into a single, last-ditch plea. *"No* one will be hurt if we reach her in time. But time is of the essence, and we can't reach her if we don't know where she is."

Ann worried the issue for several minutes longer, her eyes filled with concern, her lips clamped tightly together. Her gaze slid from Lauren to Matt and back to Lauren, asking questions for which there were, as yet, no answers.

Just as Lauren was about to scream in frustration, Ann straightened her shoulders, took a deep breath, let it out in a sigh and surrendered.

CHAPTER ELEVEN

A single long shadow stretched across the grass behind him as Ted Prinz stood in his garden staring out over the hills. Absently he lit a cigarette and dragged deeply on it. Pensive, he narrowed his eyes through the tunnel of smoke.

So Susan was in Washington, D.C. That made sense. He could picture her trying to hook up with a politician who had enough clout to protect her.

He grinned. She'd never make it. His men would make sure of that. At this very moment Kruger and the girl were being staked out at the Hay-Adams House. When they moved, his men would, too.

And Susan would regret the day she'd been born.

"Whaddya think?" Matt asked, looking at his watch. "Should we make a stab at it tonight?"

Lauren pressed a hand to her chest. "My heart is pounding. I can't believe we've found her."

"Don't believe it until you see it. There could be a catch yet."

But Lauren was shaking her head. "Ann said she'd spoken to her just last week. Oh, she's here all right. I can *feel* it."

Slinging an arm around her shoulder, Matt tugged her close. "My eternal optimist." He popped a kiss on her nose. "So. What will it be? Tonight, or tomorrow morning?"

Lauren pondered the choice. "If we go tonight, it'll have to be to her apartment. Ann said it's a nice place, which means there will be security guards—"

"Who call up to announce your arrival and get permission to let you in. Susan doesn't know us. She'll never allow it. No, I think we'll have to take her by surprise. Any advance announcement of our presence will put her on guard and, in turn, put us at an immediate disadvantage."

"On the one hand," Lauren mused, "I hate to wait. The sooner we get to her, the sooner we'll all breathe freely. But another twelve hours, after all this time . . . it can't hurt."

Matt nodded his agreement. "We know where she works. If we surprise her there tomorrow, she won't have a chance to turn us away sight unseen. And if she gets scared and tries to run, we can stop her."

"But we need time with her, time to explain what we're about." Lauren ran her tongue back and forth over her lower lip, then expressed her thoughts aloud.

"She's a beauty consultant, Ann said. That figures. From what we've learned, she has a way with makeup and color and style. What if I call first thing in the morning and make an appointment? If we just drop in, she's apt to be with a client. On the other hand, if I can guarantee us a piece of her time . . ."

A slow grin spread over Matt's face. "Smart girl. I *knew* there was a reason why I brought you along."

Lauren grabbed his ears, tugged him down and kissed his yelp away. She lingered to savor his returning kiss, her fingers tangling in his sun-kissed hair. At last she dropped her arms to his waist and pressed her cheek to his chest.

They were silent for a time, enjoying the closeness. But Lauren's thoughts of the day to come refused to stay in abeyance for long. "Poor Susan. If she only knew tonight what was in store for her tomorrow."

"Save your sympathy, sweetheart," Matt murmured. "Susan Miles may still put us through an ordeal. Confronting her is one thing, convincing her that we're on the level is another, but selling her on the idea of going to the police may be a different can of worms entirely."

Michele Sloane, as Susan now called herself, had set up her business in fashionable Georgetown. Lauren got the phone number from directory assistance and started calling at eight-thirty in the morning on the chance that the shop opened early for the prework set. It wasn't until nine that she got through.

Luck was with her. Michele had a cancellation and

could see her at eleven-thirty.

The minutes ticked by with agonizing slowness as Lauren and Matt pushed their breakfasts around their plates in the hotel dining room. Then, to expend nervous energy, they went out for a walk. But while the White House, the Mall and the Lincoln Memorial should have inspired awe, they were too preoccupied in anticipation of the coming meeting to award these sights their due.

Ten o'clock came and went, then ten-thirty. Back in their hotel room, Lauren began to pace the floor. By eleven she was ready to jump out of her skin, but it wasn't until eleven-ten that she and Matt left the room, rode the elevator in silence, walked calmly through the hotel lobby and climbed into the cab that the doorman had whistled up. They'd calculated well for the traffic. It was eleven-thirty on the dot when the cabbie pulled up at the address they'd given him.

For a minute Matt and Lauren stood before the stately brownstone on the ground floor of which was Susan's shop. The sign on the front window, a contemporary logo in burgundy, read "Elegance, Inc." Smaller letters, far below, advertised fashion advice and salon services.

Taking a collective breath for courage, they crossed the sidewalk, descended three steps to the door and entered the shop. An aura of quiet dignity surrounded them instantly. The reception area was done in shades of a soothing pale gray and peach. Soft pop music hummed in the background, low enough to create a modern mood yet be unobtrusive.

A woman sat in a chair reading a magazine, apparently awaiting her appointment. Lauren and Matt made their way directly to the receptionist.

"May I help you?" she asked politely.

"Yes. My name is Lauren Stevenson. I have an eleven-thirty appointment with Michele Sloane."

The receptionist consulted the large book open before her, put a tiny dot next to Lauren's name, then smiled up at her. "Why don't you have a seat? Michele is just finishing up with another client. She'll be with you in a minute."

Lauren thanked her and settled into one of a pair of chairs farthest from the receptionist. She crossed her legs, folded her hands in her lap and leaned closer to Matt, who'd taken the chair immediately on her left.

"When was the last time you were in a place like this?" she whispered in an attempt at levity.

His soft grunt was the only answer she got, the only thing that betrayed his mood. He looked self-confident and composed. Taking her cue from him, she breathed deeply and straightened her shoulders. They were so close, so close. . . .

Moments later another woman entered the shop, checked in with the receptionist and was sent directly through to one of the back rooms. Lauren stared after her, noting a long hallway sporting two doors on the side she could see. She assumed another two doors were on the opposite side.

Just then, from that blind side came the soft murmur of conversation. It was immediately followed by the appearance of two women, but Lauren's eyes homed in on only one of them.

Susan Miles was everything she'd been built up to be. She was indeed stunning. Very much Lauren's own height and build, she wore a pale yellow dress whose shoulder pads gave a breadth that narrowed, past a hip belt, into a pencil-slim skirt. Chunky beads hung around her neck. A coordinated bracelet ringed her wrist. Whether she wore earrings was not immediately apparent, for her chin-length hair was a mass of thick waves that framed her face in haphazard tumble.

The entire look was chic without being ostentatious. Lauren, who mere moments before had felt sufficiently confident in her own stylish tunic and slacks, was envious.

She was also puzzled. Susan Miles looked very much like her, yet very different. Apparently the receptionist had missed the resemblance. Now, studying Susan, Lauren could understand why.

Susan's hair was far lighter than Lauren's, for one thing. It had obviously been colored, though there was nothing obviously doctored about the blond, sun-streaked tangle. It blended perfectly with Susan's skin tone and makeup and looked completely natural.

Makeup. Yes, another difference. While Lauren wore it lightly and for simple enhancement, Susan's makeup sculpted her face, shading and contouring with a skill that was remarkable. Plastic surgery? Lauren doubted it. Yet there was something about the nose . . . a small bump . . .

The woman who'd been with Susan left. Susan bent over the desk to examine the appointment book, then followed the receptionist's finger to Lauren and Matt. She smiled as she straightened and approached them, but her smile wavered as she neared. Lauren thought she saw a faint drain of color from Susan's face. The smile remained but was more forced.

Lauren stood up, finding solace in the warmth of Matt's body by her side. If Susan was playing a part, she herself was doing no less. She held out her hand, willing it not to shake. "Michele?"

Susan met her clasp. "Yes. You're Lauren. And . . ." Her gaze slid to Matt.

"Matt Kruger," he said with a smile.

Susan nodded, but she was already looking back at Lauren. She folded her hands at her waist, hesitated a minute too long, then cleared her throat. "Well. You're here for a consultation. Why don't you come back to my office?"

They followed her down the hall to the last door on the right. The office they entered was simply decorated and furnished, exuding the same quiet dignity as the front room had. Large semi-abstract watercolors—one of a woman's face—hung on the walls. Had it been another time, Lauren would have paused to admire the pictures themselves, if not their matting and framing, but she was too busy trying to organize her words and thoughts to handle anything else.

They were all three seated—Susan behind her desk, Matt and Lauren in comfortable chairs before it—when Susan spoke. "What can I do for you?" she asked. Her tone was thoroughly cordial, even warm. The wariness in her eyes was subtle enough to go unnoticed by any but the most watchful of observers. Lauren and Matt were that.

Lauren went straight for the heart. "You've noticed the resemblance, haven't you?"

Susan frowned. "Resemblance?" Her expression was one of confusion, but it was studied. A second, almost imperceptible drain of color from her face betrayed her.

"I have a problem," Lauren explained softly, her eyes never once leaving Susan's. "I was hoping you could help me. Several months back I had plastic surgery, reconstructive work, actually, to correct a long-standing medical problem. The work was extensive, and when it was done, I looked like a new person. But after I returned to the States—the clinic where I had the surgery was in the Bahamas—I ran into trouble. Things started happening. Odd things. Dangerous things." She gave several examples, then paused, looking for a reaction in Susan. But the latter, aside from her underlying pallor, remained composed, so Lauren went on.

"Matt and I put two and two together when I began to get letters addressed to Susan Miles. We realized that I was being mistaken for someone else, but we couldn't find a Susan Miles in the area and we didn't know what to do next. Then, just about a week ago, I was abducted, forced off the street into a car by two men who firmly believed I was Susan Miles."

Susan blinked. That was all.

"They drove me around for hours, finally brought me to an abandoned warehouse and told me their plan.

They meant to set me on fire and watch me burn. They had every intention of seeing me dead, as their boss wanted me to be." Lauren paused again, this time out of necessity. Her voice began to shake, whether from remembered terror or the utterly bland look on Susan Miles's face, she didn't know.

Matt came to her aid. "Lauren managed to escape. But we don't know if they're still out looking for her or if they actually let her go because she managed to convince them she wasn't Susan. The police have nothing to go on, at least nothing that's leading them anywhere, and Lauren can't live under guard indefinitely. We realized then that our only hope was in finding Susan."

For the first time, Susan stirred. She propped her elbow on the arm of her chair and rested her chin on her knuckles. Her fingernails were beautifully shaped and painted a sheer pink non-color. "I'm not sure I understand. I'm a beauty consultant, not a detective. Why have you come to me?"

Lauren resumed speaking, more calmly, now, and briefly sketched the course of their search. She concluded with a soft "Ann Broszczynski sent us here."

Susan's eyes were blank and she was shaking her head, but her knuckles had curved into a fist. "None of those names mean anything to me. Ann—whoever she is—must have been wrong. I have no idea why she sent you here."

"I think you do," Matt challenged. "You saw the resemblance to your old self the minute you looked at Lauren, and we saw the resemblance the minute we looked at you."

A hoarse laugh tripped from Susan's throat. "This is ludicrous! I don't know why I'm even sitting here listening to you." But she didn't move. "Do you really expect me to swallow the story you've told? I'm sorry. Even if I believed it, which I don't, I don't know why someone would have sent you to *me*. And as far as the resemblance is concerned, you're mistaken—"

"No." Matt spoke softly, trying his best to understand her fear as he tamped down his own impatience. "We're not here to hurt you. You have a problem, and because of that, Lauren has a problem. I, for one, don't think it's fair that she's been saddled with it. She did nothing but try to correct a medical deficiency, and now she's being punished. We know that Theodore Prinz is at the root of the problem. We also know that unless you agree to go to the police and testify along with Lauren, he'll snake his way free." Susan's telephone chirped melodically. Matt ignored it. "It's only a matter of time before he finds you—Ann realized that—and he may well kill Lauren along the way."

When the phone on the desk chimed a second time, Susan picked it up. Her every movement was carefully controlled. "Yes? . . . She's back? . . . No, no, don't let her go. I'll be there in a second." Replacing the receiver, she rose from her seat and headed for the door. Matt was instantly on his feet, but she held him off with a hand. "There's a problem at the front desk. I have to see to it, but I'll be back. Please don't go anywhere. I'd like to hear more about this Theodore Prinz."

With that, she left the office. The door had no sooner closed behind her than the phone rang again, that same soft tinkle. Matt stared at it and frowned. When he made a move toward it, Lauren was one step ahead. Their lines of sight merged on the keyboard. A red dot flashed beside the bottommost number, one that was separate from the others, one totally apart from that marked "X" that would connect the interoffice line.

"Damn it," Matt barked, heading for the door, "she's gone! That wasn't the receptionist. It was someone on her personal line, someone who's calling back now to find out what in the hell she was talking about." He was in the hall, looking first one way, then the other, with Lauren by his side. "I'll take the back, sweetheart. It probably leads to an alley. No, you take the back. I'll circle around and head her off." He burst into a run toward the front of the shop.

Brushing past the white curtain at the end of the hall, Lauren raced through the back room, threw open the door and dashed up the steps. Yes, there was an alley, a long, long alley strewn with trash cans and miscellaneous other debris. Susan Miles was about halfway down its length and running.

"Michele!" Lauren screamed as she, too, broke into a run. "Wait!"

Susan wasn't waiting. She was running as if the devil himself were at her heels, and would have long since made it to the end of the alley had it not been for the dodging the obstacle course demanded.

"Michele! Wait! It's dangerous!"

But Susan had no intention of stopping. Had it not

been for Matt's timely appearance at the end of the alley, she'd have escaped. As it was, when she saw him, she whirled around, saw Lauren, whirled again and made for the nearest doorway. Matt reached her before she made it.

Capturing her bodily, he swung her up and wrestled her back until he'd pinned her to the nearest brick wall. "I am *not* going to hurt you, Susan," he gritted out between breaths, "but neither . . . neither am I going to let you get away. Not . . . after all we've been through to find you, not after all Lauren's been through *because* of you."

Lauren came to a breathless halt just as Susan sagged lower against the wall. Matt simply shifted his grip, veeing his hands under her arms and propping her right back up. She'd tricked him once. Lauren agreed with his caution.

"It wasn't my fault," Susan gasped. Her composure had vanished. There was near panic in the eyes that skipped from Matt's face to Lauren's and back. "I'd been with Ted for two years before I discovered who he really was. I wanted to leave him then, but he wouldn't hear of it. For a year, a whole year, I tried, but he threatened awful things and I kept giving in until I hated myself nearly as much as I hated him. I was desperate . . . so desperate that I tried to kill myself."

"A suicide attempt?" Matt drawled. "We knew about the accident, but that's a new twist to the story."

"Why else would I drive over a cliff? You thought I wasn't in the car when it went over the edge? I was. *I was*. But I was thrown free when the car began to roll." Trembling, she shoved the hair from her forehead. Just below her hairline was a three-inch scar. "I broke an arm and several ribs, but I could breathe and think and feel, and it was then that I realized I'd been given a second chance. So I let them think that I'd died, and I ran. Don't ask me what hospital I went to—it was in some godforsaken town in northern Arizona."

"How did you get there?"

"I hitchhiked."

"Talk of ludicrous stories!"

"It's the truth. At the time, nothing was more dangerous than staying where I was."

"Why didn't you go to the police? If Prinz threatened you—"

"Ted *owns* the police, or half of them, and what he doesn't own he has connections to. I know what I'm talking about. I've seen him buy his way out of serious investigations. That was what tipped me off in the first place!"

Lauren entered the conversation at that point. She was beginning to feel sorry for Susan. While she understood Matt's anger, she wanted to put the other woman at ease. They still needed her cooperation. "Okay," she said gently. "You felt you couldn't go to the police. Where did you go? What did you use for money? The two men who kidnapped me mentioned furs and jewels."

"I had both. Ted had given them to me. As far as I was concerned, I'd earned them."

"But how did you get them? You'd have to have gone back to Los Angeles."

"A friend did it." Susan's voice softened. "He was a little old man who used to sell flowers on a street corner not far from the boutique. I liked him. He reminded me of my father—or what my father would have been like if he'd lived beyond forty," she added in a whisper. "Sam was kind and gentle. I knew he'd do anything for me." She averted her gaze. "Maybe it was wrong of me, or arrogant. I knew Sam was dying. He'd told me that he'd been given six months to live. I figured that he wouldn't mind the risk, that he'd take pleasure in helping me out." Her eyes met Lauren's. "And he did. He told me so in a note he stuck inside the pocket of one of the coats."

"An old man, breaking into your apartment and stealing your things?" Matt was clearly skeptical.

"He didn't steal them," Susan shot back. "He simply returned to me what was mine. As for breaking into my apartment—he had friends who would have done anything for him, just as I would have."

"But you never got the chance," Matt concluded sarcastically, only to be instantly corrected.

"I did. After I sold the very first ring, I sent him a large chunk of the money. I know he received it, because I called him to make sure." Susan took a ragged breath. "Whether he lived long enough to enjoy it, I'll never know. I've tried to call him again, but there's been no answer. He may be using the money to travel, or he may be . . . well, I'll never know."

Matt stared at her. "Prinz's men may have had him killed."

"Do you think I don't know that?" Susan cried. "I've *seen* Ted in action—"

"Isn't it about time you did something about it?"

The air between the two sizzled. Lauren set about diffusing it. "We're getting ahead of ourselves. Did you come directly to Washington from Arizona?"

Susan was leaning against the brick on her own now, Matt having released her and stepped back. She took several calming breaths. "I made a few stops. I wasn't sure where I wanted to settle. But each time I stopped, I felt I was still too close to Ted, so I kept going. When I reached Washington, it was either stay or swim. So I stayed."

"What about your nose?" Lauren frowned as she leaned to the side for a profile view. "We assumed you'd have plastic surgery to change your looks. Prinz's men assumed the same, which was how they got onto me."

"I figured they'd think that, so I avoided it." Susan gave a self-conscious half shrug. "My nose had been broken in the accident, and I didn't trust the doctors in that hospital to do more than tape it up. When the bandages came off, I saw the bump. It was subtle enough to change my profile just that little bit. I told myself it'd give my face character." She snorted. "Obviously it didn't fool you."

"We started with an advantage." It was Matt speaking, more gently now. "We had your name and knew where to find you. Even before you walked into that reception area, we were primed to see Susan Miles."

With an air of helplessness, Susan raised her eyes to the sliver of sky above. "Well, you saw her. And you have her cornered. I suppose I knew that someday someone would find me. In some ways, it's a relief that it's you."

"Then you do trust us?" he asked.

Her gaze met his. "Trust? Maybe that's going a little too far."

Lauren grasped her arm. "But you do believe that what we've told you is the truth."

Susan studied her for a long time. "The resemblance . . . it's amazing. What did you look like before?"

Dropping Susan's arm, Lauren glanced awkwardly at Matt, who nodded. "I was awful." Lauren proceeded to paint a brief, if blunt, picture of her former self. "Richard took care of it all, bless him." She winced. "Then again . . ."

Matt curved his hand around her neck. "No, no, sweetheart. From a purely medical standpoint, it is a blessing, what he did. And as for this other, we'll work it all out. Susan will go to the police with us—"

"Whoa. I never said that."

"But you have to!" Lauren cried. "It's your only chance. Sooner or later those guys will find you—"

A deep voice cut her off with an ominously sarcastic "Hel-lo, hel-lo."

All three heads jerked around. Lauren and Susan gasped in tandem. Matt grew rigid.

"What have we here?" drawled the man whose face

and voice Lauren would never in a million years forget. He stood several yards away, a human wall with a gleaming gun in his hand. "Matthew Kruger, Lauren Stevenson . . . and if it isn't the elusive Miss Susan Miles."

"What do you want, Leo?" Susan demanded. Her eyes were hard, glittering more with disgust than with fear.

Leo grinned, that ugly grin Lauren remembered so well, and looked first at Mouse on his left, then at another thug on his right. The eyes he refocused on Susan were nearly black. "You know what I want. I want you."

"I'm not available."

"Seems to me you are." He cocked his head toward Lauren and Matt. "These two don't want you, that's for sure. You've been a thorn in their sides."

"I'd pick her any day—" Lauren began, only to be silenced by the restraining hand Matt put on her arm, and by his own retort.

"You've got the three of us, and you know damn well that if you so much as touch Susan, we'll go straight to the police. Do you plan a triple murder?"

"Wouldn't bother the boss any. I have his okay."

"Think, Leo, think," Susan urged. "There are too many people involved now. If you do something to Matt and Lauren, someone *else* will go to the police. This isn't another one of your little in-house jobs. If you kill one of your own, you're doing us all a favor. But to kill me—and these two, who are totally inno-cent . . . The police will get you one day, Leo. And if you think Ted will come forward on your behalf, you're crazy."

Leo laughed. "The police won't get me. I'm good at what I do. We'll have it arranged so it looks like you shot the others, then killed yourself. Very clean."

"Very simpleminded," Susan retorted. When Leo made a move toward her, she slipped into a half crouch, arms raised. "I think it's only fair to warn you that I've learned karate."

Lauren and Matt glanced at each other, then at Susan. Leo threw back his head and laughed louder. "Talk of simpleminded. That threat's the oldest in the book, and in your case it's empty. You haven't had the time to learn enough karate to protect yourself."

"I'm a quick study."

"Against a gun?"

Susan had no answer for that, and Matt and Lauren said nothing. They were concentrating on the gun, measuring the distance between Leo and his accomplices, peripherally evaluating the potential weaponry within reach.

"Gotcha there, don't I?" Leo said. He took a step back. "Okay, I want the three of you to start moving. Straight to the car at the head of the alley." He gestured at Susan with the gun. "You first."

Lauren swallowed hard. She had no desire to be in a car with Leo and company. She knew the helplessness of that. No, if a move was to be made, it had to be now.

Matt's hand remained on her arm, but it was steadily tightening. He agreed with her. She waited for his signal.

Slowly Susan moved forward. She hadn't taken two steps, though, when her ankle turned and she buckled over.

"Ah, hell," Leo moaned. "That's the corniest move I've ever seen. It won't get you anywhere, Susan, and if you think I'm going to carry you, you're nuts."

"These heels," Susan gasped. "They're too high."

Matt's hand tightened all the more on Lauren's arm. They both knew from personal experience how well Susan could maneuver, high heels or no. Internally coiled and ready, they watched her unstrap the thin buckles and remove the shoes.

"Come on, come on. We haven't all day—" Leo's words were abruptly cut off by a totally unexpected, lightning-quick move. As Susan straightened, she hiked her slim skirt high on her thighs, spun around and delivered a kick that would have made her instructor proud.

The gun went flying, as did Matt, who barreled into Leo's midsection, knocking the burly man to the ground. Susan, meanwhile, turned her attention to the other men, throwing strategically placed kicks with such speed that they barely knew what hit them. When Mouse doubled over in pain, she whirled around and into his pal, and by the time she was done with him, she was aiming lethal chops at Mouse again.

Lauren came to her aid. Grabbing a heavy shovel from its resting place beside a nearby trash bin, she slammed it repeatedly against the back of whichever man Susan wasn't battering. Each slam vented a little more of her anger, and she might have actually enjoyed herself if she hadn't shot a glance at Matt.

He and Leo were fighting hand to hand, tumbling on the filthy pavement, each landing his share of punches.

Dropping the shovel, Lauren scrambled along the alley, returning seconds later to put an end to the fray. *"That's it!"* she screamed. *"Enough!"* She stood a safe distance back with her feet planted firmly, both hands curved around Leo's gun. The fact that she didn't know how to use it was secondary to the proprietary air with which she held it. Her chest was heaving, the only part of her that betrayed any weakness.

Later she realized that if she'd had to shoot, she'd never have been able to separate Matt from Leo, so fast were they shifting. But her strident yell brought all heads up in surprise. Matt took advantage of the precious seconds to free himself and stumble to her side. He grabbed the gun and turned it on the trio.

"Susan! That's enough!" he ordered. She'd been poised to deliver another side-handed slice to Mouse's head, and only with reluctance did she lower her arm and move back.

Matt motioned with the gun toward the three. "Okay, up! And if you think I don't know how to use this, think again. I'm an avid hunter." His knees were bent; both hands were on the gun, holding it aimed and steady. Not once did his eyes leave the men. "Lauren, go back inside the shop and call the police—"

The sound of shoes clattering on the pavement interrupted him, and seconds later the police themselves rounded the corner and entered the alley with their guns drawn. Slowly Matt straightened. He didn't lower his arm until each of Prinz's men had been handcuffed.

"Mr. Kruger?" one of the officers asked. He was the only one not in uniform and was obviously the man in command. "I'm Detective Walker. Phil Huber gave me a call and told me to keep an eye out. He sensed there might be some trouble."

"How did you know where to come?" Matt wondered. His voice shook. He shot a glance behind him to make sure Lauren was safe.

Walker smiled and cocked his head toward Susan, who stood warily at the side. "Miss Miles's receptionist gave us a call when she found out that something had gone awry with your, uh, beauty consultation. Sorry we didn't get here sooner." He studied Matt's face. "We might have spared you a little of that."

Gingerly Matt fingered his cheek, then his mouth. In the next instant, he reached out for Lauren and hauled her close. She was eager to support him; he'd fought valiantly and had to be uncomfortable.

"Those three thugs intended to kill us," he said.

Lauren pointed. "Those *two* were the ones who kidnapped me back in Boston."

"No doubt," Matt added, his eyes filled with venom, "the third is another of Prinz's men."

"His name is Hank Ober, but he's called Rat," Susan stated stiffly. "The one with the ugly nose is Leo

Charney, and the other, Mouse, is Malcolm Donnia." She watched as the three men were hustled off. "What will you do with them?"

The detective faced her. "Book them for attempted murder."

"Then what?"

"They'll be arraigned, and if they can post bond, they'll be released until their trial."

"*Released!* Do you know what they'll do once they hit the streets? They'll disappear. But before they do that, they'll finish off one or another of us, if not all three!"

"Susan . . ." Matt took her shoulder with his free hand. "That won't happen. The police won't *let* it—"

"The police! If they're not already in Ted's pocket, they will be soon!"

"Just a minute now," Walker growled. He took a menacing step closer. "I have never been, and will never be, in anyone's pocket, and I can safely vouch for three-quarters of my men."

"And the other quarter?"

"They won't be allowed anywhere *near* this case. The Ted Prinzes of the world would like to believe they can buy their way out of trouble, but it won't work here."

"You know of Ted?" Susan asked, wavering.

"Every major law-enforcement officer in the country knows of him. It will be one of the greatest thrills of my career to nail him, but I can do that only if you're willing to testify."

"You have to, Susan," Lauren begged. "Once and

for all, it has to be put to rest."

Matt echoed her sentiment. "Lauren's right. If the three of us work together, we can do it. Lauren and I alone . . . well, it'll be tougher."

"He'll still come after me. It won't matter if he's in prison."

Walker spoke up. "He won't *dare* come after you. Nor will he send anyone else. He knows we'll be watching his every step. I've seen how these men work, Susan. Revenge may eat them alive, but in the end they opt for survival. Prinz will be signing his own death warrant if he comes near you again. He'll know that. Believe me, he'll know it."

Susan swallowed and looked from the detective to Matt and Lauren. "I want to believe. Really I do."

"Trust him," Matt urged. "Trust *us*. But then, you already do, don't you?"

"What makes you think that?" she returned, but there was a softness in her tone.

Matt smiled, then winced when his bruised lip protested. He soothed the spot with his finger. "You really do know karate, but you don't try it on me. One kick, and you'd have escaped. The fact that you didn't try it had to mean something." He ventured a second smile, this one more carefully. "How *did* you learn it so quickly?"

Susan shrugged and gave a tentative grin of her own. "Like I told Leo, I'm a quick study."

Matt chuckled softly. Reaching out, he drew Susan to his side at the same time that his arm tightened around Lauren. "You'll work with us, Susan, won't you?"

Susan moistened her lips, but it was Lauren she was looking at. "After all you've gone through for me, I guess I'll have to." She jerked her head toward Matt. "Where did you even find this big lummox, Lauren? Do you think maybe he has an identical twin stashed away somewhere?"

Lauren grinned up at Matt. "I don't think there's another man like him on the face of the earth. He's pretty special, isn't he?"

Purpled cheek, bruised lip, battered ribs and all, Matt sucked in a deep breath and threw back his head. "Ahhhh. Paradise. One pretty lady on the left, one pretty lady on the right . . . if only my buddies at the beer hall could see me now!"

"The beer hall? You never talked about a beer hall. For that matter," Lauren said, scowling, "you never said you were an avid hunter." They were back in the hotel room after spending the afternoon at the police station. Lauren had insisted that Matt take a long, hot bath to soothe his aching body, but now she had him in bed, exactly where she wanted him.

Matt looked up at her through one half-lidded eye. "Where did you think construction workers went for fun?" He steeled himself against an attack that never came.

"Did you get drunk?" Lauren asked.

"On occasion."

"What were you like . . . drunk?"

He shrugged the shoulder she wasn't leaning against. "I don't know. I was too far out of it to tell."

She grinned. "And the hunting?"

"Wooden ducks at an amusement park. We should go sometime. I'll win you a huge stuffed teddy bear."

Lauren settled onto him, gently and with a sigh. "Thanks, but I've already got one." She rubbed her ear against the tawny hair on his chest and stilled only when he began to stroke her back.

"You're pretty special yourself," he murmured. "The way you thought to go for that gun, and then the way you held it . . . I thought for a minute that *you* were the one with experience."

"All a bluff. I've never held a gun in my life."

"Not even a water gun?"

"Nope. My parents were pacifists. Dead set against weapons of any kind. That's one of the things that drove them crazy about Brad. He used to make guns out of whatever toys he had handy. Some of them were pretty creative."

"Lauren?"

She took a deep breath, inhaling the clean, male scent of his skin. "Mmm?"

"What will your parents say about me?"

"That depends," she said softly and raised her head. "It depends on what I tell them first."

"How about you tell them that I love you and want to marry you?"

"How about I tell them that you're fearless and strong, or that you've got brains as well as brawn, or that you saved my life?"

"I didn't save your life. You escaped from the warehouse on your own. Then, today, you were the one who saved all of our lives."

"You saved my life."

"How did I save your life?"

"You gave it deep, deep, lasting meaning. A good job is fine. So's a good house, even a pretty face. But the thing that really pulled it all together was you. I love you, Matt. Love is what counts. Always has been, always will be."

Matt cleared his throat, but his voice still came out hoarse. "How about you tell them that I love you and want to marry you?"

"They'll hit the roof, but you know something?" Lauren asked, pushing her chin out. "I don't care! If they love me—and I'm sure they do—they'll come around in time. So. Any other questions?"

"Just one. Aren't you worried about where we'll live?"

She turned the tables on him. "Are you?"

"No."

"Why not?"

"Because I've already decided that if my boss won't open a permanent Boston office, I'm quitting. I've made enough contacts here to get another job. And I love the farmhouse in Lincoln." He paused, narrowing his eyes. "But you knew that. You've known all along. You're too smart, that's what you are. You've got me wrapped around your little finger. Y'know, maybe I ought to rethink this. If I'm going to be led around by the nose for another fifty or sixty years—"

Lauren's lips silenced him, and within seconds he was fully involved in the nonverbal give-and-take of love. Belying the punishment he had taken that day, he rolled over to cover her with his body. Hands buried deep in her hair, hips poised above hers, he whispered thickly, ". . . for another fifty or sixty years, I'll love it . . . every . . . sweet . . . minute."

Center Point Publishing
600 Brooks Road ● PO Box 1
Thorndike ME 04986-0001 USA

(207) 568-3717

**US & Canada:
1 800 929-9108**